the further adventures of

SHERLOCK HOLMES

DEATHLY RELICS

the further adventures of

SHERLOCK HOLMES

DEATHLY RELICS

SAM SICILIANO

TITAN BOOKS

THE FURTHER ADVENTURES OF SHERLOCK HOLMES:
DEATHLY RELICS

Print edition ISBN: 9781803361840
E-book edition ISBN: 9781803361857

Published by Titan Books
A division of Titan Publishing Group Ltd
144 Southwark Street, London SE1 0UP
www.titanbooks.com

First edition: January 2023
10 9 8 7 6 5 4 3 2 1

A CIP catalogue record for this title is available from the British Library.

Printed and bound by CPI Group (UK) Ltd, Croydon, CR0 4YY.

To L. Frank Baum, Walter R. Brooks, Robert Heinlein, Edgar Rice Burroughs and the other authors who provided me with a refuge from all the trials and tribulations of my youth.

The story in this novel takes place before that of
The Devil and the Four.

Chapter One

Sherlock Holmes took off his top hat, and the brilliant April sun shone down upon his long sloping forehead, his prominent nose and slicked-back black hair, glossy with pomade. He wore a fine black frock coat, a guide book forming a bulge in its side pocket, and held a silver-headed stick in his hand. The shrunken pupils of his gray-blue eyes looked thoughtfully down upon the skeletal circular ruin of the Roman Colosseum.

Formed of travertine, crumbling brick and concrete, the Colosseum was all reddish-brown and gray, mixed with the greens of moss, grasses and other plants. A sand-covered wooden floor had once formed the circular arena where the spectacles and combats took place, but it was long gone, revealing fragments of pillars and theatrical mechanisms in uneven rows. Gone too were the rows of seats, although two stories of stone with gaping black arches still formed great circles above. The highest level had partly broken off, and only about half still stood, a semicircle set against the bright blue sky, the rectangles of its vacant windows revealing that same blue sky. In the very center of the Colosseum, a glaring anachronism had been erected, a tall black cross which commemorated the Christians martyred there.

A cool breeze touched our faces; the temperature must have been in the mid-sixties. Holmes eased out his breath in a long sigh. "One cannot help but contemplate mortality and the swift passage of time in Rome. Everywhere there are reminders of the brevity of life and of empires, and none is more representative than this vast ruin."

"Yes," I said, "but it is not so much a monument to glory as to barbarism. Perhaps there has been a rough sort of progress, after all, in two thousand years. At least we no longer gather in great crowds to watch animals and people be ruthlessly slaughtered."

Holmes's narrow lips curved upward, his ironic smile rather gentle. "Bravo, Henry! You have found a silver lining to this particular cloud. Still, the weight of history is heavy here in Rome. Every street has some reminder—if not an actual Roman structure, then a newer edifice built with materials scavenged from the past."

Scattered about the two curving circular floors of the Colosseum, I could see the tourists, men in dark suits or frock coats, all wearing hats, and women in red, green, blue, or purple, their colors vivid against the dreary ruins. Some were kneeling at the stations of the cross set up around the perimeter of the arena. "It makes you wonder what London will be like in a millennium or two," I said. "And that in turn makes you recall London wasn't much of a place when this grand monstrosity was constructed."

Holmes nodded. "Yes. But regardless of what remains of London in the future, you and I will be long forgotten."

I smiled. "Your fame as a detective is likely to outlast your lifetime."

"Perhaps. But two thousand years?" A bark of laughter slipped from his lips. "I think not. A few decades at best."

"I don't know. Watson's writings have given you a certain literary notoriety."

"'Literary' is the key word there, as in 'fictional.' Regardless, the only fictional, or semi-historical characters who have lived on for more than two millennia are those from the epics: Aeneas, Odysseus, Achilles. I would hardly compare the feeble efforts of Watson and myself with the great heroes of the epic poets."

I was still smiling. "I suppose not."

Holmes put his hat back on. "I think I have had enough of the Colosseum and melancholy reflections on the transience of all things for one day. Shall we have a look at the Arch of Constantine? It stands right next door, so to speak. The Etruscans and the Romans were the first to perfect the arch. According to my guide book, that of Constantine dates from about AD 350, while the Colosseum was completed earlier, around AD 80."

"I am ready to move on." I glanced a last time at the ruins before us. "This would have been quite a sight in AD 80. It's hard to imagine how it must have appeared all new and filled with thousands of shouting people."

"All of them long dead, and most reduced to dust. *Sic transit gloria mundi.*"

"*Tempus fugit.*" I smiled. *Time flies* was one of the few Latin phrases I could recall.

Holmes nodded. "A pity I cannot quite quote Shelley's poem 'Ozymandias.' All I recall is 'look on my works, ye mighty, and despair!'" We stared gravely at one another, and then, as if on cue, we both laughed. "Enough of this nonsensical morbidity! A quick look at the arch, and then I think it will be time to find a small trattoria and drown all such gloomy reflections in some good red wine accompanied by a plate of spaghetti."

"Now there is something which has lasted even more than two thousand years, and undoubtedly will endure as long as humans walk the earth!"

"Spaghetti?" He spoke with mock gravity.

"No, wine! It is surely a gift of the gods!" I exclaimed.

"Bacchus, to be exact." Holmes started for the arched entranceway which led to a stairway down to the exit.

I followed. "And soon, I hope, you will at last tell me the object of our visit, the person whom we are going to see."

"If you wish, but would you not rather wait and be surprised at the last moment?"

"When I agreed to accompany you to Italy, you swore that this would be a minor diplomatic mission and that, unlike nearly all of our other trips, dead bodies would not begin to pile up."

"Have a guess," he said.

We had reached the shadowy interior which was much cooler. "Well, if it's diplomatic, the British ambassador to the Italian state would be the obvious suspect."

"Obvious, but wrong."

"Perhaps someone not British, but rather, a representative of the Italian government, possibly the prime minister."

"You are on the right track, but higher still."

I was frowning. "You can't mean King Umberto himself?"

"Warmer still, but a potentate of a different sort, one with a more universal realm."

My lips parted in both surprise and dismay. I seized his arm and stared at him. "You cannot mean...?"

The corners of his lips rose in a quicksilver smile.

* * *

Two Swiss Guards in their outlandish, archaic regalia—baggy pantaloons and tight jackets with broad stripes of yellow and blue, silver cuirasses and helmets topped with scarlet plumes—led us through a labyrinth of marble corridors with high ceilings and colorful paintings of cherubs and saints. Finally, they stopped before two towering doors with an elaborate bas-relief pattern carved into the oak. One of them rapped lightly, and a moment later the door swung inward.

A short, stout man stood before us. His black soutane had purple trim, and the sash about his waist was also purple, marking him as a monsignor in the Catholic Church. He had a round face and thick spectacles which slightly shrank his dark brown eyes. "*Entrate, signori.*" We went through the doorway, and the two guards followed us.

The room had a high ceiling with more celestial beings painted there, towering windows along one wall which let in the bright sunlight, and many tall bookshelves lined with fat tomes. At the end of the room near a desk stood a small slight man dressed all in white: white cassock with a row of tiny white buttons, white skull cap—or *zucchetto*, as it was called in Italian—and a white sash round his waist, the band cincture with golden fringe at the hanging bottom. The toes of the red slippers that peeped out from under the white skirts of the soutane provided a jarring contrast. A jeweled pectoral cross on its chain hung almost to his waist. He raised his two hands with fingers open by way of greeting and smiled at us.

Holmes strode boldly forward, paused to bow, and then shook the man's hand. "*Santo Padre, è un grande onore. Mi chiamo Sherlock Holmes, e questo è il mio cugino ed amico, Dottore Henry Vernier.*"

The pope gave me a curious look. "*Vernier e non Watson?*" Italians rarely use the consonant *w*, and when they do, it is generally pronounced as an English *v*, so he said "Vatson."

"Vernier," I said firmly, and then I also bowed. We had discussed beforehand whether I should kiss the ring. Holmes was not Catholic, so he needn't, but I had been baptized and confirmed in the Church. However, I had long since stopped attending Mass regularly and no longer thought of myself as much of a Catholic, so I had decided I would follow Holmes's lead. Thus, I also shook the pope's hand. Both Holmes and I towered over him; he must have been only three or four inches over five feet.

"*Anche un grande onore per me, Santo Padre,*" I said.

"*Benvenuto, gentiluomini. Preferreste parlare in italiano o francese? Sfortunamente non parlo inglese.*" He gave us the choice of Italian or French since he didn't speak English.

Holmes spoke Italian fairly well, I, less so, but Holmes's French was excellent. As for me, having been raised in France by an English mother and a French father, both English and French were my mother tongues.

"*Francese, per favore,*" Holmes said.

The pope nodded. "*Comme vous voulez.*" The conversation which followed was all in French, and we soon discovered that the pontiff spoke the language almost like a native Parisian. He gestured toward the priest who had followed us in. "This is my secretary, Monsignor Arnone." Holmes and I also shook hands with him. "And now, I believe you have something for me, Mr. Holmes."

"I do indeed—for you, and you alone."

Holmes withdrew a large bluish envelope from his inside coat pocket and handed it over. On it was the circle of a red wax seal. The pope broke the seal, set the envelope on the desk, and unfolded the contents. He put on some spectacles, read briefly, noted the signature at the end, then gave the papers to the monsignor, who put them back in their envelope. The pope set down his spectacles of thin gold wire with their thick lenses. He gave Holmes an appreciative nod.

"You have saved both your government and the Holy See a great deal of embarrassment in recovering this document. You have my thanks."

Holmes bowed slightly. "It was an honor to be able to assist both you and her majesty."

The pope smiled faintly. The former Cardinal Vincenzo Pecci of Perugia had become Pope Leo XIII in 1878 at the age of sixty-seven, so that put him in his early eighties. Still, he seemed quite spry, almost gnomish even, if a trifle bent at the waist. On either side of the *zucchetto*, thick white hair swept back hid the tops of his long ears. His wide mouth, lips thin with age, was perpendicular to a long, slender, prominent nose. His piercing dark brown eyes provided striking contrast, and the few dark hairs in his eyebrows were a reminder of hair that must have once been black.

"I may wish to send something back to England with you, Monsieur Holmes. Where in Rome are you staying, should we need to contact you?"

"I am at the Hotel Eden near the Villa Borghese gardens."

"Ah, an establishment of high repute." He sat down in a massive throne-like chair near the desk, then gestured toward us. His fingers were elegant and graceful. "Seat yourselves, *messieurs.* I wish to speak with you briefly." It had more the tone of a command than a request. He nodded toward Arnone and the two tall guardsmen behind us. "Leave us." They trooped out even as Holmes and I sat in two more modest chairs near the dais.

A certain hesitancy showed in the pontiff's dark eyes. "Have you worked in Rome in the past, Monsieur Holmes?"

"I have, Saint Père. Certain cases have brought me here before."

"And have you any contacts in the Roman police?"

Holmes eyed him cautiously. "A few."

The pope's lips pursed briefly. "Your reputation is not unknown to me. Monsignor Arnone also told me something of your accomplishments. *Le Avventure di Sherlock Holmes* was recently published in Italy."

Holmes eased out a slow sigh. "I hope he didn't believe everything in the book. It is a work of fiction over which I have no control."

"Even so... you *are* the world's foremost consulting detective." He used the words *détective conseil*, a rather literal translation.

Holmes's lips curved upward slightly; he was not immune to a certain vanity. "Perhaps."

The pope raised his hand to touch the knuckles of his right hand lightly to his lips, then lowered it. "And you frequently find lost things–things like that document which you brought me?"

"Yes."

"Something has gone missing, something of inestimable value." He sank back into his chair. "As you may know, relations are strained between the Italian state and the Holy See. Ever since 1870 when the Italian soldiers marched in and took over Rome, the Holy Father has been, so to speak, a prisoner here. Since that date, neither my predecessor Pius nor I have left the shelter of the Vatican, and we have made our displeasure at the theft of our lands and properties known to the government and to the Italian people." His voice had become quite stern.

Holmes nodded. "So I have heard."

"All the same, since so many of our churches, convents and shrines remain in Rome, we must often work with the Roman police, especially when it comes to criminal matters. In this case, we contacted them immediately, but they have been of no help. Regrettably, too, our loss was reported in the newspapers."

Holmes's eyes were curious. "What is missing?"

The pope inhaled slowly through his nostrils, lips tightly compressed. "The forefinger of Saint Thomas."

Holmes's eyes widened, even as one corner of his mouth rose in what was obviously the beginning of a smile. He struggled for control even as his eyes shifted briefly to mine. I was equally puzzled. It must be a joke—but it could not be! Surely the supreme pontiff would not jest about such a thing.

Holmes managed to look grave. "The finger of Saint Thomas. How exactly…?"

"It is one of the most precious of all relics, the small bone from the tip of the blessed apostle's finger. You are not a Catholic, Monsieur Holmes, but surely you must know the story of Saint Thomas from the Gospel?"

"Certainly—'doubting Thomas.' The other Apostles told him that the risen Christ had appeared while he was absent, but he would not believe them. Not until I can put my finger in his wounds and feel them myself, he said. And when Christ next appeared, he had Thomas touch his wounds. Thomas did so and said, 'My Lord and my God.' And Jesus said, 'Because you have seen me, you have believed: blessed are they that have not seen, and yet have believed.'"

The pope was clearly relieved that even members of the Protestant opposition knew something of scripture. "Exactly so. And the very finger with which Thomas touched the wounds is one of Christendom's most precious relics. It was kept along with five other relics from the crucifixion in a chapel at Santa Croce in Gerusalemme: pieces of wood from the true cross, other wood from the scourging post, a nail from the cross, two thorns from the crown of thorns, and the *titulus crucis*, the rectangle of wood with 'Jesus, the Nazarene King of the Jews' inscribed upon it. Saint Helena, the mother of Constantine, brought them to Rome from the Holy Land in the fourth century. Do either of you know the church of Santa Croce? It is not far from the main train station of Rome."

Holmes and I both shook our heads.

"A pity. It is a beautiful church, and with its relics..."

I was frowning. "Who would have possibly stolen such a thing?"

"Certainly not a devout member of the Church," the pope said. "He would know that this is not mere thievery, but sacrilege as well, and as such, a doubly grievous mortal sin. A true Catholic would realize he was condemning himself to Hell."

Holmes's forehead had creased. "I suppose there must be some market for precious relics."

"Not among faithful Catholics." The pope's voice was again stern.

I knew Holmes well enough to see a faint skepticism in his gray eyes. "When did this happen?"

"Five days ago. The rector of the church, Monsignor Nardone, discovered it was missing first thing in the morning. It must have been taken overnight."

"I assume the relics are secured?"

"They are kept in a locked case with a thick plate glass in front. There were six beautiful golden and silver reliquaries containing the sacred objects. The one with the finger was gone, even though the padlock was in place and appeared untouched. Its key was also in its usual place."

"So, someone took Thomas's relic, but left the other five behind?"

"Exactly so. Monsignor Nardone was alarmed, and he immediately checked the other reliquaries. They and their contents were still there."

"How odd," I murmured. "Was the relic of Thomas more valuable than the other ones?"

The pope stared gravely at me. "One cannot put a cost on sacred objects. They are all equally valuable—all are invaluable."

Holmes placed the tips of his fingers briefly together. "Henry does have a point. Why would someone choose that relic over the other five? Interesting." He nodded mechanically. Again, I knew him well enough to see that he was uneasy about something.

The pope's dark brown eyes were piercing. "Monsieur Holmes, you are not a Catholic, so I cannot command you. All the same, I would be most grateful if you could help restore this precious object to us. Naturally, too, we would see that you are financially compensated for your efforts."

Holmes frowned. "Money is not a consideration. In this case I might offer my services gratis, but all the same… there are other grave matters which occupy me at the present time, matters I am not at liberty to discuss."

"Nothing can be graver than this theft. At least not to my mind." The pope sighed softly. "But I suppose I cannot expect you to share my feelings."

"I doubt, too, that I would be the best person to pursue the thief. Although certain intrigues have brought me to Rome, I have never actually had a case originate here. I have only a passing familiarity with the city, and then there is the language barrier. My Italian is passable, but little more."

"That had occurred to me. There is a certain prelate that works here in the Vatican. Originally from England, he has been in Rome for thirty years. He is something of a polyglot, and speaks Italian like a native. I could assign him to you and let him assist you in your efforts."

Holmes slowly eased out his breath. "I am grateful for the honor you do me, Saint Père. All the same, I do have other commitments at this time. I shall see if certain matters may be rescheduled, but I do not wish to encourage false hope. Most likely I shall be occupied, and I must also depart for England early next week."

The pope shook his head. "A pity."

I knew of no such grave matters occupying Holmes. Either he hadn't told me, or more likely, he simply did not want to take on this particular case.

The pope grasped the ring on the finger of his right hand and began to turn it back and forth. It was made of gold, a square setting with what must be a round red ruby in its center. His eyes peered off into the distance. Despite his diminutive size, he had an overwhelming aura of command and authority. Finally, he sighed and lowered his hand.

"Regrettable. All the same, if you can reschedule your affairs, write me at once, and I shall have Monsignor Greene summoned— he is the English priest I mentioned. I would also provide you with a papal letter commanding all Catholics, laity and clergy alike, to assist you in your efforts."

"I shall see what I can do, Saint Père." Holmes's tone of voice was not encouraging.

The pope nodded. "I shall hope for the best, and perhaps… Sometimes God works in mysterious ways." He smiled faintly. "It would be curious indeed if our Lord sent a Protestant to help us find Saint Thomas's precious relic."

He rose, indicating our audience was finished, and Holmes and I quickly stood as well. He started for the grand baroque doors, and we followed. "I shall hope to see you again, Monsieur Holmes, but if not I must thank you once more for your help in recovering the documents. You have done the Holy See and your country a great service."

"I am glad I could have been of help."

We paused before the doors. "The guards will show you the way out." The pope hesitated. "Might I give you my blessing?"

"We would be honored." Holmes knelt, and I did the same.

The pope murmured some words in Latin, ending with "*In nomine Patris et Filii et Spiritus Sancti,*" even as his hand made two passes through the air shaping a cross.

Holmes bowed his head, then rose. "Thank you, Saint Père."

"Yes, thank you," I said.

"You are most welcome." His dark eyes were fixed on Holmes. "*Arrivederci.*"

Holmes opened the door, let me leave first, then followed. Monsignor Arnone and the two Swiss Guards were waiting. Arnone nodded at us, then went back into the room, while Holmes and I started down the vast corridor after the guards. I had the sense of being in a vast elaborate maze, everywhere decorated with ornate cornices and friezes, the walls and ceilings teeming with paintings of cherubs, angels, and saints, all adorned with golden halos.

Soon we stepped out into the bright sunshine and started for Saint Peter's Square, where cabs would be waiting close by. Holmes had put on his top hat, and the ferrule of his stick made regular taps as it struck the strip of the pavement.

"All right," I said, "what is the serious business that so occupies you? I thought we were to be idle tourists for a week. Michelle is coming next week, and you were to leave on Wednesday."

Michelle, my wife, was also a physician, a very popular and busy one, but she had arranged for some holiday time with me in Rome. Sherlock would be with us briefly, and then just the two of us were to spend another week together in Italy. She had joked that she wanted Holmes to leave promptly because she, too, was worried about corpses accumulating.

Holmes smiled at me. "You do not consider my company and our visits to the sights of Rome an urgent undertaking?"

"Ah, I suspected as much. You did not want to take the case."

"Even so, Henry."

"And why not?"

He gave an odd sort of laugh. "Must I explain? Is it not rather obvious? Seeking out an ancient fragment of bone which almost certainly does not come from the historical Saint Thomas is hardly my line of work. Although I am no longer a frequent churchgoer and although my inclination is agnostic rather than religious, I was raised an Anglican, and as such, this Roman Catholic fascination with relics confounds me—as does their gullibility! Pieces of the true cross, thorns from the crown of thorns, bones from various apostles... Simple logic says that after nearly two thousand years, they must have crumbled to dust! Worse still is their inclination to divide the remains of the saints. As I recall, Saint Thomas's finger is here in Rome, but the rest of him is somewhere else! And the cathedral at Siena has the distinction of having Saint Catherine's mummified head while other pieces of her... Have you seen that head, by the way?"

"No, I have not."

"I have—unfortunately! I found it a truly disgusting sight. The human body is a sacred-object, and its remains should rest whole and undisturbed in the earth, not put on ghoulish display all encased in gold and jewels. It does verge on idolatry."

"I absolutely agree with you. I may have been raised a Roman Catholic at my father's insistence, but something of my mother's Anglican mistrust remains. Then, too, ever since the

Enlightenment, the French have been split between the forces of reason and skepticism, and those of the Catholic Church. In my case, that French skepticism has largely triumphed."

"The idea of searching for some old bone which probably came from the skeleton of a poor beggar in a mass grave strikes me as absurd. Of course, I could not say that to the Holy Father, nor could I simply refuse outright."

I laughed. "No, I suppose not. Although... surely even he cannot think that every relic on display is genuine? Someone, I believe, once made a joke about how all the fragments of the true cross would be enough to create a forest."

We had passed through the arched north entranceway into the immense square of Saint Peter's, the great white pillars curving around in a row on either side of us, Bernini's sculptured figures staring down from their perches on high, the many saints set against the blue sky.

"I suppose we should be more charitable, Henry. As a practical matter, if it gives comfort to believers, it cannot be all bad." He smiled. "Nevertheless, chasing after lost relics is hardly a fit occupation for Sherlock Holmes."

"It is an interesting sort of mystery, though. Why would anyone steal relics? And that one in particular?"

"The first question is more easily answered than the second. There must be a lucrative black market for stolen relics. I suspect there may be some Roman Catholics who somehow convince themselves that the benefit of the relic outweighs the sinfulness of the theft. Such a person might not much concern himself with notions of sacrilege. In the past, competing monasteries, and also cities, vied over certain saintly relics and would often steal them back and forth from one another. Perhaps some devout person wants to return the finger to its original resting place." His voice was faintly ironic.

I smiled but shook my head. "How nonsensical! Well, if you were to take the case, where on earth would you begin?"

"Isn't that obvious? With Monsignor Nardone."

"Do you actually think he might have done it? Isn't that a little *too* obvious?"

"Yes, but it must be someone who knew where the key was kept. Nardone could tell me who else had knowledge and access to it."

"Well, it almost certainly cannot have been a priest: he would know the gravity and the sacrilegious nature of a such a crime."

Holmes shrugged, smiling slightly. "I doubt we shall ever know the answer." He paused and looked around the vast square, which on a map had been revealed as more keyhole-shaped than square: a round circle, with a flared rectangle opening onto the steps up to the basilica. He raised his stick and pointed at the tall obelisk in the exact center of the circle. "It's hard to believe that monument came from Egypt and has actually been moved two or three times. Caligula had it brought to Rome, and its last move was to that spot there in the sixteenth century when the basilica was completed. Moving it would have been quite a feat of engineering in itself."

"Its original creators in ancient Egypt could have never imagined such a fate."

Holmes smiled. "So, we return to the folly of empires. I wonder where it will be a thousand years from now."

I shrugged. "The Catholic Church may not have the legions of soldiers the Romans did, but I suspect it may last for at least another millennium or two."

"Yes, perhaps so, but you are wrong about the legions—Rome swarms with papal troops."

"What do you mean? The Swiss Guard? There aren't that many of them."

"No, no, not the Swiss Guard. These warriors do not wear armor or helmets—although they have various standard headgear—and their uniforms are black, the officers with colored piping."

I smiled. "Ah, I see: the clerics. Sometimes their uniforms are gray, though." A tonsured friar passed us, probably a Franciscan, in a gray hooded robe and sandals, a corded rope tied round his waist.

It was late afternoon, and the bright sun bathed most of the square, one curving side in blue-gray shadow. Many well-dressed pilgrims, both men and women, were scattered about the square, taking in Bernini's statues up on high or Saint Peter's great facade and ornate dome. Mingled among them in more ragged clothing were beggars cadging alms, mostly children or the elderly.

There was also a throng of priests and sisters in every variety of habit. A proud monsignor strode by in full regalia: a black cassock with purplish piping and buttons, a red pompom on the oddly shaped hat, the biretta with its three blades, and a flamboyant reddish-purple cape which matched the banded sash round his waist. A flash of purple stocking showed between his black pant cuff and shoe as he walked. Two short, stout priests in black cassocks and wide-brimmed black hats were speaking Italian and eagerly waving their hands about. Some nuns had the all-white "butterfly" headwear, while others wore various black veils over white cloths which hid all their head and neck, leaving only the ovals of their faces exposed.

I shook my head. "You are right about the legions. There are even female soldiers with their own distinctive uniforms. Not even Notre-Dame de Paris had this many religious in the square before it."

"Little wonder. Rome is far smaller than London, only four hundred thousand inhabitants, or so I believe, and even in Italy, Naples and Milan are far more populous. However, the greatest concentration of priests and nuns in the world must be here at the

Church's capital and spiritual center." The brim of his top hat hid his eyes in shadow as he gazed slowly round about us. Finally, he shrugged. "It is curious, Henry. Theirs is a world unknown to me, a society completely apart from that which surrounds us in England. Frankly, I don't know what to make of these devotees. That is another reason the case of the missing forefinger did not appeal to me. I cannot fathom their inner lives, their private thoughts, their motives."

"Nor can I, exactly, and I was raised a member of the Church. I especially cannot understand..." My voice faded away.

Holmes looked at me more closely. "Cannot understand what?"

"Well, if you must know... I cannot understand celibacy."

Holmes laughed softly.

"I wonder if..." I began. "Priests do stray, you know. There was a scandal once in our parish."

Holmes's smile was rather humorless. "I know something of celibacy—not so much by choice, as by... accident. All the same, even though it may be my fate to pass my life alone—"

"You will never convince me of that!" I exclaimed.

"All the same, I could never swear such an oath. Perhaps, again, it is my Anglican upbringing once more rearing its head, but it seems inhuman. To cut oneself off from love and affection, the most basic of human needs..."

I gave a fierce nod. "We agree on this."

Holmes was staring at the two Italian priests talking. "As I said, it is all a mystery to me, although I suppose... for these priests the situation must be similar to those adolescent school days away from home when one dwells only with other boys and has all men for teachers, and the only women about are maids and the cook, and one's mother is far, far away."

"I hadn't thought of that, but you are right. Hopefully most men outgrow that suffocating stage and find a woman to love and cherish."

His smile was rather forlorn. "That is indeed the hope. And that is why I could never swear a vow of perpetual chastity. But enough philosophizing! Rome, ancient and modern, does bring forth these ponderous thoughts and reflections. May the bizarre universe of Leo XIII and the papal legions remain a mystery to this particular stalwart Englishman!—and may investigating the theft of lost relics go to someone far more suitable. It is time, instead, to ponder that most delightful of questions: where shall our next Roman dinner take place and what new delights shall we sample?"

"I liked the restaurant very much where we ate last night."

"Then return to it with Michelle, you must! But in the meantime, I demand that we keep with the holiday spirit of adventure and try someplace new!"

I smiled. "As you wish. The choice shall be yours."

We found a small unpretentious trattoria near our hotel, and Holmes, to my horror, ordered one of their specialties, *trippa alla romana*, tripe Roman style. The mere sight of the dish with its chunks of honeycombed cow stomach in a spicy red sauce made my own stomach lurch. Normally I would taste almost anything, but not that particular dish. Instead, I went with the lamb shank in a tasty brown gravy. We accompanied our dish with a bottle of Apulian red wine made with the *primitivo* grape, and both of us were well satisfied with our choices.

Afterwards we strolled the Roman streets for a while before returning to the hotel. The man behind the desk saw us come in and raised his hand. "Signor Holmes. Is something for you."

He handed Holmes an envelope.

"*Grazie mille,*" Holmes said, even as he opened the envelope.

He unfolded the letter as he stepped into the lobby and then began to read. A smile pulled at his mouth, then suddenly an explosive sound burst forth, something between a laugh and a snort. "Oh, very droll," he exclaimed.

"What is it?" I asked.

"It is from the British ambassador to Italy, Lord William Humphrey. He and I are old acquaintances. He mentions the delicate balancing act the crown must negotiate between the Italian government and the Holy See, the necessity of trying to keep on good terms with the two antagonistic parties. He received an emissary from the pope asking if he could facilitate my assistance in the case of the missing relic of Saint Thomas."

I gave my head a shake. "So, the Holy Father will not take no for an answer. But what is so amusing?"

"Lord William assures me that if I take it on, 'The Case of Doubting Thomas's Digit' will surely become one of my most celebrated adventures."

I smiled. "Very good! Perhaps 'The Case of Doubting Thomas's Disappearing Digit.'"

"Please, Henry—do not pursue this jest any further!"

"Well, what will you do? I must admit that my selfish desire to have you visit the sights of Rome with me outweighs my patriotic feelings as an Englishman."

"I shall try to steer a middle ground. Let us go ahead tomorrow with our planned excursion to Tivoli—after all, we have our train tickets—but I shall write to the pope and tell him we shall be at the Vatican the following day at nine ready to investigate this business for a day or two. I suspect it may not really be very complicated, but unfortunately, that does not necessarily mean it will be easy to solve. Then, too, it promises to be quite... original, very different from anything I have done before. Who knows?" His smile was ironic. "Perhaps it will become one of my most celebrated adventures."

He put one hand over his mouth, stifling a yawn. "It has been a busy day, and I am ready to turn in. We must be up early to catch our train. It will be agreeable to breathe the fresh air of the countryside and be away from Rome for a day. There is a certain gloom and decay which hangs about this ancient city of ruins and monuments."

Chapter Two

Tuesday, we had a splendid day in nearby Tivoli, but Wednesday morning at nine, we stood before the Papal Palace in the Vatican. Soon we were following the Swiss Guards through the labyrinth of ornate corridors and stairways, this time to a more formal, more ornate, reception room. Dressed all in white, as before, the pope stood before a tall window, and at his side were two contrasting figures in black soutanes, one the short rotund Monsignor Arnone with his thick-lensed spectacles and wide reddish-purple sash round his belly.

The other man was tall, thin—gaunt, even, his cheeks sunken under high prominent cheekbones—and those features, along with his glaring black eyes, gave him the appearance of some haunted saint from an El Greco portrait. The bright red zucchetto above his high bald crown, as well as the red piping on his soutane and the red band cincture were emblems of his rank as cardinal. We had not yet met, but somehow our mere presence seemed to inflame him; anger smoldered in his eyes and stiffened his narrow mouth and thin lips.

Holmes and I bowed and shook hands with the pope. He nodded toward the tall man. *"Messieurs,* this is Cardinal Cicogno. He is head of the Congregation of Rites, one of the administrative departments in the Roman Curia, the governing body of the Church. Among his many duties is the care and authentication of relics."

Holmes bowed formally and murmured, *"Eminenza."* Again, I followed his lead.

The pope gestured with his long fingers. "This is Monsieur Sherlock Holmes, of whom we have been speaking, and his companion is…" He stopped and gave me a questioning look.

"Vernier," I said. "Dr. Henry Vernier."

"Thank you, Dr. Vernier. My memory for names is not what it used to be. Cardinal Cicogno and I were just discussing the theft of the relics."

Cicogno shook his head savagely. "The theft of holy relics is the most blasphemous and sacrilegious of crimes." His dark eyebrows had scrunched together over his long, curiously twisted nose.

The pope sighed. "As the guardian of holy objects, the cardinal is most upset—as are we all. And he is correct: this is a very grave matter." He set his hand lightly on the cardinal's arm. "Carlo, we shall discuss this further later."

"As you wish." As Cicogno spoke, he seemed to snap ferociously at the very air. His eyes shifted again to Holmes and me. "I do not particularly approve of nonbelievers meddling in the affairs of the Church, especially since diabolical influences may well be at work."

"As I said, Carlo, we shall speak of this later." The pope did not raise his voice, but his authoritative tone made it clear who was in charge.

The cardinal bowed slightly, then turned and strode across the multi-colored marble floor toward the tall oaken doors. One of the guards opened a door for him, then closed it behind him.

The pope gave us an apologetic smile. "Cardinal Cicogno is distraught. Given the uncertain political situation with the Italian government, he has been worried about the relics in Rome for many years, and now his worst fears seem to be coming true." He glanced at the monsignor. "Would you fetch Monsignor Greene and send him in? And have the guards wait outside."

"*Certo, Santo Padre.*" Arnone nodded to us. "*Arrivederci, signori.*" He headed for the door, and soon we were left alone with the pope.

He gave a weary sigh. "Monsieur Holmes, I thank you for rearranging your schedule to assist us in our investigation of this crime. If anyone can restore the missing relic, it is you."

"Thank you, Saint Père. I shall do my best, but you must not expect too much from me. My time is, unfortunately, limited, and I am not, after all, a miracle worker." A flicker of a smile came and went. "That would be more in your department than mine."

The pope took a white envelope from a nearby desk and offered it to Holmes. "I have prepared the letter I spoke of before. It states that you are acting on my behalf and that all those of the Catholic faith should help you in any way possible."

Holmes took the envelope and slipped it into the inside pocket of his frock coat. "Thank you. I am certain it will prove useful."

The far doors opened, and we turned to see another monsignor approaching in his black cassock and reddish-purple sash. Like Arnone, he was on the heavy side, but instead of the dark olive skin and brown eyes of a southern Italian, Greene had pale skin and the ruddy cheeks so typically English. His eyes were a vivid blue, and his hair—what remained of it—was a sandy reddish-brown. He extended a plump freckled hand, his smile both enthusiastic and genuine.

"I am Monsignor Richard Greene." He shook Holmes's hand eagerly. "You are, of course, Sherlock Holmes." Next it was my turn. His grip was impressive. "And you must be the mysterious and little-known Dr. Vernier." He gave me a mock serious frown. "It must be difficult always living in Watson's shadow."

"You don't know the half of it!" I exclaimed.

He smiled, then turned, knelt before the pope and kissed his ring. He switched from English to perfect French: "Holy Father, I thank you again for your trust. I know this is a serious business, but all the same, for me it is the chance of lifetime—to actually work with Sherlock Holmes! I could never have imagined such an opportunity."

The pope nodded. "You were the obvious choice, Monsignor." He turned to us. "And now, *messieurs*, other duties require my time. I shall leave you in Monsignor Greene's good hands. He has a full report on the theft and can either assist you directly or contact any necessary parties. However, before we part, let me give you my blessing."

Holmes, Greene, and I knelt. The pope raised his thin graceful right hand. "Heavenly Father, bless these men and their undertaking. Watch over them, protect them from harm, and help them to bring the holy relic of your Apostle Thomas back to your Church." He made a vertical and horizontal pass in the shape of a cross. "*In nomine Patris et Filii et Spiritus Sancti.*"

We stood, bowed slightly, then backed toward the doorway, turning at last to follow Monsignor Greene. He opened the big doors for us, waited, then stepped out and closed them. The two tall Swiss Guards were standing on either side. He smiled at them. "*Guten Tag meine Herren.*"

The taller one with a blond beard smiled back. "*Salve, Monsignore.*"

Greene started down the corridor. "I have an office here in the palace on the first floor. After I make a brief stop, we can go directly to Santa Croce and see Monsignor Nardone. He's expecting us. I assumed you would want to start at the scene of the crime."

"Exactly," Holmes replied.

Greene abruptly stopped walking, and we did the same. He gave us a quick smile, then grasped us each by the arm. "Come, gentlemen—the game's afoot!" I laughed, and Holmes gave him a brief sardonic smile. He let go of our arms. "I've always wanted to say that." We resumed our walk through the wide marble hallway.

Greene took us into his small, cluttered office to fetch his hat, the so-called *saturno* favored by practical priests in Rome. Black felt, with a rounded crown, a sort of half sphere, it had a brim about three-inches wide. Its name came from its resemblance to the ringed planet. When we stepped out into the sunlight, he placed it firmly over his thinning hair. Even with the local headgear, he still looked quite obviously English rather than Italian.

As we rode in a four-wheeled carriage across the Tiber and into Rome proper, we talked with the monsignor. He had indeed been in Rome for nearly thirty years, having arrived in the early 1860s when Pius IX was still pope, and he could remember when the Italians had marched into Rome and taken over the city in 1870. While he was happy to actually converse in English, he told us he had long ago begun to think in Italian and Latin, and now he had to search for certain words in English.

The cab soon came to a stop, and we stepped out onto the square before the church. Greene smiled at us. "Lovely day, isn't it? Are you weary of being tourists, or would you like me to act as guide while we proceed? I know the basilica quite well."

"Please do," Holmes said. "We have not visited Santa Croce before."

Greene pointed at a tall, ancient wall of red-orange brick. "That's one of the best-preserved sections of Roman wall, and beyond it lies the remains of an amphitheater. Supposedly, in the fourth century, the Roman palace of Saint Helena stood here at the very site of the church. She had returned from the Holy Land with her relics of the crucifixion and some actual soil from Jerusalem. She built a chapel to hold the precious objects, and over time it became the church of Santa Croce in Gerusalemme. It is 'in Jerusalem' and not 'of Jerusalem,' because of that soil. The old square bell tower of brown brick in back there, was constructed in the twelfth century, the clock added on in the eighteenth. Pope Benedict also had the white marble facade with the four sculpted pillars constructed in the eighteenth century. Up top are the statues of various saints and angels. To the left is Saint Helena with a cross, and on the right with his laurel wreath and Roman armor is the Emperor Constantine."

Greene started forward, and we followed. "A monastery for Cistercian monks connects directly with the church on the right side. Since the church has no rectory, Monsignor Nardone has a room in the monastery and takes his meals with the monks. A cardinal priest is always assigned to basilicas and is titular head, but Nardone serves as pastor and says most of the daily and Sunday masses."

Greene used the brass knocker on the tall doors under a stone arch, and almost immediately the door swung inward. A tonsured monk stood before us in his robes of contrasting color: the habit was pale undyed wool, but a rectangular dark brown, almost black scapular hung down in front and in back, cinched at the waist by a rope.

"*Buon giorno, fratello,*" Greene said. "*Monsignor Nardone, ci aspetta.*"

The monk put his hands together as he bowed, then turned and walked into the shadowy interior.

Within a minute or two, a tall priest in the usual black cassock and monsignor's reddish-purple sash, approached us, a smile on his thin aristocratic face. He looked to be about forty, balding in front, his light brown hair swept back over his prominent ears. He had a certain precise, meticulous air about him.

"Ricardo," he said to Greene, and continued in Italian, "What a pleasure to see you. And this must be the famed Sherlock Holmes." He shook Holmes's hand, then mine, his grip brief and adequate, rather than firm and assertive. "And you are?"

"Vernier. Dr. Henry Vernier."

"I'm sorry I don't speak English, *signori*."

"We speak Italian," Holmes said in Italian, "and Monsignor Greene can help with any difficult vocabulary."

"Excellent! I hope you can help us, Signor Holmes. It is a sad day for all of the faithful when the beloved relics of the Apostles are not safe even in the middle of Rome. I suppose you will want to see the remaining relics?"

"Even so, Monsignor."

"It shall be my privilege to show them to you." He turned and led us to the doors of the basilica, then opened one to let us in.

We went through the vestibule into the church proper and continued toward the altar. The church had massive pillars along the nave on either side, and the floor between the pews showed a spectacular swirling circular pattern of dark and light marble in the Cosmatesque style. Holmes was between Nardone and Greene, the Italian speaking so softly I couldn't understand him. Even so, his voice echoed faintly overhead in that vast, dim enclosure. The church was mostly empty with less than a dozen people seated.

As we advanced, a soft incessant sound coalesced off ahead to my right where a woman and a man sat together. Given what I could see of a black garment covering his broad shoulders, as well as its narrow black collar, he looked to be a priest. She also wore black with the faint sheen of silk, and her hat and its plumes were equally somber. I could hear the gentle rumble of his baritone voice murmur something even as he set his hand on her shoulder, but if anything, the other sound grew louder. It was weeping. She was crying as if her heart were broken, with a certain fierce edge, probably from trying to mute the sound. I felt a twinge of pity and wondered what could have upset her so.

I lingered slightly behind my companions, turning briefly after we had passed the two. I saw the white notch of his Roman collar—a priest indeed, but his face was turned away from me. Her eyes caught mine for only an instant. Her lips tried to form a smile—or at least remain neutral—but instead twisted involuntarily as she lowered her eyes and sobbed anew. She had light brown hair and a pale, beautiful face—angelic, almost, or perhaps it was only this setting that made me think of angels. I walked more briskly to catch up with the others. Someone so young shouldn't be so unhappy, I thought.

We all genuflected before the elaborate baldaquin which rose before the altar. It had pillars about fifteen feet high, marble with veins of various colors running through them, and on top was some elaborate bronze sculpture. Monsignor Nardone turned right and led us through an arch and down a long sloping passageway with broad steps. We came out in a small chapel all ablaze with the light of many thick candles. Set into one wall in an arched opening was a life-size statue of a woman holding an actual wooden cross taller than her, and above the arch was a circular window providing light. But dominating the room was a glass case at the far side, which contained five elaborate reliquaries. In some pews, several pilgrims were on their knees praying. One man in a black suit lay prostrate upon the floor before the case, his arms outstretched to form a cross of his own.

A short robust man with a huge black mustache stood next to the relics, one hand resting just over the other. He was wearing a worn black suit and a white shirt. Obviously, he was a guard for the relics. He looked bored.

Nardone led us forward, his voice hushed. "The relic of San Tommaso was there on the top shelf, alongside two reliquaries containing a fragment of the scouring pillar and two thorns from the crown of thorns. In the middle shelf are the fragments of the true cross, and on the bottom are the *titulus* and one of the nails hammered into our Savior's flesh."

Each relic was encased in ornamented creations of gold and silver, but the cross was obviously the main attraction. Its reliquary was over twice as tall as the others. An elaborate cross rose above a golden box, while two silver angels holding spears stood on either side of the base of the cross. Holmes took a quick look, then stepped toward an object I knew he must find more interesting: a large, sturdy gray padlock which secured the wooden door and its thick glass plate to the wooden frame.

Holmes bent to examine the lock, twisting it to get the light from the nearby candles onto the back. "Facchelli. Obviously in Italy one would use an Italian lock, but I'm not familiar with the manufacturer."

Nardone smiled enthusiastically. "I chose the lock myself. I am Milanese, and Facchelli has their factory in Milan. They are the best."

Holmes turned it slightly in his hand. "I can see that you didn't scrimp. The lock is obviously well made. It also does not appear to have been tampered with."

"It was not. I tested it: it opens and closes normally."

"Are the relics ever taken out of this case?"

"Yes, for certain special occasions."

"When was the last time you had opened the case there?"

"For Easter Mass, only a little over a week ago. We had the fragment of the cross on display under the baldaquin during the high Mass."

"And where do you keep the key?"

Nardone looked about suspiciously at the people seated nearby. "One cannot be too careful." He leaned over and whispered something into Holmes's ear. He straightened and said, very softly, "You must be a tall person to reach it."

"And who knows about its hiding place besides you?"

"Cardinal Indovino. He is in charge of Santa Croce."

"Have you no assistant pastors assigned here?"

"No, the church is not a regular parish. Technically I am a rector and not a pastor. However, occasionally young priests from the nearby theological college are assigned to assist me with the masses."

"Who would that be, most recently?"

"Fathers Silva and Blackwell. You must meet Father Blackwell. He is English, too."

"Is he now? And is he tall?"

Nardone had been smiling, but he suddenly appeared grave. "Yes, but he is an exemplary priest. He would never be involved in any crime, especially a sacrilegious one."

"And Father Silva—is he tall?"

"No. To the contrary."

"Did either of them help you say Mass on Easter?"

"Actually, the cardinal officiated on that most special of all feast days. I assisted him—along with Fathers Blackwell and Silva."

Holmes nodded. "Interesting. I shall want to meet them both."

"Would you like me to show you the actual location of the key?"

"In a moment, please." Holmes took a step back, dropped his top hat onto the seat of a pew, then folded his arms and began to slowly scrutinize the chapel; his eyes swept back and forth like those of some great bird of prey soaring high above a field and searching for game.

I sighed and folded my own arms. I knew this could take a while. Monsignor Greene leaned over and took my arm. "Do you see the statue of Helena there?"

"She's rather a formidable dame, quite robust. With those flowing robes she does look quite Roman."

Greene smiled. "She should—she was originally Juno. The old Roman statue was repurposed to become a saint."

I smiled. "Nothing of ancient Rome ever seems to go to waste around here."

Holmes was still peering about, and I found the chapel stuffy. The many candles seemed to take all the oxygen out of the room. An old woman in black was also moaning in rather melodramatic ecstasy before the relics.

"I think I'll have a look around the church proper," I said to Greene. "I'll join you a little later."

He nodded. "I shall stay with Mr. Holmes in case he needs something translated for Monsignor Nardone."

Holmes's eyes flickered ever so briefly as I turned away and started back up the passageway.

I came out near the altar and stared out at the interior of the church, the pews all in shadow. The priest and the young woman were still sitting together toward the middle. I couldn't hear her crying, but that might just be because I was too far away. I stepped nearer the altar and its baldaquin. Over it was a domed ceiling, and around the top was a painting of the Holy Land and deserts; in the center a female saint hovered within a bright blue circle, probably Saint Helena again. She was certainly everywhere in the basilica.

I sighed softly. As a skeptic, I found all these elaborate churches of Rome with their statues, marble, and gilt faintly depressing. To me, they were monuments without meaning. Then, too, I was already starting to have a sort of church fatigue: you could only admire so many before they all began to blend together. And I found more of a sense of the presence of God out in nature—in mountains, woods, or the ocean—rather than in any human structure. I considered leaving the church and wandering about Rome on my own, but I could not abandon Holmes, even though this case seemed faintly nonsensical.

I scratched at my cheek and lowered my hand. There was a kind of thump, and a woman shrieked, "*Dio!*" even as a man cried out, "Anna!"

I quickly turned, then strode forward. The young woman had collapsed on the marble floor near the pews, and over her stood the priest, hands outspread. Because he had been seated, I had not realized quite how tall he was. He glanced briefly at me, his eyes desperate, then knelt down. An older woman in black made her way along a pew to join him. We all came together over the fallen figure in her black silk dress lying on that cold intricate marble floor.

The priest gently raised her head. "Anna," he murmured. He looked up at me. He was strikingly handsome: square-jawed, a cleft in his chin, black-haired but with brilliant blue eyes.

He didn't look very Italian, so I decided to try English with him. "I'm a doctor," I said. "Did she hit her head?"

"No, I don't think so. She just crumpled."

"*Lei è caduto,*" said the old woman. "*Posso aiutarvi?*"

"No, *grazie,*" I said. "*Sono un medico.*"

"*Poverissima,*" murmured the old woman sympathetically. "*E si bella.*" She shook her head, then stepped back into a nearby pew.

"Help me get her up," I said. The priest took one arm, I the other, and we lifted her up and got her onto the end of the pew. She weighed hardly anything. She moaned softly, her head lolling about. Her hat had tumbled off and was still lying on the floor, and a strand of her light brown hair had come loose and curved round her cheek. Her skin was pale. She was quite beautiful, but thin and wan. "Do you know why she might have fainted?" I asked the priest.

He gave a shrug, his mouth grim. He had sat down beside her and clung tightly to her arm. "I don't think she has eaten or slept for almost forty-eight hours."

"Good Heavens," I murmured. "Has she at least been drinking water?"

"I doubt it."

"Little wonder she fainted. What on earth was she thinking of?"

The priest gave me a reproachful look. "Her father died early yesterday morning. She has had a hard time of it."

I felt the shock of it myself. "Oh. Well, all the same…"

Her eyes suddenly opened. They were a deep dark brown that you wouldn't expect for someone with such fair skin and light hair. They were also extremely bloodshot, her eyelids reddish and swollen. "What has happened?" she murmured in English. She had a brown mole near the right corner of her small mouth with its full lips.

"You've had a faint," I said.

I saw understanding and despair come back into her eyes and face. "Oh God," she murmured. A weary tear seeped from her eye. "I just want to die."

The priest shook his head savagely. "You mustn't say that." He gave her arm a squeeze, then let go.

She stared at him. "I'm sorry."

"I'm a doctor," I said. "He told me you haven't eaten or slept for forty-eight hours. Is that true?"

She had to think about it. "I suppose so."

"And have you had anything to drink?"

She had to think about that, too. "Not that I can remember."

"He explained about…" I began, but stopped before saying, "your father." I didn't want to start her crying again. "You've had a difficult time, but you must take care of yourself. It won't do to make yourself ill. That won't help anything—it will only make you feel worse."

"Will it?"

"Yes." I looked down at the priest. "Before anything else, she needs to eat and drink a little something. Then she should go home and get some sleep."

"I won't ever sleep again," she said.

My mouth tightened. "Oh yes, you will."

I had a sudden idea and glanced again at the priest. "There must be wine for communion in the sanctuary—and unconsecrated hosts. It really would be a good idea to get some food and drink into her."

"I don't want to leave her when she is like this."

"I can watch her while you…"

"Edward, what has happened?" It was Monsignor Greene. He had come up behind me, along with Holmes and Monsignor Nardone.

"Signorina Antonelli fainted." The priest hesitated. "The count died yesterday morning."

Greene stiffened. "So, it has happened at last… May he rest in peace." He crossed himself, then glanced down at the girl. "Anna, I'm so sorry."

She gave a slight nod, her eyes going all liquid. I stared past Greene at Monsignor Nardone. "Monsignor, could you bring some of the unconsecrated sacramental wine and communion wafers? She has not eaten or had much to drink for two days. I'm afraid if she tries to go anywhere in her current condition she will just collapse again."

"Certainly." Nardone turned and strode back toward the altar.

A certain stubbornness showed in her eyes. "I don't want anything. I'm not hungry or thirsty."

"That doesn't matter. Consider it medicine."

She sighed and sat upright. "I think I feel better."

"And you'll feel still better after you eat and drink."

Greene touched her lightly on the shoulder. "Anna, be sensible, please."

She stared up at him, then slowly drew in her breath. "I shall try."

Holmes had been watching intently. He spoke to the priest. "Would you be Father Blackwell, by any chance?"

The man gazed at him. "I would. And how do you know my name?"

"Monsignor Nardone said he had an English priest assisting him named Blackwell."

Blackwell's smooth brow creased. "And who might you be?"

Greene smiled. "Ah, forgive me! Let me do the introductions. Father Edward Blackwell, this is Mr. Sherlock Holmes."

Blackwell stiffened, his lips parting ever so slightly, his eyes going curiously blank. "Sherlock Holmes?" he murmured in awe.

"You must have heard of him."

Blackwell nodded but did not speak.

"Edward has been in Rome for over a year, and we English priests have to stick together here amidst all these Italians! Besides, we have the same alma mater, the College of the Immaculate Conception at Spinkhill." Greene pointed in my direction with his chin. "And this is Mr. Holmes's traveling companion, Dr. Henry Vernier." Blackwell and I gave each other a nod.

"Gentlemen, this is Signorina Anna Antonelli. Her father was Count Tommaso Antonelli, patriarch of one of the oldest and noblest Roman families." He gave his head a regretful shake. "And also one of my oldest and dearest friends in Rome. I spent many a happy hour in his home, and I watched this beautiful young lady grow up."

The girl gave a pained laugh. Her eyes shifted to mine, and she managed a brief smile. "Thank you for helping me, Doctor."

"The pleasure was mine."

She drew in her breath and sat more upright. "I think I would like to go home now." She looked toward the distant altar, her eyes curiously vacant. "I am done here."

I was still standing beside her at the end of the pew. "Not just yet." I turned toward the altar and saw Nardone emerge from the back.

He strode toward us, a water glass in one hand, a folded napkin in the other. "Here we are," he said.

I took the glass from him. It was half full of red wine. "Drink some of this."

She took the glass and sipped at it. She took a bigger swallow, then sighed. Nardone gave me the napkin, which I unfolded to reveal a clump of the round white wafers used for communion. I reflected that I had swallowed many of these, but never actually held one. Only a priest could touch the consecrated host with his fingers. I gave her one. "Eat this."

She turned to Blackwell, who had let go of her arm. "Is it all right?"

"Certainly. They are unconsecrated—only lumps of bread."

She took one and chewed thoughtfully. "It's almost like a cracker." She took another. "I was always taught to swallow them at communion without chewing. They don't have much taste."

I laughed gently. "You can have something more flavorful later on. Take another swallow of wine." She did so, and I handed her more wafers. An odd smile suddenly twisted at her mouth. "What is it?" I asked.

"I never thought I'd have a sort of picnic in the basilica."

Greene laughed, but Father Blackwell was not amused.

"How is it," I asked, "that you speak English so well, Signorina Antonelli?"

"Oh, my mother was English, and I also went to school for many years in England." Her brief good spirits vanished. "She's dead, too."

"I'm a half-breed myself. My mother was English, my father French."

Her dark eyes stared at me, the black pupils enormous in the dim church. "Just like me, almost." She took another swallow of wine, then sighed. "I do feel better."

I nodded. "I knew you would once you ate and drank. Will you promise me to go home, eat something more substantial, and then go straight to bed?"

"I don't think I can sleep."

"Well, you can lie down and try. Perhaps I shall stop in later to check on you, and I can bring my medical bag along. If you are still awake, I can give you something."

She put her hand over her mouth to stifle a yawn. Now that she had eaten, drunk and unwound slightly, I could see just how exhausted she was. Shadows showed under her eyes, and her mouth drooped slightly.

I glanced at Blackwell. "She must have a cook or servant who could prepare some food for her."

"Yes, she does."

"Good." I wouldn't have trusted her in a restaurant, exhausted as she was. "Can you get her home, then, and…"

He gave a brusque nod. "I certainly can. And I shall see that she eats before I leave."

Her eyes widened slightly. "I don't want to be alone."

"I shall come back later," he said. "I must… I have let everything go for too long."

Her lips pursed. "Of course you have—you've done so much for me. Without you, I… Don't worry about me." She drew in her breath. "I think I will be all right now."

"I really would like to check on you myself," I said. "Where do you live?"

"Via San Antonio, *numero* 22. It is not far from here."

"Excellent. And Signor Holmes and I are staying at the Eden Hotel should you wish to contact us."

She looked at me, faintly puzzled. "You are so much nicer than Dr. Rancole."

Holmes had folded his arms, and he was staring at Blackwell. "And I shall want to speak to you soon, Father."

The priest sighed, his face tensing briefly, then relaxing. "Must you? I haven't been to the college in over a week, and there is—" his eyes shifted warily toward Anna "—there is a funeral to arrange."

Holmes said nothing, but Greene spoke. "Mr. Holmes is here at the invitation of the Holy Father himself. It concerns a very grave matter. He…"

Blackwell sighed. "The missing relic, I suppose. That's obvious enough."

"Yes, so you see why you must see him as soon as possible."

While Anna had finally seemed to relax, the priest still seemed prey to some fierce energy. "I shall try to–I shall try to arrange a time. I shall send you a note at the Eden, Mr. Holmes."

"Thank you, Father Blackwell. I am not exactly sure how urgent it really is. Get some rest yourself before you come to see me."

Greene looked confused. "Not urgent–what do you mean?"

Holmes shrugged his shoulders. "Sometimes cases take odd twists and turns."

Blackwell stood. "Are you ready, then, Signorina Antonelli?"

"Yes."

"Finish your wine first," I said.

She drank it down, then handed me the glass. She stared past me at Monsignor Nardone. "Thank you for your generosity, Monsignor."

"Not at all, child! I am happy to see you looking so much better. And I know you are in good hands with Father Blackwell."

She nodded mechanically, and for the first time some color showed in her cheeks. She stood up and set one hand on the pew. Father Blackwell and I were both ready to catch her if necessary, but she seemed steady on her feet. I bent down, then handed her her hat.

"Thank you." She smoothed back a strand of hair, then put on the black hat with its wide brim and swooping plumes. She stepped out into the aisle, and Blackwell followed. She touched my arm lightly. "Thank you again, Dr. Vernier."

"I'm glad I could have been of help."

Blackwell's mouth pulled taut as he smiled at me, then he turned and followed her toward the entrance.

"Quite a bit of excitement for one day," Greene said. "Poor

girl. It must have been very difficult. Her father had some wasting disease, probably a cancer, and he was in a great deal of pain. Even the morphine didn't seem to do much for him any longer."

I frowned. "I wonder if they were giving him an adequate dose. One cannot scrimp in such cases, especially if the outcome is in little doubt."

Monsignor Nardone raised his long, graceful hand. "God's mercy and grace are more powerful than any human medicine."

I said nothing, although I did not agree.

Holmes was frowning slightly. "Was the count very devout? Would his faith have carried him through?"

"Certainly!" Nardone exclaimed. He seemed appalled that Holmes would even ask such a question.

Greene, on the other hand, looked rather grave. Holmes had noticed his expression. "Monsignor?"

"Father Blackwell attended the count in his final illness. I did call upon him a few times, and... he did have his doubts. I can only hope that they were resolved in his final hours."

"What happened to the girl's mother?" I asked.

Greene shook his head. "So many afflictions in such a short time! I saw the three of them a little over a year ago—it was, in fact, when I introduced Father Blackwell to them. They seemed the very picture of happiness and health. Shortly afterwards, the countess was killed in a freak carriage accident while they were vacationing in the south. Anna and the count were devastated."

"She has indeed had a hard time of it," I said. "And does she have any other family to help console her?"

"Only an aunt or two in England. Her father was the last of his family. Anna's sister and brother died in their youth, and the count's parents are gone."

Nardone looked somewhat impatient. "Would you still like to see the key, Signor Holmes?"

"Yes, thank you."

We started toward the altar, genuflected, then went to the right and through a door into the small sanctuary room. Monsignor Nardone turned and raised one hand sternly. "Dr. Vernier, Monsignor Greene, I must ask you to wait outside. It is not that I mistrust you, but this is a secret known only to me and the cardinal."

Monsignor Greene smiled. "Certainly. I understand." He turned and went back through the door.

I was about to join him, but Holmes grasped my arm. "Monsignor Nardone, if you are going to trust me, you must trust Dr. Vernier. We are working on this case together, and he has my utmost confidence."

Nardone drew in his breath slowly and stared at me. "And you swear to tell no one?"

"Of course."

"Very well." He looked at Holmes. "I suspect you know where to find it."

"Yes."

Holmes walked over to the tall antique armoire. Dark walnut, with six sculpted doors, it was a beautiful piece of furniture. One door was open, and we could see vestments hanging inside. Its top was very elaborate, flaring outward in layers, but in the center the wood had an elegant rising arch, in which were sculpted some flowery ornamentation and a shield with a cross on it. Holmes went to the middle, rose on his toes, and felt around behind the arch. He soon withdrew a key, then lowered his arm and turned the key to look at the round end.

"F for Facchelli, I presume."

"Exactly so. You must admit that it a good hiding place. To an outsider, the key might be anywhere in the basilica. They would be more likely to suspect it was somewhere in the chapel itself and not so far away."

Holmes stroked his chin. "I suppose that is so. You did say you had tried the key and it functioned normally? Very good." He stood up on his toes once more to put the key back where he had found it.

"Someone would have to be tall indeed," I said.

Holmes smiled and pointed at a chair next to a small table. "Or they might simply stand on a chair. Concerning the location of the key, would Fathers Silva and Blackwell have known it was somewhere here in the sacristy?"

Nardone actually scowled. "Must you pursue this ridiculous line of inquiry? Both of them are good and faithful priests. They would never steal a precious relic."

Holmes shrugged. "Perhaps not, but could you please answer my question? Did you ever ask them to remain outside while you fetched the key?"

"No, I did not. That would have been far too obvious."

"All the same, might they have noticed you come out of the sacristy with the key in hand?"

Nardone still appeared very stern. "It is possible."

Holmes nodded. "Thank you, Monsignor. I think we are finished here."

We went back into the church, then to the baldaquin where we all genuflected. Monsignor Greene had joined us. We turned and started for the far doors. Again, I examined the elaborate circular design of the floor made up of small inlaid pieces of different colored marble. We went through the doors into the great domed area which served as vestibule for the basilica. Standing there was the black-bearded Cistercian monk from the monastery in his dark and light-colored garments, and beside him was a short man in a blue uniform and cap holding a big package wrapped in brown paper.

The monk pointed at Monsignor Nardone. "That is the monsignor," he said.

"*Grazie*," the man said, then stepped forward. "A package for you, Monsignor. You must sign for it." He had a heavy accent of some kind, and I could hardly understand his Italian.

"Can't this wait?" Nardone asked.

"This was to be delivered to you alone and signed in acknowledgment."

"Oh, very well."

Nardone took first the package, then a piece of paper which he set upon the box. He took the pencil offered and scrawled his signature on the bottom. The man took the paper and tore off half to give the priest. "*Grazie mille.*" He turned and left through the entrance doors.

Nardone's mouth formed a downward curve, and then he held the package forward, offering it to the monk. "Could you take this, *fratello*? I'll see to it later when I have finished with my guests."

The monk took the package, but Holmes stepped forward and raised his hand. "Wait. Were you expecting a package, Monsignor?"

"No, not that I know of."

Holmes smiled faintly. "I think I would like to see the contents of this particular package."

Chapter Three

T he monk departed the vestibule for the for the monastery. Holmes set the package on a small table, then took out a penknife, cut open the brown paper and pulled it open. Next, he cut a strip of sealing tape holding the two flaps together. Stepping back, he folded the blade and put it away. "Have a look, Monsignor."

Nardone appeared faintly puzzled. The contents of the box were hidden in crumpled newspaper. He thrust in his hands, felt around, then withdrew a metal object, scattering paper all about. "God be praised!" he exclaimed.

He held up what must be the missing reliquary. Made of gold and silver, it had a base and a thin stem like that of a goblet, then a metal circle covered with glass on both sides that was surrounded by a sort of silver halo in a woven leaf pattern. Between the glass circles was a fixed silver object shaped vaguely like a finger with long slots along the sides. Through the slots you could see a loose, single grayish white fragment which must be bone. The whole thing appeared grotesque to me.

"The saints preserve us," Greene muttered.

Nardone clutched the reliquary to his chest, clearly unwilling to have it leave his grasp, and dug about in the box with his other hand, pulling out crumpled newspaper. Finally the box was empty. "I thought there might be a note of explanation." He gave a deep sigh. "Regardless, some sinner must have repented of his sacrilegious theft."

Holmes nodded. "That is likely."

Greene stared curiously at him. "You don't seem particularly surprised."

"No."

I shook my head. "Well, I am surprised! I wonder... From a more cynical perspective, perhaps the person discovered there was no great market for a stolen reliquary. Well, regardless of the motive, all's well that ends well, as they say in English."

Nardone looked puzzled, but Greene translated the phrase for him.

"I suppose we'll never know who really stole it," I said.

Holmes lips formed a familiar sardonic smile, and I gave him an inquiring look.

Nardone held the reliquary tightly with both hands. "I shall get the key and put it back in the case immediately. I cannot rest until I know it is safe in its customary place."

Holmes's dark brows came together. "I saw that you have a guard over the display case."

"Yes, and now we lock the church up at ten o'clock at night, and as an added precaution since the theft, we keep a guard there all night long in the chapel. We don't want any more precious relics to go missing."

Holmes nodded.

Greene smiled at us. "Well, I have somewhat mixed feelings. I am happy to see the relic restored so quickly, but I was looking forward to spending some time with you, Mr. Holmes, and you, Dr. Vernier. I was also looking forward to seeing Sherlock Holmes in action!"

"I am not disappointed to see the case resolved," Holmes said.

Greene was still smiling. "Who knows. Perhaps the thief got wind that Sherlock Holmes was on his trail and became so fearful, that he decided to return the reliquary."

"Well, I must get this under lock and key," Nardone said.

"And I think we shall be on our way," Holmes said. "We must return to the Vatican."

"You needn't trouble yourself," Greene said. "I can be the bearer of the good news. Although I am certain the pope will want to thank you for your efforts."

"Oh, we shall come along. The reliquary may have been restored, but there are still some… trifling details which need resolving in my mind. A visit with Cardinal Cicogno might be helpful."

Greene gave him a bewildered look. "A curious choice—a visit to the dragon's lair! If you wish."

"Perhaps we might fortify ourselves with some lunch first."

Greene smiled. "A good idea. A visit with Cardinal Cicogno is not something one does unfortified."

Holmes bowed toward Nardone. "It has been a pleasure, Monsignor."

Nardone seemed reluctant to let go of the reliquary, but he did shake Holmes's hand and then mine. "I am glad to have met you, Signor Holmes, but I am happier still that your services were, in the end, not needed."

Holmes shrugged faintly. "Let's hope so."

* * *

A young priest ushered us into Cardinal Cicogno's large office. The cardinal rose from behind a well-worn mahogany desk and approached us. Monsignor Greene genuflected, then kissed his ring. Holmes and I bowed slightly.

"We are the bearers of good news, Eminence," Greene said. "The relic of Saint Thomas has been returned to us."

Cicogno's thin lips parted, even as the well-worn creases deepened in his high broad forehead below the red zucchetto. "Is this true?"

"I would not jest about such a thing."

Cicogno quickly crossed himself. "Thanks be to God." He actually smiled, his dour face briefly transformed. He glanced at Holmes. "Perhaps I was wrong to discourage your efforts on our behalf."

"I cannot take the credit, Eminence. The reliquary arrived in a box sent through the post while we were visiting Monsignor Nardone."

"Was there a note or any kind of acknowledgment?"

"None," Greene said.

Cicogno stroked his chin with his long, elegant fingers. "How curious. Still, this is a great relief." His smile wavered, then vanished as he sighed. "However, no sacred objects are ever truly safe in this wretched city." He glanced at a nearby table. "Would you care to sit for a moment?"

"I did have a few questions," Holmes said.

The cardinal sat first, and we took the other chairs round the circular table. Holmes set his elbows on the chair arms and placed the tips of his fingers together. "Some Anglicans believe that Roman Catholics worship relics in blatant idolatry; however…"

Cicogno's eyes burned. "That is nonsense—that is…"

Holmes raised one hand. "However, I was going to say, that is a misunderstanding, I believe. While Catholics may honor relics, the honor truly belongs to the saint, and ultimately to God alone."

Cicogno stared incredulously. "You know something of our theology, Signor Holmes—more than some ignorant Catholics. While certain of the faithful mistakenly pray to saints begging for favors or ask magical cures of relics, true Catholics know that saints and relics are only intercessors with our Savior. While some cures may be associated with relics, it is not the objects themselves which have restorative power, but only the Supreme Being Himself. Saints and relics cannot perform miracles: only God can perform them. Prayers to the saints or homage to relics should always be with that understanding. Otherwise, it verges on idolatry, a grave sin and often a form of unintentional heresy."

"Still, I presume holy relics are associated with miracles, even though they may not be the actual cause?"

Cicogno nodded. "Exactly so. In fact, generally for holy relics, there must be documented examples of miraculous cures or resurrections. For example, Saint Helena was said to have recognized the true cross in the Holy Land because it raised someone from the dead." He stopped suddenly, one side of his mouth curving upward. "There—see, I made the same elementary error! I said *it* raised someone from the dead. The relic did not raise someone from the dead—God did."

I reflected that such theorizing and all these types of fine quibbles were one of the main reasons I had drifted away from the Catholic Church.

Holmes was tapping his fingers together. "All the same, according to doctrine, the relics do somehow make it more likely that God will answer the prayers of the faithful?"

Cicogno briefly mulled the question. "Yes, I suppose that is true."

"These are all rather subtle distinctions," I said.

Cicogno glanced sternly at me. "Human existence and the mysteries of life and death are not simple."

Holmes smiled. "I think we can all agree on that."

Greene also smiled. "Amen to that!" He had been listening with a sort of fixed pleasant look, rather mechanical somehow, his hands clasped together. As only a lowly monsignor, I suspected he did not want any trouble with the cardinal. Then, too, Cicogno was clearly imperious and short-tempered.

"There is something I am curious about," Holmes said. "What might the penalty be for a priest who committed the sacrilegious act of stealing a holy relic?"

Cicogno's face darkened. "It would be grave indeed. I would surely be involved, and I would demand the maximum penalty. Are you familiar with the concept of canonical *degradatio*, to use the Latin term?"

Greene's pleasant expression vanished.

"Is that degradation?" Holmes asked. We had been speaking Italian, and he used the word *degradazione*.

"Even so."

Holmes shook his head. "I am not."

"The term is also used in the army when an officer is officially stripped of his rank and privileges for some grave misconduct. And as with the military, there is a formal ceremony, a sort of Holy Orders in reverse, wherein the miscreant is dismissed from the priesthood along with all its powers and benefits, and he is also literally stripped of the vestments of his office. At the end, he is turned over to the civilian authorities for prosecution of his crimes."

Greene looked shocked. "That would be the maximum penalty indeed."

Holmes tapped the chair arm lightly with his fingers. "But what if the priest took the relic because... oh, say, he wished to somehow protect it?"

The color faded slightly from Cicogno's face. "Obviously that would be a different matter altogether."

"Protect it from what?" I asked.

Cicogno stared at me as if I were some sort of imbecile. "From all the forces of evil and stupidity which abound in the world around us!"

"The pope mentioned your concern about the relics in Rome," Holmes said.

Cicogno set both hands flat on the table and leaned forward. "We in the Vatican are under siege, surrounded by hostile powers. The so-called Italian state and the unbelievers who comprise its ranks—they have stolen our lands, our churches, our schools—they would take everything! The Vatican hangs by a thread. At any moment they could march in and claim all that remains—including Saint Peter's itself—for themselves. The pope would truly become their prisoner. I have pleaded with the Holy Father... The Holy See need not remain in Rome. We should move someplace we are not surrounded by enemies." His voice had risen, but he let out a sigh. "If such a place exists."

"And does it?" Holmes asked.

"I believe so. France, Germany, and Italy are lost, beset by heretic rulers and crazed parliaments. All three nations have declared virtual war against our faith. However, Franz Joseph, the emperor of Austria-Hungary, is a true son of the Church. I also have great hopes for Spain. Its regent Maria Christina is devout, and her young son, the future Alfonso XIII, shows great promise."

I shook my head in disbelief. "You would actually have the entire Church pack up from Rome and leave for... for Austria?"

"Of course not! Not everyone. Some would need to stay to administer to the faithful who remain and to care for the many historic churches. But the governing bodies and the pope, *yes*. The Holy Father has considered it. Regardless, even if we do remain here, then the most precious relics such as those at Santa Croce in Gerusalemme should be sent somewhere safe. This latest theft has shown, once and for all, how perilous Rome is."

Holmes nodded thoughtfully. "But the Holy Father, I take it, does not agree?"

Cicogno inhaled slowly. "I shall try once more to persuade him. At the very least, we might lock the relics up in some secure hiding place."

"But then the faithful would be deprived of their beneficent influence," Greene said warily.

"Which would also occur if they were stolen! No, far better they are out of harm's way. They could always be brought forth again should the wretched Italian government and its evil king collapse, and better days arrive." He shook his head. "But I am not hopeful. We live in a wicked time. People have moved away from their traditions of faith and devotion. They deny all authority. Instead, they promote the tyranny of the people, and rather than God, they worship notions of progress and science."

I hesitated, thinking I should know better. "There have been genuine advances in medicine. Anesthetics like ether and chloroform, as well as the practice of antisepsis, have transformed the art of surgery."

Cicogno stared contemptuously at me. "But that has done nothing for the care of the soul. No, no, more has been lost in our times than has been gained. The old verities—faith, respect...

"Let me give you one extraordinary example. A little over a

decade ago, the body of our departed pope, the blessed and beloved Holy Father Pius IX was being moved from Saint Peter's to a more fitting final resting place at another church, La Basilica Papale di San Lorenzo fuori le Mura. When the cortege approached the Tiber, it was confronted by a screaming Roman mob cursing the Church and shouting, 'Long live Italy!' and, 'Death to the priests!' Only the arrival of a militia stopped them. They actually wanted to throw the pope and his coffin into the river! Who can imagine a greater sacrilege than that? Such wickedness is hard to fathom. Truly that mob was made of savage beasts, not of men. And these are the people who surround us here in Rome! Can you blame me for wanting to leave?—and for wanting to secure all our precious relics from the great mob of unbelievers?"

"I see your point indeed, Eminence." Holmes drew his watch from his waistcoat pocket. "This has been most interesting, but we do not wish to take up too much of your valuable time."

"I do have another appointment this afternoon." Cicogno rose, and we did the same. "You are more... sensible than I had imagined, Signor Holmes. Perhaps involving you in this matter was not such a bad idea after all. We do appreciate your help in trying to resolve this gravest of crimes."

Holmes's mouth formed a brief playful smile, and he gave a quick nod. "*Mille grazie, Eminenza.*"

The cardinal followed us to the doors, but let us open them. Just outside, the young priest was waiting with another man. Not very tall and with thinning hair on top, perhaps by way of compensation the gentleman had grown one of the largest black mustaches I had ever seen, its curling waxed ends extending out past his cheeks two inches on either side. In Rome I had noticed photos of the Italian king Umberto with his own giant mustache;

this gentleman must wish to rival or acknowledge his sovereign. He was exquisitely dressed and held a gray Homburg in his gray-gloved hands.

"*Il barone, Eminenza,*" the priest said.

The baron dropped down on one knee to kiss the cardinal's ring. "*Eminenza.*" He rose, then greeted Greene. "*Monsignore.*" He glanced at Holmes and me.

"These are two Englishmen who wished to assist us with the search for the missing relic—which—" Cicogno again actually smiled "—has been found, Giuseppe!"

The baron quickly crossed himself. "Praise be to God Almighty! And do we have the culprit in chains as well?"

Cicogno's visage grew somber again. "No. His identity is still unknown, but he must have repented and decided to return the reliquary. It does not completely free his soul from the burden of so grave a sin, but it is a start." He turned to us. "Monsignor Greene, you know the baron. Mr. Holmes, Dr. Vernier, this is Baron Giuseppe Marullo. His is an old and distinguished family of Naples which has always faithfully served the Church. Not for him republics and atheist kings!"

Marullo gave his head a fierce shake. "No, indeed!" He sighed. "I still remember as a boy when good Ferdinand was king, before that devil Garibaldi came and bewitched our people. It was a sad day for Naples when the Kingdom of Italy was born."

"And a sad one for the Church as well," agreed Cicogno.

The baron squinted at us. "English, you say? But I suppose you must be Roman Catholics?"

Holmes smiled faintly, gave me a quick side glance, then said, "I'm afraid not."

The baron turned to the cardinal. "I don't understand."

"Mr. Holmes is a famous detective from London. He has recently assisted the Holy See in another matter, and the Holy Father thought he might be able to find the relic. However, thankfully his services are no longer required."

"Thankfully indeed." He made a slight smile which was mostly lost in mustache. "Perhaps someday you English will come around again to the true faith."

Holmes was still smiling. "Perhaps."

The cardinal nodded at us. "*Addio, signori.*"

I suspected his use of *addio* was not accidental; it was much more final than the usual *arrivederci,* which meant "see you again."

"Good day, then," Marullo said. He followed the cardinal into his office.

Soon we were walking down one of the vast elaborately decorated hallways. Monsignor Greene half turned his head back in the direction we had come, then gave a great sigh and smiled. "I must admit I am generally happier *after* a meeting with Cardinal Cicogno than before."

We had a few brief words with the pope, who was pleased indeed that the relic had reappeared, then we left the Papal Palace. Monsignor Greene told us how sad he would be to leave us so soon and offered to act as our guide for what remained of the day. We were glad to take him up on his offer. We walked to the historic Castel Sant'Angelo, then strolled along the bank of the Tiber. The late afternoon sun glinted yellow all along the water, dazzling our eyes, and many boats and barges passed by. One was obviously a tour boat with well-dressed passengers lining the railing, and two small children waved eagerly at us. Smiling, I waved back.

We decided to return to the far side of Rome so I could check on Signorina Antonelli, and since that was near Santa Croce, Holmes suggested a quick stop there for a last look at the restored relic. Greene eagerly told us of his favorite restaurant in that same neighborhood and suggested we have dinner there. With our plans made, we took a carriage over one of the bridges on the Tiber and headed east.

Baron Haussmann had transformed Paris, opening up the city with grand boulevards, and someday Rome might undergo a similar transformation. For now, however, it is difficult making one's way through the narrow, crowded streets of the city center, especially so late in the day. We had to wait at one point while two loaded wagons pulled by draft horses tried to get past one another. However, every so often the narrow street would open up into some sprawling piazza with a fountain or an obelisk, and nearby, a tall church. We also passed that famed remnant of ancient Rome, the Forum, with some worn splotched pillars still standing and jumbled marble blocks strewn upon the barren turf. Looking about, you could generally tell the difference between the fashionably dressed tourists and pilgrims, and the locals in their rough-cut plain clothing.

We stepped out at last onto the cobbled street before a great square building three stories high, its exterior an orange-tan stucco, the tall windows set at regularly spaced intervals. A small balcony protruded over the towering paneled double doors, and on either side were stone columns.

Monsignor Greene examined the facade. "Palazzo Antonelli was built in the seventeenth century, I believe. It's a bit worn now, but still quite something." He went forward, hesitated, then rapped lightly with the bronze door knocker. "I hope Anna is asleep in her bedroom, and we won't wake her."

The door soon swung open, revealing a thin, stooped man with white hair billowing about his large ears, a great white mustache and long wispy goatee. He wore a formal dark blue morning coat with two rows of gold buttons, a purple velvet waistcoat, spotless white linen, and gloves. He smiled at Greene. "Ah, Monsignor, welcome. Enter, enter!"

We stepped into an enormous vestibule, nearly as large as my sitting room at home. High overhead were painted angels and heroic naked figures, and the floor was an intricate pattern of colored marble squares.

"Is Signorina Antonelli available," Greene asked, "or is she sleeping? We absolutely do not wish to wake her."

"She is still asleep, I believe. The poor girl was exhausted." The servant's face became very grave. "The count... It was very difficult."

"Well, we will come back another time and see how she is doing."

"Did she eat something before she slept?" I asked.

The servant gave me a curious look. "This is Dr. Vernier," Greene said. "He was attending to your mistress."

"She and the good father did eat something before they slept."

Greene gave him a slightly startled look, and the servant quickly said. "She is in her room, of course, but Father Blackwell fell asleep on the sofa. We did not have the heart to disturb him. We..."

A tall figure in black stepped slowly forward from the nearby doorway. Father Blackwell's eyes were only half open, his dark hair tousled, one lock hanging in a black comma almost to his eyes. "What time is it?" He looked incredibly groggy, and his cassock was rumpled.

Holmes looked at his watch. "Five of six," he said.

Blackwell shook his head, blinked twice. "Good heavens. I fell asleep around one, just after lunch—I should have been gone long ago. I have so much to do."

Greene touched him lightly on the shoulder. "I'm sure the rest did you good. I'll wager you had little more sleep than Anna the last few days."

Blackwell nodded. "You would win that bet. I had better get back to my lodgings. The other priests will wonder what has happened to me."

Greene raised his hand abruptly. "Oh, it almost slipped my mind—the lost relic has been found!"

Blackwell's mouth twitched. "Has it?"

"Yes. Someone boxed it up and sent it back to the church."

Blackwell sighed. "Well, that's a relief." His eye shifted toward Holmes. "In that case… do you still need to see me, Mr. Holmes?"

"Yes, I do. I have some questions about Santa Croce you may be able to help me with."

"Monsignor Nardone certainly knows far more about the church than me."

"We shall see."

Blackwell slowly drew in his breath. He had a broad, massive-looking chest. "Very well, if you insist. Perhaps tomorrow in the late afternoon I might have a few minutes. You were staying at the Eden? I could meet you there at, say, five in the afternoon."

"Very good. We shall be expecting you."

Blackwell lowered his blue eyes. He still didn't look quite awake, but his tightly compressed lips showed a certain tension. "I must be going." He nodded at the servant. "Good day, Francesco."

He took a step forward, but the old man grasped his arm tightly. *"Grazie padre—grazie per tutto."*

"I only wish I could have done more." Blackwell drew in his breath slowly and glanced at Greene. "Richard, the funeral will be the day after tomorrow, Friday morning around ten at the little church down the street, San Giovanni."

Greene nodded. "I shall be there, Edward."

Blackwell's gaze was faintly troubled. "Good day, gentlemen."

"We were just leaving, too," the monsignor said.

"I'm afraid I must almost literally run." Blackwell turned, slipped through the door, and was gone.

We said good day to the aged butler, then stepped out onto the street. The church wasn't far so we decided to walk. Greene knew his way through the maze of narrow twisting streets, but after a couple of turns, I had completely lost any sense of direction. We came out into the piazza before Santa Croce and were immediately beset by beggars: a hunched and crippled old crone all in black, a one-legged man with a wooden crutch, and a plethora of thin, barefoot children. Most had tin cups, and their differently pitched voices joined in a cacophonous din of Italian.

Greene quickly strolled by them, paying no attention to the children nipping—so to speak—at our heels. His black *saturno* hid most of his balding crown, but his eyes beneath its brim were regretful. "I've learned to mostly ignore them, God help me. There is no way to give all the poor of Rome the charity they need."

We went through the domed entry portal, then through another set of doors into the basilica proper. I again admired the beautifully designed marble floors along the center of the nave. We turned right to take the passageway down to the chapel of Saint Helena.

Its candles cast a feeble flickering light compared with that coming from the arched window above the statue of Saint Helena. At this hour, only two women were seated in the pews, but standing near the glass case with the relics was a giant of a man. He appeared twice the size of the guard who had been there in the morning. His black jacket barely spanned his barrel chest, his white collar was sunken into his great neck, and he had a wooden truncheon like that of a British bobby strapped to his side. His black hair was curly, and of course he had the usual Italianate mustache, one of a size which matched the rest of him. He gave us a curt nod.

We went to the case. The relic of Saint Thomas was back on the top shelf alongside the thorns and nails from the crucifixion. Briefly, I was struck by an odd sense of absurdity. Certainly, the French rationalist skeptical outlook in me had triumphed over naïve religious piety. Putting ancient nails and thorns in these gaudy reliquaries of gold and silver seemed ridiculous, and it made the objects–despite what the cardinal had said–practically beg for worship!

Holmes stood before the glass, his thin hands behind his back, holding both his stick and his top hat. His brow was furrowed, his gaze intense, and I wondered if he was reflecting much the same thing as I. However, I could not break the silence of the chapel or make a mockery of Greene's faith by asking Holmes directly.

At last Holmes turned to the guard. "Are you here all night, *signore*?" Holmes asked in Italian.

The guard looked slightly puzzled, then nodded. His somewhat hoarse whispery reply was a rushed liquid flow, of which the only word I recognized was *notte*: "night." Holmes looked at me, and I saw that he hadn't understood either.

Greene smiled. "That is Calabrian dialect. We had a cook who was Calabrian, and she taught me some of it. He said he is indeed here all night."

Greene said something to the guard, which made him look grave. As he replied, he lifted both hands, then raised and lowered them twice for emphasis, his sausage-like fingers parted slightly. Finally he patted the club at his side with his right hand.

Greene clapped the guard on his upper arm. "*Si bravu cristiano!*"
He turned to us. "He says no one is going to take any relics while
he is on duty."

I gave my head a shake. "I believe him."

Holmes's lips flickered in and out of a brief, humorless smile.
He was staring again at the relics. "I wonder... The cardinal made
a fairly compelling case for his fears."

Greene shook his head. "I don't think it's quite as bad as he
thinks. It's only a crazy few who want to throw dead popes into the
river. Most Italians still believe in God and the Church, even when
they don't come to Mass every Sunday. Catholicism is in their
blood. If the Church were willing to go half way with the Italian
government..." He shrugged. "Someday a pope will come along
who is willing to be a spiritual ruler alone, and not a temporal one.
There will be an agreement."

Holmes smiled. "You should perhaps be a diplomat, Monsignor,
rather than a priest."

"No, thank you, Mr. Holmes! Let me say a brief prayer—devotion,
after all, must take precedence over appetite—and then we shall be
on our way to the restaurant."

Greene sat in the front row of the pews, put his hat next
to him, then clasped his hands together and bowed his head.
Holmes and I stepped away from the relics and went over to the
statue of Saint Helena. Holmes glanced overhead. "Those are
rather spectacular mosaics."

Christ in a blue robe framed by an ornate oval was in the center,
and four saints were similarly framed in ovals. Blue, and especially
gold, were the predominant colors in the ceiling. "I didn't even
notice them last time." I lowered my gaze, then glanced again at
Greene. His face showed an unaccustomed seriousness.

I looked about again, then sighed. I was tired of churches and chapels—and especially of relics like that odd little fragment of gray-white bone encased in that glittering monstrosity of a container. I held up my hand and examined my index finger. At least back home in England, I should be safe: no one would dig up my bones and put pieces of them in trophy cases! I lowered my hand.

"Thinking your finger is, after all, safe?" Holmes murmured.

I jerked my head toward him. "You have taken up mind-reading!"

"Oh Henry, it was obvious enough. You were staring at your finger, your gaze contemplative." He held up his own hand, raising his slender finger and twisting it slightly. "I too am rather fond of these old digits. I would not want this one to end up in a reliquary." He lowered his hand. "I wonder who the poor man was whose fingerbone ended up in there? The rest of him must be dust by now. How ironic: that one tiny piece of him which remains must be more famous and well known than ever he was in his life." Again, his lips flickered upward. "A strange sort of immortality."

I felt that restlessness and uncertainty and fear that came whenever I contemplated my own mortality for too long. "Let's wait for the monsignor upstairs. I'm tired of this chapel."

"A good idea, Henry." However, he paused at the entranceway for a last look back. "I hope this is our last visit for a long time." He sounded faintly doubtful.

"I suppose the thief might strike again."

He shook his head. "No, not that one, at any rate."

I stared intently at him. "Can you...? You sound as if you knew who the thief was."

"Oh yes, Henry. I think I do."

"But how possibly...?"

His eyes had an odd distant look. "Some things are only too obvious."

"Who, then?"

"Wait another day, and you shall have your answer, I think. Be patient, Henry. At least there are no corpses yet." His smile vanished. "I mustn't joke about such things—it is bad luck."

"Now you believe in luck?"

"You are not the only one to be affected by these relics. There is a certain melancholy aura which encompasses them, at least for skeptics like us." He looked about and found some wood in the door frame, which he rapped with his knuckles. "Knock on wood." He stepped past me, and I followed him up the sloping passageway.

Monsignor Greene with his plump ruddy cheeks, his blue eyes, his sandy-colored hair shot with gray and parted on the right side to cover a balding spot, his matching bushy eyebrows, and his slightly pudgy hands spotted with freckles, might appear the quintessential Englishman, but he ate spaghetti with all the skill of a native Italian. He wrapped several red-drenched strands skillfully round the fork, then put the whole thing in his mouth, chewed briefly and swallowed. His eyes showed his innate good humor, and indeed a well-cooked plate of spaghetti did seem one of the simple joys of life. He raised his glass and sipped at the red wine.

"*Eccellente,*" he said with gusto.

Holmes also took a large mouthful of spaghetti, doing so with his usual grace and elegance. "This is very good. I have not had this spaghetti *all'amatriciana* before. Is there bacon in it?"

"Very good, Mr. Holmes! It is smoked *guanciale* from the cheek of the pig. *Amatriciana* is, like so much of the Italian cuisine found in Rome, a simple peasant dish, in this case from the town of Amatrice to the northwest. There is much of England that I miss, but one cannot deny the general superiority of Italian cooking. I definitely do not miss steak and kidney pie or jellied eels."

I made a mock shudder. "Some of us who live there also do not miss them!"

Greene swirled his wine glass slightly, then sipped again. "What I do lack is the company of genial Englishmen like yourselves! English priests are still a rarity in Rome. There are intermittent visitors, but few long-term residents like myself. Oh, there is an Irishman that works for the cardinal secretary of state, but he hardly counts! I know the languages well enough to socialize with the French, Italians, Spanish, and Germans, but there is still nothing like conversing in one's mother tongue with fellow countrymen. That is one reason Edward and I have become such good friends."

"When you first arrived, did you ever imagine you would stay in Rome for thirty years?" Holmes asked.

"Not at all! I came to study theology one autumn when I was only twenty-seven, and somehow I never left."

"Somewhat like Father Blackwell, I suppose?"

Greene's eyes showed a faint wariness, even as he smiled. "I must confess that even in my prime I was no young Adonis like Edward." He hesitated. "Such handsomeness can be something of a burden for a young priest. All the same, he is a very worthy and devout young man." His look was almost reproachful.

"I do not doubt it," Holmes said. "And do you think he will stay on for thirty years?"

"No. He wants to be a simple parish priest back home, not an odd jack of all trades like me."

I had finished my spaghetti, and I dabbed at my mouth with my napkin. "What exactly do you do, Monsignor?"

"Whatever the Holy Father tells me! Seriously, though, I am a sort of... investigator, and problem solver. I suppose my work is not unlike yours, Mr. Holmes. When certain difficulties arise, he sends me off to have a look, then to report back and advise him. I just had a stay of a month in Vienna."

Holmes nodded. "I see. And do you think a red hat may lie in your future?"

"The saints preserve us!" Greene downed his glass of wine, then shook his head again.

I was surprised. "You don't want a promotion?"

"Not in the least. It has been broached in the past, but I have made it clear that purple is enough for me. I never was partial to red. It does not really go with my pinkish complexion."

I laughed at this. Greene raised the wine bottle and poured more into my glass, Holmes's, and finally his own. "We must have another bottle, I think, for the *secondi piatti*. You will not regret ordering the veal *scallopini*. It is exquisite here. A *vino bianco* would be best, perhaps a *pino grigio*."

Holmes smiled. "We are in your very good hands, Monsignor."

"I am certainly glad..." I began, but hesitated.

"Out with it," Greene said.

"Well, I am glad you are not an ascetic, some fanatic who has no use for the earthly pleasures of fine dining."

"Ah." Greene set both hands before him on the tablecloth; the small red buttons of his cassock made a neat vertical row down his chest. "You have noticed my one weakness. I am hardly a Saint Francis—more a Friar Tuck, I fear!"

Again, I laughed.

"In the past, I tried fasting on occasion, but it only seemed to fuel an already unhealthy obsession with food. I do try not to let my appetite get the best of me, but it is difficult in Rome. I hope to retire to England in a few years, and there will certainly be fewer near occasions of sin there."

Holmes looked thoughtfully at him. "So you would really leave Rome?"

Greene gave a brusque nod. "Oh, yes."

"And why exactly is that?"

Greene's brow furrowed, his lips clamping together. He did not speak for a few seconds. "It would be better for my soul if I returned home. Living in Rome, being at the center of things, being always around cardinals and bishops and seeing how they treat one another, all the scheming and struggling..." He sighed. "Let us just say that it is not always an edifying spectacle. Men of God do not always behave like men of God. If one is not careful... one begins to doubt. I have to remind myself that all those people I knew at our little village church, the poor farmers or shopkeepers, were just as much Catholics as all these men in Rome who wear purple or red."

"I understand you perfectly," said Holmes. "In my profession I have dealt with the entire span of human society from highest to the lowest. However, the most corrupt always seemed to dwell amidst the upper classes."

"We do understand one another," Greene said. He hesitated.

"What is it?" Holmes asked.

"Promise me one thing: promise that you will be gentle with Edward. He is very young. And very innocent–shockingly innocent."

Holmes nodded. "I promise."

I eyed the monsignor thoughtfully. "Weren't you equally innocent at his age?"

Greene sighed. "No, I was not. The difference is that I grew up in a poor family, not a wealthy one. The poor know more about the unsavory side of life, about bad tempers and cruelty, about all the little infidelities which surround us. The children of the rich can grow up in a make-believe world where evil barely exists. But enough of this—we are becoming serious, grim even—which is forbidden at a meal like this!" The waiter arrived with three steaming plates which smelled wonderful and set them before us. "*Un'altra bottiglia, cameriere,*" Greene said, "*qualche vino bianco di buon gusto, per favore.*"

Upon my plate, amidst the small slices of browned meat, were pieces of lemon, tiny green capers, and sliced mushrooms. The waiter soon returned with a bottle of wine, quickly broke the seal, and pulled the cork. Another waiter came with three new glasses, which he set before us, even as the first waiter poured out the wine. It was a pale yellow.

When we had all been served, Greene raised his glass. "To England, gentlemen, and especially to its most celebrated detective! Your very good health."

We all clinked glasses, then sipped the wine. It was cold and delicious.

Chapter Four

After our meal, we lingered at the table awhile sampling Italian *digestivi*, various strong-tasting liqueurs which were supposed to aid digestion. One was a clear sharp liquid with a liquorish-like base of fennel, while another, *concerto*, was dark brown, very complex, and almost chocolatey, a mix tasting of many spices.

We agreed to spend much of the next day again with Monsignor Greene. Indeed, he was at our hotel first thing in the morning on Thursday, to join us for breakfast, and since the restaurant catered to English travelers, he was delighted to discover he could order bacon and eggs instead of the usual meager Italian fare. He had brought along a Roman newspaper with a headline about the relic being found. The article mentioned the valuable assistance of *il investigatore illustre inglese*, the illustrious detective Sherlock Holmes.

Holmes shrugged. "I suppose I should not complain about getting credit even when it is not deserved. It is good for business, after all."

After eating, we headed off for the other side of the Tiber and the Trastevere district which was south of the Vatican. Monsignor

Greene had been eager to show us more churches or, possibly, the Roman catacombs, but I had seen enough gilded altars, swooning saints, and fat cherubs! I wanted to be out of doors if the good weather held, which it did. We wandered for a long while in a botanical garden, making our way gradually uphill to a spot which had a spectacular view of the city and the dome of Saint Peter's. We descended and visited a *mercato*, the local market set up along the narrow streets where boisterous vendors sold fruit, vegetables, and nearly every variety of trinket imaginable. I had learned not to try to bargain with the Romans; I was putty in their hands.

By then we had worked up an appetite for lunch, and of course, the monsignor knew of the perfect restaurant nearby! At the market, we had admired huge globes of fresh artichokes heaped in crates, their leaves colored a spectacular purple and green, so Greene ordered side dishes of baked *carciofi alla Romana*. He also recommended another local Roman specialty dish, *tonnarelli con cacio e pepe*, a sort of square-shaped spaghetti with flavorful *pecorino romano* cheese and black pepper. It was delicious, but I reflected that if I continued to eat like this every day, I too would end up as plump as Greene. We walked about the district after lunch, and around four, the monsignor left us to return to the Vatican.

Before parting, his face below the brim of the black *saturno* showed an unaccustomed gravity. "Is it really necessary that you see Father Blackwell, Holmes? I could keep you occupied, and I am sure he would not be disappointed if you skipped your appointment."

Holmes slowly drew in his breath. "I need to speak with him, Monsignor."

Greene shrugged. "As you wish." He turned to go, then turned back to us. "Remember what I said—he is an innocent. As a matter of doctrine, it is arguable whether one can be *too* innocent, but as a practical matter in dealing with the world, that can greatly complicate things. *Arrivederci*, then, and I shall see you tomorrow."

We found a carriage to take us back across the river and through town to our hotel. Somewhat worn out from all the fresh air and walking, I half-dozed during the ride. Holmes was mostly silent, his slender face staring gravely out the window at the streets of Rome. We arrived well before five, and I yawned as we walked into the main lobby.

"I am half tempted to take a nap. Must I be there when you speak with the priest?"

Holmes gave a curt nod. "Yes, your presence may be helpful."

I fought off another yawn. "Very well, as you wish."

Holmes and I had a suite on the top floor of the Eden with a well-furnished sitting room, and promptly at five came a rap at our door. Holmes walked over to open it.

Father Blackwell stepped into the room. His brow was furrowed, his mouth taut. He nodded at me. Alongside Holmes, it was clear that indeed he had an inch or two of height on my cousin. As usual he wore a plain black cassock. His black hair was slightly tousled, and I reflected that his handsome looks—that square jaw, well-defined cheekbones and hazy blue eyes—must prove distracting to some female worshipers, especially the younger ones. I wondered briefly if Signorina Antonelli was immune to his charms, then realized that would be the last thing the poor girl was thinking about during her father's final illness.

Holmes gestured at a velvet armchair with an elaborate pattern of red and gold. "Please have a seat."

Blackwell stared gravely at him, as if this was the oddest suggestion he had ever heard and one which demanded deep reflection. At last he sat, but leaning slightly forward in the chair, his forearms poised on its arms, as if ready to spring up at any moment.

Holmes sat on the other end of the sofa from me. "Thank you for coming, Father."

"You're welcome." Blackwell's eyes were fixed on him, his expression still grim.

Holmes stared back. "I think you know why I wanted to see you."

Blackwell opened his mouth, then closed it, even as he brusquely shook his head.

"Come, come, Father. We needn't play games. I promise I mean you no harm."

I frowned at Holmes, wondering what harm Blackwell could possibly fear from us.

Blackwell hesitated, then lowered his gaze. "I had hoped that your reputation might be exaggerated. What is it...? Why do you want to see me?"

"To discuss the theft of the relic and clear up a few details. You took it, didn't you?"

Blackwell caught his breath, appearing grimmer still, and in his face, you could see the reflection of a brief inner struggle. "Yes."

I sat up very straight. "What! Why ever would you do such a thing?"

Blackwell smiled bitterly. "Mr. Holmes?"

"Oh, Henry, isn't that rather obvious? They hoped for a miracle cure. Given the count's name, it may have seemed almost divinely preordained."

"You are talking about Count Antonelli?" I asked. "I don't see the connection."

"No, Henry, not his surname, but his first name–Tommaso, the Italian for Thomas. Would San Tommaso not come to the aid of his namesake?"

A brief smile pulled at Blackwell's mouth. "I see your reputation is not exaggerated in the least."

"You may have hoped for a cure, but if not a cure, at least… Perhaps the count's religious faith wavered with the approach of death. He had not only the saint's name but his temperament: he was also a doubting Thomas."

"Very good, Mr. Holmes. Very good indeed."

"You hoped the relic might give him some spiritual consolation."

"Yes."

"Did it?"

Blackwell gave a great sigh, his blue eyes suddenly tormented. "No. Not in the least. To the contrary…" He swallowed, then sagged back into the chair. "We were so certain. We had prayed together for a long while, and Anna had totally convinced herself that it would work. I went to the basilica in the middle of the night. The key to the case was not difficult to find. I knew it was somewhere in the sanctuary, most likely somewhere high up. Monsignor Nardone is not skilled at subterfuge.

"Anna and I took the reliquary to the count in his bedroom. He was so gaunt and pale, hardly the man I knew. And unshaven—I don't remember when he had last shaved. I had wrapped it up, and she triumphantly pulled away the towel to reveal the reliquary. He stared at it a long while without speaking. We hoped for the best, but soon it became apparent… At last he told us to get it away from him. Somehow it frightened him. He could not really shout, but his voice was hoarse and strained. And then, he whispered…"

Holmes waited a few seconds. "What did he whisper?"

"'This is what I will soon become. Bones.'" Blackwell put his hand on his forehead. "There could be no greater punishment for my sin."

"Sin?" I asked.

He let his hand drop and nodded. "I knew it was wrong, deep

inside I always knew it was wrong, but I managed to convince myself... It was pride, it was spiritual arrogance, it was..."

"It was because you wanted to help him," Holmes said. "He was suffering, and you wanted to help him."

"All the same, I am a priest. I should have known better. Relics are not magical. I of all people should have known that. We could have prayed to Saint Thomas even without the relic. In retrospect, that would have been better—he would not have been so frightened. And the fear seemed to stay with him, to hover always at his side."

Holmes regarded him closely. "I suspect you also did it for her."

Blackwell clutched at the chair arms with his big brawny hands. "She had nothing to do with it! The fault is mine—all mine! I should have tried to discourage her. I should have told her—I should have *insisted*—that it was the wrong thing to do. I see that now."

An odd variation of Holmes's sardonic smile briefly pulled at his lips. "It was worth a try."

Blackwell shook his head again. "No, it was not! And now I must pay for my crime."

Holmes stared at him. "I told you I meant you no harm. Your secret is safe with me."

"I have committed a serious crime, and I must suffer the consequences. I shall go to the Vatican constabulary—I shall go this very day!—confess everything and accept my punishment." His voice had risen in a dramatic crescendo.

I had a sudden memory of Cardinal Cicogno's face flushed with righteous anger. "You cannot do such a thing!"

"I must," Blackwell said.

Holmes sat back in the sofa. "That would be most unwise, Father Blackwell. I think you—and the lady—have suffered enough."

"She will not suffer! I will make it clear that it was all my idea, that I and I only am responsible. How ever?–why ever?–would they want to punish her? No, no, I alone stole the relic, and I alone shall pay the price."

"And do you know what the price is likely to be?"

"I… perhaps they will simply turn me over to the Roman police. I am willing to spend time in prison if that is their judgment."

"Are you familiar with the term *degradatio*, Father? Cardinal Cicogno was telling us what would happen to a priest if one was involved in the theft, and of course the cardinal is the ultimate authority over matters involving saints and relics."

Blackwell's lips parted perhaps half an inch, his face going pale. "He said that? *Degradatio*?"

"You Catholics do not use the term 'defrocking,' I believe, but that is what degradation amounts to. Do you really think that is what you deserve?"

Blackwell seemed unable to speak.

"Perhaps you made a mistake, but that is no reason to ruin your life and abandon your vocation. You certainly never meant to keep the relic, did you? You always intended to return it?"

"Certainly! I…" A brief pained smile appeared. "We said–I said–I was only borrowing it. I tried to tell myself that borrowing it for a good cause was not sinful."

I gave a sharp nod. "And you were right! Don't be ridiculous. You may have made a mistake, but this was no terrible sin."

Blackwell bit briefly at his lower lip.

"I would tend to concur with Henry's appraisal, Father. Confess everything to Monsignor Greene and let him absolve you. Then consider the matter closed and put it all behind you."

"You… you tempt me."

"With all that has happened in the last few days," Holmes said, "I doubt that you can think clearly just now. Don't do anything rash or foolhardy. Greene seems a sensible man. I suspect he, too, has figured this all out, and you can go to him for advice. But first you must get some rest, see to the funeral of the count, and above all, you must not torment yourself. What is done is done. After all, no one was harmed in any way by the theft. Oh, several people were greatly consternated, but they will get over it—as will you. Get on with your life and be done with it."

Blackwell's face sagged, and then an enormous yawn contorted his face, even as his hand rose to cover his mouth. "I am so tired. Could it really be so simple?"

"Sherlock is absolutely right," I said.

His brow was furrowed. "But is it... is it really the *right* thing to do? I don't know if..." His face contorted into a smile. "Are you a good angel offering consolation, or a bad one merely tempting me?"

Holmes smiled. "I am hardly any sort of angel. I am only human. But while I may not be traditionally religious, I do have a strong moral sense. It is imperative in my profession if one is to survive without being corrupted. In this case, I assure you, not pursuing the matter with the authorities is surely the right thing to do."

I could see in the priest's face that he was still struggling. "As I said, Sherlock is right—leave well enough alone. I suppose, too, that you haven't been eating or sleeping normally?"

Again he fought with a yawn. "No. I thought I knew what I must do—turn myself in, but I was... I was afraid." His eyes showed a kind of dumb vacant misery.

"Well now that you know what you really must do—which is definitely *not* throwing yourself before the tender mercies of Cardinal Cicogno—you need no longer be afraid. You need to eat a good dinner and get a good night's sleep before you do anything else. I'm a doctor, remember, and that is my official advice. Will you follow it?"

"I have so much to do. I've neglected my studies, and there is the funeral tomorrow."

"Well, another day or two won't make much difference in your studies, and the best thing you can do to prepare for the funeral is get a good rest tonight—all right?"

The fearful energy driving him had visibly faded, and now he looked absolutely exhausted. "I suppose you're right."

Holmes nodded. "Indeed he is, Father Blackwell. I second all that he has said. Moreover… it is not in the least helpful to consider what you did a crime. Believe me—I know all about crime. I have seen its every variety and manifestation from the petty to the horrendous. Borrowing the relic, as you put it, does not really qualify, especially since you so promptly returned it when you were done with it."

Blackwell ran his hand through his black curly hair. "I don't know what to think."

"Then don't think!" I exclaimed. "Do as I tell you. Eat something and then go straight to bed. You can always torment yourself tomorrow should you so desire."

Holmes smiled at this, and even Blackwell looked briefly amused. "All right." He sighed. "Are you done with me, then?"

"Not quite," Holmes said, even as he stood. "I think we could all use a brandy."

"I don't generally take strong spirits," Blackwell said.

"Well, in this case," I said, "consider it doctor's orders."

Holmes had gone to the sideboard and poured from an elaborate cut-glass carafe. He brought Blackwell and me a glass, then returned for his own, which he raised. "To… to 'let bygones be bygones,' gentlemen."

I nodded, sipped, and felt the liquid warm its way down. Blackwell hesitated, then finally took a drink. "It's very good," he said.

Holmes swirled his glass slightly. "Indeed it is." He sat back down. We were all briefly quiet.

Holmes took another sip. "Monsignor Greene said you had both attended the same preparatory school, I believe, one near Sheffield."

"Yes, the College of the Immaculate Conception at Spinkhill."

"And what seminary did you attend?"

"Allen Hall in London."

"Ah yes, I have often passed by there."

We were all silent again sipping at our brandy. Finally I asked a rather obvious question. "And did you always know you wanted to be a priest?"

He stared at me with those deep blue eyes. "Yes, I suppose so." His mouth briefly twitched upward. "I never had any doubts. Back then."

"You must come from a religious family."

"My mother was very devout. She always encouraged my vocation."

"How old were you when you went off to the Immaculate Conception school?"

"Twelve."

I shook my head. "It seems very young."

Blackwell shrugged, but said nothing. He drank more of the brandy. "Everything went so smoothly for years and years. I was always a good student, especially with languages. Not perhaps as good as Richard–Monsignor Greene–but close. And then…" He was staring blankly into space. "I wish I had never come to Rome."

I was frowning. "But you have done nothing wrong."

"Haven't I?" he murmured.

"I thought you understood that taking the relic was not some terrible sin."

His eyes shifted at last to mine. "Yes, I suppose I do, but…" He inhaled slowly through his nostrils. "There are other… troubles."

"What troubles?"

He stared at me, a certain haughtiness appearing in his expression. "They are not your affair."

"As you wish." I was annoyed, but tried not to show it.

He was still staring at me. "Are you married, Doctor?"

I hesitated before answering. This must be a tit-for-tat sort of thing. "Yes."

"And you, Mr. Holmes?"

"No, I am a seasoned bachelor." He shifted his gaze to me. "The fair sex remains a mystery to me. Henry is the expert on all matters concerning them."

"Hardly," I said.

Blackwell gazed curiously at me, then looked down at the brandy. He raised his glass and downed the last of it. "Can I go now?"

Holmes set down his glass and stood. "Certainly you may." He walked over to the priest, who had also risen, and extended his slender hand.

Blackwell stared at him, then his own larger hand swallowed up Holmes's. "Thank you, Mr. Holmes." Blackwell also shook my hand. "And you, Dr. Vernier. Also, I haven't thanked you properly for helping Signorina Antonelli at the church when she fainted. I was alarmed, and I didn't know what to do."

"I'm glad I could be of assistance. I hope she is feeling better. I plan on visiting her later today."

"She is much better, but…"

"But what?"

He drew in his breath. "She knew I was coming to see you, and that has her worried. I didn't exactly tell her I meant to turn myself in, but I think she suspects as much."

"Well, that is one less worry for her, then," I said.

"Yes." He swallowed. "I... I did so dread this meeting, but now... Again, thank you both!" He turned and strode resolutely to the door, closing it behind him after he had stepped outside.

I glanced at Holmes. "So when exactly did you figure everything out?"

"Things don't often come to me in a flash, but this was the exception. We had already heard that the girl's father had died the day before, and when Greene introduced us and mentioned that her father was named Tommaso Antonelli, I had virtually all of it at once. Any doubts were resolved when the reliquary arrived via the post. With the count dead, I knew it would no longer be of any use."

I shook my head. "I'm the Catholic—or raised as one, anyway— and yet you are the one who figured it out so quickly."

He shrugged. "Evidently miraculous relics are not to your taste."

"Poor things! To go to all that trouble, and to have the relic not only not work in any beneficial way, but instead, to actually frighten the poor man! Life can play cruel tricks on us."

"Indeed it can, Henry. However, people's sensibilities differ dramatically. You saw the man yesterday prostrating himself before the relics, while both you and I found that small gray piece of bone in its ostentatious reliquary repulsive."

I sat back down and took another swallow of brandy. Holmes also sat and drank the last of his. He drew his watch from the pocket in his waistcoat. "Barely six. Too early for dinner, especially by Italian standards. Normally I'd suggest a stroll, but we have already walked a great deal today."

I covered my mouth as I yawned. "That nap I considered earlier is still a possibility, although it's getting rather late to nap. All the same..." A rather feeble rap sounded at our door. "Who could that be? I wonder if Father Blackwell forgot something."

"I shall see." Holmes stood, walked over, and opened the door. "Ah," he murmured. "Come in, *signorina.*"

Anna Antonelli stepped into the room. I quickly rose to my feet. A red flush simmered in each cheek, and she held her head high and upright on her long thin neck. She was again dressed in mourning—she wore another stunning black silk dress, one with an elaborate damask pattern, and even her hat had a black plume. The dress made the pallor of her skin, other than her cheeks, stand out, and again I was struck by the contrast between her fair skin and light-brown hair and those dark brown eyes with the black pupils.

"He was here, wasn't he?"

Holmes nodded. "Yes."

"I waited until he had left, but I made sure he didn't see me." She reached out to touch Holmes's forearm with her fingertips. "Please—you must keep him from doing anything foolish. It is all my fault! I was the one who persuaded him to take the relic. He thought it was a bad idea from the start, but I would not let him alone. He mustn't suffer for my stupidity—*he mustn't.* If anyone is to be punished, it is me." Her eyes had taken on a liquid sheen. "I—I was half crazy—willing to do anything to save my father. I couldn't sleep, and I prayed and prayed, and it seemed to me that God had answered me—that Saint Thomas had answered me—and that there was a way. Oh, I was such a fool! Perhaps, perhaps, after all it was only the Devil... Yes, in retrospect, it must have been..."

I had risen, too, and alarmed by her mounting hysteria, I reached out and grabbed her arm just above the elbow, squeezing tightly; it felt thin and bony. "Don't be ridiculous—there's no need to bring the Devil into it!"

She gave me a curious look. "No?"

"No! Of course not. You were just worn out and grief-stricken."

Her eyebrows scrunched together. "That is when we are most vulnerable to the Devil."

"The two of you!" I exclaimed. "You seem determined to torture yourselves! Be sensible, for God's sake. Leave the Devil out of it—if you loved your father, of course you would be willing to try anything."

"All the same, I couldn't bear it if Father Blackwell were to suffer on my account. He mustn't…"

Holmes raised his hand. "*Signorina*, calm yourself. We have spoken with him, and I think he finally understands that what he did was not criminal, and that he need not turn himself into the authorities."

She drew in her breath, blinked once. "He does?"

"Yes. We convinced him that he has done nothing terribly wrong."

"Oh, thank God for that! And thank you, sir—thank you so much." Her eyes almost instantly overflowed with tears, and she swayed ominously.

My hand shot out to again grasp her arm above the elbow. "I think you need to sit down."

I steered her toward the red and yellow overstuffed chair, and she collapsed into it, her black skirts squishing and fluffing out. "*Grazie*," she murmured. "I do feel a little dizzy."

I went to the sideboard, poured out some brandy, then brought the glass to her.

"I don't care for brandy."

"Drink it anyway. Doctor's orders."

She pulled off her glove, revealing her long white fingers, then took the glass and cautiously sipped. Her dark eyes stared up at me. "It's not bad, after all." She took another sip.

"And what have you eaten today?"

She did not even have to think. "I ate yesterday afternoon before I fell asleep."

"It is customary to eat three meals a day."

"Father Blackwell came in the morning and told me he had an appointment to see you. I was... I was afraid for him. He said what a dreadful thing he had done and how he should have known better, and how now he must suffer the consequences."

Holmes shook his head. "We heard all of that."

"Anyway, it took away my appetite. I couldn't let him take all the blame. I asked him where he was meeting you and decided to try to see you after he left."

"Well, now that you know there is nothing to fear," I said, "you can eat again. Unfortunately, we do not have any communion wafers available here."

That made her actually smile, even though her eyes were still teary. "You are very droll, I see, Dr. Vernier." Her amusement was more than I thought I deserved, but I was glad to see the change.

"I think there is only one thing to be done." Holmes's voice was grave. "Have you any plans for this evening, *signorina*?"

She gave him an inquisitive glance. "No."

"Are no family members in town for your father's funeral?"

"No, there is no one. My father—like myself—was the only child in his family to survive into adulthood, and his parents are long since deceased. My mother was estranged from her mother and father. They did not approve of her marrying an Italian, and they too are dead. Only my one aunt remains, my mother's older sister.

We did send her a letter when my mother died, and she replied offering her formal condolences."

"Well then, perhaps you would join us for dinner. The hotel restaurant is quite good. That way we can have the pleasure of your company and also ensure that you eat a hearty meal."

She gave a long sigh. "Oh, I would be happy to join you! It will be nice... to have some company."

I nodded at Holmes. "An excellent idea. A pity we can't have Father Blackwell come along to dinner as well. He, too, could use a good meal."

"That would have been nice," Anna said rather forlornly.

Holmes had picked up my glass and his own. "More brandy, Henry?"

"Yes, just a splash."

He poured, then handed me my glass. We both sat on the sofa, and he raised his glass. "To your very good health, and to... better days."

"Oh thank you, sir." She raised her glass, then sipped at the brandy.

"As Henry noted yesterday, *signorina*, your English is certainly perfect. You speak it like a native."

She nodded. "It's as I said. My mother always spoke English with me so I would be bilingual, and then I went to a Catholic girls' school in England for four years."

"Where was that?" I asked.

"Near London–Saint Teresa's Academy, run by the sisters."

"I suppose your mother must have been a Catholic, too," I said.

"Yes. A convert." Her smile was bittersweet. "It was rather ironic. My father was raised a Catholic, but he was always rather lax, while my mother who had been a Protestant became the devout one."

Holmes tapped lightly at the sofa arm with the fingers of his left hand. "And which of them do you take after?"

"My mother. I suppose."

"But you are not sure?" I asked.

Her dark eyes regarded me gravely. "After all that has happened in the last year... I don't know what to think any longer."

I nodded. "Ah. That I understand."

She was still staring at me. "You said your father was French, your mother English. You too must have been raised as a Catholic."

"Yes, but in my case, as they say, it did not exactly stick."

"No?" This seemed to worry her.

"It's not that I would not like to believe. I am, in truth, a sort of agnostic Catholic."

She glanced at Holmes. "And you, Mr. Holmes?"

He smiled. "I am, in truth, a sort of agnostic Anglican."

She lowered her gaze. "I was so certain... once upon a time. There was an answer for every question... a grand edifice of towering marble pillars, golden domes and grandiose facades, a beautiful construction, a... theory, an explanation, of absolutely everything. But in the end, I'm afraid... it may all be a mirage." She wilted before our eyes.

Worried, I said, "Come now, I don't think it's as bad as all that. There are the hard times, but there are the good times as well. Someday I am certain you will meet someone and marry and..."

She shook her head. "Oh, I shall never marry."

"Why on earth not?" I asked.

A flush showed in her cheeks. "It is not my destiny. I had thought of becoming a sister like those at the school, but after all that has happened, I can no longer consider it, not now anyway."

I was frowning. "Good! That would be an utter waste." She gave me an incredulous look, and I felt my own face heat. "I'm sorry. I may be an agnostic in many things, but I do believe in marriage. My own marriage is the best part of my life, the one certainty in an uncertain world."

"What is your wife like?"

"She is a redhead, tall and beautiful, witty and intelligent. I am a very lucky man."

Holmes smiled. "I can vouch for all that he said."

"I wish I could meet her," she said.

"And so you shall, I promise. She arrives early next week."

She turned to Holmes. "And you, Mr. Holmes, are you married?"

"No, but as they say, hope springs eternal within the human breast. I have not yet abandoned all hope." I knew he must be thinking of Violet Wheelwright.

Again the fingers of his left hand drummed lightly at the sofa arm. "But you surprise me, miss. Has not some young man been interested in you?"

Her expression grew troubled as she stumbled for words. "Not… not exactly."

"What do you mean?" he asked.

"There have been some who pestered my father, but none of those appealed to me in the least. And…" she spoke more eagerly, "there was Giancarlo. We were madly in love when we were eight years old."

Holmes was still regarding her. "And these spiritual doubts of yours, have you discussed them with Father Blackwell?"

Her dark eyes opened wide in horror. "I could never do that!"

I gave my head a shake. "But I thought that was what priests were for—counseling the faithful during their times of trouble."

"I… I could never tell him how I feel. He is the noblest and finest of men. I can't imagine how I could have ever survived the last few months without him. He was always there when I needed him, and he was so kind to father. He would… he would be so disappointed in me. No, he is the last person I would ever talk to."

"Perhaps Monsignor Greene, then," Holmes said. "He seems an old friend of your family."

She seemed relieved. "Yes, perhaps so. He is indeed an old friend."

"Enough of this," I exclaimed. "All cares and woes must be set aside for an evening—you deserve a respite. You have had enough of sadness and despair. You must be happy this evening even if it kills you!"

She actually laughed. "I shall try, Dr. Vernier. For your sake, I shall try."

We did have a very agreeable dinner with Signorina Antonelli, and indeed, all unpleasantness was briefly set aside. She asked Holmes about some of his cases and wanted to know more about Michelle. As was generally the case, she was greatly surprised when I told her Michelle was a physician like myself. Lady doctors were unheard of in Italy.

Anna's beauty was not exactly the kind to turn men's heads, but when she smiled, when she became animated, there was something about the set of her mouth, those full lips along with the mole near the corner, and those dark eyes, that was very appealing. She might be small in stature, probably two or three inches over five feet, but she had a powerful kind of energy, a real dynamism, that added to that appeal.

When the waiter refilled all our wine glasses, she hesitantly took hers by the stem, raised it, and looking at me, asked if we might drink a toast to her father. "Or is that bringing up cares and woes?"

I told her that we could certainly drink to her father. We all clinked glasses, saluting the count, then sipped. "I wish you could have met him," she murmured as she sipped her wine.

I asked her what her favorite memories of her father were as a child. She thought for a moment, then laughed. There were two games that they had played intermittently for a long time: horse and tiger. When her father was the horse, he would get down on all fours and go about with her on his back. When he was the tiger, he became ferocious and would chase her growling and roaring. The only refuge from the savage beast was her bed or the sofa, and he would pace about roaring and snapping at her with his jaws.

She smiled as she spoke, but when she finished her eyes filled with tears. "I'm so glad he is at peace at last." She glanced at me. "Sorry, Dr. Vernier."

"That's quite all right," I said.

Holmes asked her how long her family had known Monsignor Greene. She told us her mother had met him when she first came to Rome and was studying to become a Catholic, some twenty-five years ago. As an English priest, he could help her learn both theology and the Italian language. Ever since then, he had been a friend and occasional visitor, often joining them for Sunday dinner. He and their cook Angelina were great friends.

"And Monsignor Greene introduced you to Father Blackwell, did he not?"

Something changed in her expression, and she took a big swallow of wine, flushing slightly, then smiled at us. She told us how Father Blackwell had also become a good friend and a frequent visitor. "My mother used to joke about him." Her smile wavered, then vanished. You could tell she regretted mentioning this detail.

"How so?" I asked.

She hesitated, "Well, she said it was a shame so handsome a man was a priest. Of course, she was only being facetious. The priesthood is a sacred calling, a true sacrament. She, of all people, understood that."

Father Blackwell had been a great comfort after her mother died and had become very close to her father. The two men had long conversations together while they walked through the streets of Rome. Having his wife suddenly snatched away from him had taken away the last remnants of the count's religious faith. She and the priest had occasionally talked about what might be done to help him. Sometimes they prayed together. Again Anna looked at me. "But we mustn't talk about that."

She told us about her time at school in England, how very strict the sisters had been. She had finished there about two years ago. "Which would make you about twenty," Holmes said. She nodded. She had gotten along well with her classmates, but her English best friend was married now, had a baby, and lived in London.

I noticed that Holmes was glancing past her, his dark brows coming together. Finally, he said, "Signorina Antonelli, do you know that young man at the table in the corner, the one with the rather fantastical mustache?"

She and I both turned. Indeed, there was no ignoring that mustache! The Italians certainly favored mustaches, but this one was extravagant even by their standards. He had a narrow face with gray eyes, his brown hair combed back to reveal his broad forehead, but the mustache completely hid his mouth. It looked to be about three inches long in front, the sides even longer, coming to great waxed points which curved upward and outward on either side of his face. Baron Marullo had an impressive mustache, but this one was even grander. Somehow, it didn't exactly fit the rest of his face.

He looked to be about twenty-five and was well dressed, but with a certain dandyish flair. His velvet jacket was a dark burgundy color, his cravat a navy blue with a pearl in the center. He stared calmly at us, then his gaze shifted to Anna, and he gave a polite nod.

She frowned, then gave a minuscule nod in return, even as her cheeks began to color. "I've never seen him in my life. I could not forget such a mustache."

Holmes was still frowning. "No, you could not—which may be the point."

"What do you mean?" I asked, but he only shrugged. I looked at the young man again. He was still staring at Anna, his male interest obvious enough. "Well, he certainly isn't very subtle. I think you have made a conquest, *signorina*."

"It's not my fault," she murmured with a shake of her head.

Our stout waiter appeared before us with a bottle in his hand. He set it on the table, then withdrew a corkscrew. Holmes gave him a puzzled look. "What's this?"

"A bottle of *Marsala vergine oro*, one of our very best sweet wines, with the compliments of the gentleman with the mustache." He nodded toward the corner table. "He thought you might enjoy it with dessert."

I scratched at my chin. "Why *vergine*?" The word was Italian for virgin.

"That just means it is aged several years, *signore*. At least five." He had the cork out and poured some into a clean glass. It was yellow-white, rather than the usual red of marsala. "Oro" was gold and must refer to the color. He hesitated, then offered the glass to Holmes to taste.

Anna's face was quite flushed, and she set her hand on Holmes's wrist. "Can't we send it back?"

The waiter recoiled in horror. "Oh no, *signorina*! It is open now, and it is wonderful! You will see."

Holmes raised the glass and sipped the wine. "It is very good indeed, sweet but not cloyingly so."

The waiter poured Anna and me a glass. She eyed hers warily. She would not look at the young man. His eyes were still fixed on us. Since the mustache completely hid his mouth, I couldn't tell if he was smiling. I tasted the wine. I usually didn't care for Marsala, but this yellow variant really was exceptional. Anna was staring apprehensively at her glass. "Try it," I said. "The waiter was right, it is wonderful."

She sipped it, then gave an appreciative nod. However, she turned her chair slightly so the young man was even further out of her line of vision.

By the time we had finished dessert, and each had another glass of the Marsala, Anna did look actually happy, her dark eyes glowing. She held the glass with its golden elixir in her long slender fingers and smiled at us. While her face might not be dazzling, she certainly did have beautiful hands, her fingers exquisitely shaped, the blue veins showing in the pale skin below her knuckles.

I smiled at her. "You've done very well."

"I cannot recall when I've last had such a good time." The sadness came back into her countenance, her mouth wavering. "I don't want it to end. I... I am dreading tomorrow."

"We shall go out again, I promise—when Michelle is here. By then the funeral will be long over with. The four of us can go out for dinner together."

"Oh, I would like that!"

When, at last, we walked toward the exit doorway, she scrupulously ignored the young gentleman with the mustache. Holmes, on the other hand, peered at him sharply. In response, he waved goodbye, then touched his fingertips to his mustache. A typically Italian male, I thought—although the wine had been remarkable.

Out front a coach with the Antonelli coat of arms on its side had been waiting, and we waved farewell to Anna as it pulled away. We turned to go back inside and saw a tall figure in a burgundy velvet coat and top hat stroll off in the opposite direction.

Soon Holmes and I sank down into the comfortable depths of the huge sofa in our sitting room. Holmes turned to me, and one black eyebrow rose slightly.

"What is it?" I asked.

"You are the expert on such things, not me, and as such, I would like to verify a certain hypothesis with you."

I smiled. "Whatever are you talking about?"

"Matters amatory, those concerning relationships between men and women."

"Yes? What is this hypothesis?"

"That Signorina Antonelli is deeply in love with Father Blackwell."

I opened my mouth, then closed it. "Yes, I suppose she is."

"Ah, it's good to know I am not utterly obtuse in such matters after all."

"She certainly seems to worship the ground he walks on."

"And Father Blackwell?"

"What about him?" I asked.

"I suspect he has similar feelings for the girl."

I frowned. "Does he, now?"

"You are the expert."

"I'm not sure. Perhaps you are right. He has considerable self-reserve, much more than her." I shook my head. "It's a pity he's a priest. They would make a fine couple."

Holmes took out his silver case from his inside pocket and withdrew a cigarette. "I am afraid this is one sort of intrigue which is beyond my powers to untangle."

The next morning, we were about to go down for breakfast, when someone rapped loudly at our door. I got there just before Holmes and opened it. Monsignor Greene stood before me. His face was quite red, his eyes opened very wide, his mouth agape, and he clutched his *saturno* by the brim with both of his plump hands.

"What on earth—has something happened?" I asked.

He stared past me at Holmes. "Thank God you're here! You must come at once—they're gone, taken, all of them this time—all of the relics! But worse yet—the guard—they murdered him in cold blood! He's dead!"

Holmes's smile of greeting had vanished, but another flickered back, brief and grim. "And so it begins again," he murmured.

Chapter Five

Holmes, Monsignor Greene, and I entered the Basilica of Santa Croce just after nine. A police guard was keeping the general public out, so the vast church was empty, save Monsignor Nardone at the back of the church. After the dull thud of the tall door echoed through that vast space, the priest turned, then rose and made his way to the end of the pew. Clearly he was distraught, his eyes red and puffy, his thin aristocratic face pale.

"Thank God you've come," he murmured. "It is…" He choked back a sob, managed only to say, "abomination." Slowly he drew in a breath. "The police are in the chapel. I could not—I cannot—bear to be there. Perhaps later." Tears seeped from his eyes. Greene reached over and gave his arm a squeeze.

Holmes, Greene, and I strode along the nave of the basilica, then down the passageway to the chapel. A policeman in his blue uniform with the red stripe on the trousers stood before the entranceway. Greene explained who we were and that we must see the body.

Frowning, the man turned, then said rather loudly, considering it was a church, "*Commissario!*"

His superior approached us, a tall, broad somewhat stout man of about forty in an elegant navy-blue suit, with, of course, a mustache, the usual black variety with waxed ends curling upward. His hair was parted neatly down the middle, and his eyes were large, brown, and liquid. They widened with surprise as his man said, "Sherlock Holmes." He gave us a slight, very formal bow.

"Gentlemen, I am Commissario Manara. It is a great honor, Signor Holmes."

Greene introduced himself and us in his perfect Italian, then explained that the pope was very concerned about the murder and the theft of the relics, and had already asked Holmes to look into the earlier disappearance. Manara nodded, the corners of his mouth curving up ironically into the ends of his mustache. "Ah yes, the prior theft, which would seem to have been a sort of dress rehearsal." He stepped back and turned to gesture toward the interior. "Feel free to have a look, Signor Holmes."

We walked into the chapel. Another policeman was standing before the massive form of the guard, who lay sprawled face down before the pew. A dark circular stain was evident on the back of his black jacket. Holmes squatted and touched the bloody spot lightly, then inserted his fingertip into a small tear in the jacket that was only about an inch wide. He looked up at the *commissario*. "A puncture wound, no doubt neatly through the heart."

Manara nodded. "Exactly so. A quick thrust, then a skillful twist of the blade to amplify the damage."

Holmes stood. "Did you check to see if it came out the other side?"

"Yes. It did not. The man had the chest of an ox."

"Still, a long narrow blade, I suspect. Most likely a stiletto, the classic silent weapon of the assassin."

Manara smiled. "Very good, Signor Holmes! My thoughts exactly. Monsignor Nardone told me his name is Antonio Cascone. He has a wife and two children."

Holmes stroked his chin thoughtfully. "Cascone must have been sitting in the pew, probably dozing, and his killer crept up behind him. A quick stab and it was over at once. Do you know of any in Rome who favor the stiletto?"

Manara's out-of-place good humor dissolved. "Have you heard of the Camorra?"

Holmes frowned. "Perhaps. Let me think. They are not as well-known as the Sicilian Mafia, I believe, but isn't it another Italian criminal society dominated by particular families? A society centered in Naples."

Manara gave an appreciative nod. "I can see that your reputation is not unwarranted, Signor Holmes. The stiletto is a traditional favorite of the *camorristi*. Extortion in Naples is their specialty, but something seems to be happening with the Camorra here in Rome, for what reason I know not. This is the fourth such stabbed corpse I have encountered in the last six months. Someone certainly favors a blade and is accomplished in its use. He always attacks from the back, slipping his steel just between the shoulder blade and the spine, neatly skewering the heart. His victims would have died in an instant, hardly conscious of what was happening to them."

I repressed a shudder. There was something so primitive, direct, and savage about a stabbing. It was not like a pistol which worked well at a distance. One had to be close to the victim, right next to him, and it could take several blows to kill—not in this case, however. One stab had clearly sufficed. All the same, it was difficult to believe that a single thrust could completely extinguish the life of such a large powerful man.

Holmes slowly eased out his breath. "So it would seem we have a professional at work here, an expert in the art of silent killing with the stiletto."

Manara nodded. "My thoughts exactly."

Holmes turned toward the display case. "Well, he certainly used no such finesse in breaking into the case." Shattered glass was scattered all about the floor, while some jagged shards like thin sharp teeth remained in the rectangular wooden frame. The shelves were empty now, the relics in their gaudy reliquaries all gone.

Monsignor Greene's plump face had gone very pale. "Are you done with the body?" The *commissario* nodded. "Could you gentlemen help me to turn him? It is too late for extreme unction, but I want to pray for him."

Holmes and I stooped down. I grasped an arm. It was apparent from its stiffness that rigor mortis had set in. Turning him was something of a project. I was glad we weren't trying to lift him, but we managed to roll him over. His dark eyes stared upward, and his face had the blankness, pallor, and lack of expression of death.

"Rigor mortis seems complete, so I suspect he was stabbed around midnight," Holmes said.

Manara nodded again. "Yes, I agree."

Greene knelt on the floor. He closed the dead man's eyes, then took one of his hands. It was so very large, those sausage-like fingers now deathly white. "*Poverino*," Greene muttered. He lowered the hand, then put his own freckled hand on the man's chest and began to murmur so quietly we could not make out the words. We all stood with bowed heads, the *commissario* and the policeman included. At last, Greene made two passes over the forehead with his fingertips, tracing the shape of a cross. He stood up, shaking his head. "The primal sin of Cain—murder, the blackest of all sins."

Holmes hesitated, then said, "And for what?" He glanced at me, and I could see the anger in his eyes. I knew what he must be thinking: murder for a few worthless objects, objects which almost certainly had nothing really to do with the crucifixion of Christ or the body of an apostle.

Manara's forehead had creased, his eyebrows coming together over his long aquiline nose. "The modus operandi certainly may fit a *camorrista* killer, but not the theft itself. It would not be like them to steal holy relics. The same is true for the Mafia. I've never heard of either society being involved in such thievery. Their trade is squeezing money from small shopkeepers and tradesmen, selling them their 'protection.'"

Holmes nodded. "It does seem odd." He looked about the room, searching, but then his gaze turned briefly inward. Finally, he ran his long fingers along his jaw. "Tell me, Commissario, would you know of an Italian nobleman from Naples, a Baron Marullo?"

Manara hesitated only a second or two. "Yes, I know of him. He's active in the politics between Church and state, supposedly a very devout Catholic." His voice had a faintly sarcastic edge.

"Why 'supposedly'?" Holmes asked.

"He was reputed to have a special fondness for harlots, which helped drive his long-suffering wife to an early grave. I cannot vouch for the accuracy of that, but I do know he likes to gamble. My sources have placed him in many high-stakes card games. They say that he has gambled away most of his fortune and has heavy debts."

"Ah," Holmes said. "And could he have ties to the Camorra?"

"That I cannot say. It would not be typical for one of the nobility, especially one who flaunts his religion so much. However, I would certainly not rule it out."

I had listened in puzzlement. "Who is this Marullo?" I asked.

"Don't you recall? We met him as we were leaving Cardinal Cicogno's office." Holmes turned again to Manara. "Do you know the cardinal?"

"I know of him, but Church politics is a quagmire. I have enough trouble keeping track of all the secular participants in Roman society."

"His responsibilities include the oversight of all holy relics. I think we shall need to pay him another visit very soon."

I noticed Greene's face contort ever so slightly. In truth, he and the cardinal did seem complete opposites in every way, one a thin angry fanatic, the other plump, good-humored, and open-minded.

Holmes's gaze was still fixed on the *commissario*. "*Signore*, I would assume that no ordinary Italian thief would steal holy relics. A certain superstitious awe, a fear of being cursed for sacrilege, would hold him in check."

"I agree with you, Signor Holmes. They might steal gold chalices, or some precious reliquaries, but then leave the actual contents—bones, or whatever—behind. And to compound the deed with murder…" He looked baffled. "They could have simply given the big brute there a rap on the head, then tied him up. Instead, they stabbed him in cold blood."

"Cold blood indeed," Holmes murmured. "Tell me, Commissario, given the recent theft, the church must have been locked. Must I check the doors and windows, or have you already discovered how they got in?"

"Spare yourself the trouble, *signore*. It is quite obvious. The back door to the sacristy was unlocked."

Holmes frowned. "Not by choice, I presume?"

"No. The monsignor swears he left the door locked. Ever since the first theft, he says he has double-checked everything before he leaves, to make certain all is secure."

"And was the lock forced, then? Perhaps I should have a look."

"Again, *signore*, spare yourself the effort. I examined it carefully myself. There is absolutely no sign it was forced: the plate and the keyhole have not been damaged. I even tried locking and unlocking it myself. It functions normally. Whoever opened that door was very skilled at lock-picking."

A flicker of a smile passed over Holmes's lips. "We are dealing with someone of many talents, perhaps a sort of renaissance man of crime, although of course there is no telling how many people were actually involved."

The *commissario* shook his head. "No."

"All the same... The fact that the door was left unlocked tells us something. It shows... a certain laziness, perhaps, and a certain arrogance. Someone that clever with locks could have locked the door back up when they departed. Then there would have been no way to tell how they got in. But he couldn't be bothered. Perhaps, too, he wanted to show off, to flaunt his talents. I do not think this was any common thief."

We were all silent for a few seconds, but at last Manara spoke. "I don't envy you your task, *signore*. Not that I doubt your abilities, but finding these relics... I suspect we shall never see them again."

"I would wager we will!" Greene exclaimed.

Holmes smiled at his enthusiasm, then shrugged. "I am hardly so sanguine myself. Well, all the same, let me have a brief look around the chapel before we depart."

"Be my guest."

Greene touched Holmes lightly on the arm. "Do you need me any longer, Holmes? The funeral Mass for the count starts at ten. After that there is a graveside ceremony at the cemetery. I very much want to attend."

"You must go, Monsignor. And send our regrets and condolences to the *signorina.* After we finish here, I want to see Cardinal Cicogno."

Greene looked uncomfortable. "Can't it wait until after the funeral?"

Holmes shook his head. "I think not."

"Your Italian is quite good. I think you can get by. Besides, he speaks French fairly well if need be."

"Don't worry. We shall do fine without you. Your duties lie elsewhere."

"Thank you." Greene nodded to me, then turned and left.

Holmes put his left arm behind him, took his wrist with his right hand, then stepped closer to the case and the shattered remnants of the pane.

I turned away and sank down onto the pew, only a few feet away from the corpse. The *commissario* soon joined me, sitting close by. The fact we were in a church gave us a good excuse for remaining silent. I felt oddly discouraged, and my stomach had that queer fluttery feeling that came from seeing corpses. Our talk of bodies piling up was meant as humor, but now that it was actually happening, there was nothing droll in it at all. Less than a day before, that man lying dead on the floor had been alive and breathing. He must have said goodbye to his wife and children before leaving for the church. They had not suspected that he would not return—that that was his final farewell.

And to be murdered for a bunch of worthless silly items—a fragment of bone, slivers of ancient wood, a thorn or two, and a rusty nail. How absurd! It seemed to compound the stupidity of it all. But it was not amusing. Murder never was. I was glad Michelle would be with us in another few days. She was always a comfort when I was troubled.

I sat silently for perhaps a quarter of an hour while Holmes went all round the chapel. Nothing seemed to particularly catch his interest. Finally he came over to the pews where Manara and I were sitting. We both stood up.

"I did not expect our assassin to leave any obvious trace behind, and he did not. Henry and I will be leaving. Should you wish to contact me, Commissario, we are staying at the Hotel Eden."

"Very good, Signor Holmes. It has been a great honor to meet you. Here is my card, and you can always reach me through the main Roman Questura near the train station."

"Doubtlessly we shall soon meet again: I know I shall have further questions, so *arrivederci*, Commissario."

We made our way out of the church. Monsignor Nardone was still sitting alone in a pew at the back, his face stricken. He gave us a nod as we passed him. Outside the sunshine and the noisy bustle of the plaza were welcome after that shadowy interior with its funereal silence. We soon found a cab and headed for the Vatican.

Cardinal Cicogno's young clerical assistant was obviously not Italian; he spoke the language with a rather strong accent which even I could hear. He was tall and slender, like the cardinal himself, but fair-complexioned. His hair, which was a light brown shade very close to blond, seemed to want to stand upright rather than lie flat. I suspected he was Austrian or German. He left us waiting while he went in to see the cardinal. He soon returned looking both worried and somewhat surprised. "The cardinal will see you now, *signori.*" He stood near the doorway, then stepped back, remaining outside as he closed the door behind us.

Cicogno sat behind his huge mahogany desk. I thought of the term "careworn." It certainly fitted the cardinal, his expression showing that the weight of the world lay heavy on his shoulders. He seemed a different man to the one we had seen with the blazing eyes and the fiery temper. Those black eyes had lost their glow and showed, more than anything, pain, and his gaunt face appeared even more skeletal. He moved as if to get up, but could not seem to expend the energy. He wore the usual black soutane with the red piping, along with the red zucchetto.

"You wished to see me, Signor Holmes."

"Yes, Eminence. You must have heard about the theft of the relics and the murder of the guard?"

Cicogno's eyes showed a brief flash of temper. "Yes, certainly."

"Your worries about the relics seem to have proven prescient. Perhaps now the Holy Father will listen to you."

Cicogno stared silently at him. Finally he spoke. "What does it matter?"

Holmes and I were both surprised.

"It is too late, too late for anything. And a man is dead." His gaze was fixed on us. "How exactly did he die?"

"He was stabbed through the heart, most likely with a stiletto, an assassin's weapon."

Again, Cicogno's eyes had a certain glow. His lips formed the word *assassino*, but he barely spoke it aloud. "I wish to God… We should have never put a guard over the relics. They were not worth a man's life. Truly… Satan turns our best intentions against us. He employs his hellish tricks. He knows all our weaknesses, and uses them."

Holmes briefly glanced at me. Cicogno was a changed man.

"Cascone had a wife and two children." The cardinal sighed. "At least I can see they are provided for."

Holmes was watching him closely. "Eminence, do you know of any reason why the Camorra might have been involved in the theft?"

Cicogno stared at him. "*What*? What on earth are you talking about?"

"The *commissario* from the *polizia* said the stiletto is a weapon of choice for the *camorristi*. Moreover, he has seen four other corpses stabbed in the same way in the past six months."

"Are you serious, *signore*?"

"I would not joke about such a thing."

The cardinal shook his head. "I cannot believe it! Worse and worse! The Camorra—thieves, extortionists, assassins, brigands!—the scum of the south!—what ever...?" He had set both hands on his desk, and he slowly rose to his feet. The red of the sash round his waist was like a bloody belt. "Are you sure of this?"

"Commissario Manara was quite certain."

"The theft was... sacrilege enough... but to drag the Camorra into this business..." He stumbled over his words. "The Neapolitans are crazy," he mumbled, almost to himself. Anger again showed in his eyes, the set of his thin lips. "He will pay for this—I swear he will pay!" He licked his lips, gazed again at us. "The thief, I mean—the thief—or thieves—whoever is guilty! They will pay—they are damned!" His mouth twisted into a brief savage smile. "Oh dear God," he murmured, even as he collapsed back into his seat. "Forgive me, *signori*, but I am not myself today. This theft has made me... I feel ill."

I regarded him closely. "You do not look well, Eminence."

"And I should not. I have failed. I have failed in my solemn duty. Yes, the relics were my responsibility, but I am a prince of the

Church, one also responsible for the souls of the faithful—for the soul of Antonio Cascone." His dark eyes filled with tears. "Yes, I failed Cascone. Relics can be recovered, but a life taken is gone forever."

He was so contrite I felt sorry for him. "You mustn't blame yourself," I said.

His anguished eyes turned to me. He opened his mouth, then closed it without speaking. He ran the long skeletal fingers of his right hand back along his forehead and bald crown until the tips rested on the red zucchetto. He lowered his hand and drew in his breath. "Leave me, please. We shall… we shall discuss this another time. It is… too soon."

"As you wish, Eminence. Perhaps we might return tomorrow?" suggested Holmes.

Cicogno nodded, not even looking at us. "Yes, as you wish."

We turned and started for the door. Holmes's gray eyes again shifted briefly toward me. We stepped outside, and Holmes closed the door.

The young priest was waiting for us. He looked faintly puzzled. "What did he say?"

"He is most upset," Holmes said.

The priest nodded. "I have never seen him so upset—angry, yes; furious, yes; but not like this."

"Tell me, Father, would you know where in Rome Baron Marullo is staying?"

"Why, yes. He has lodgings near the Villa Borghese and the park."

"Excellent. That would be close to our hotel. Could you possibly write out the address for me?"

"Certainly, Signor Holmes. I have it just here." He went through some cards in a small metal box and finally withdrew one. He wrote with a pencil on a small piece of paper, then handed the paper to Holmes, who folded it neatly twice and put it into his inside jacket pocket.

Soon Holmes and I were wandering down the gaudy decorated corridors. "I am astonished," I said. "Clearly he was more disturbed by the murder than the theft."

Holmes nodded. "Yes. I think the killing caught him by surprise."

I frowned. "But not the theft? Well, I suppose Saint Thomas's finger temporarily going missing must have prepared him for that."

Holmes smiled bitterly. "Oh yes."

After a leisurely lunch, Holmes and I took a cab across Rome. The two-story palazzo where the baron was staying had clearly seen better days: some of the stucco had disintegrated, leaving behind large pale blotches like some terrible skin disease, and the wooden window frames badly needed paint. A small portly man in a black suit answered the door; his mustache and what remained of his hair were equally black.

"Yes?" he asked, none too hospitably.

Holmes handed him one of his calling cards. "Signor Sherlock Holmes to see Baron Marullo, *per favore.*"

"Come in, please." We stepped into a tiny vestibule. Various small squares from the wooden parquet floor were missing. "A moment." The man disappeared into the house proper. He soon reappeared. "Follow me, *signori.*" He led us to a well-worn sitting room where the baron awaited us.

Marullo shook our hands enthusiastically. "What an unexpected pleasure to see you, Mr. Holmes! And you...?" He gave me a slightly pained look.

I quickly said, "Vernier. Dr. Henry Vernier."

"Please sit down, gentlemen."

Holmes and I sat on a red velvet couch with shiny patches on its armrests and the fronts of the cushions, while the baron sat in a matching overstuffed chair.

The baron's lodgings might be worn, but not his clothing. He wore a dark blue coat with four golden buttons, the top two fastened, along with gray flannel trousers and shoes which glistened a glossy black. The fabric of the jacket and trousers had the luxurious sheen unique to wool woven in Italy, and their cut, too, was quite different from that of London garments. His fantastical black mustache was still neatly waxed at the ends, and he touched the rigid right tip gently. "How kind of you to call on me. I suppose the cardinal told you where I live?"

Holmes nodded, his mouth grim. "I'm afraid this is not a social visit, Baron. Have you heard about the relics?"

Marullo's mouth twitched faintly, then he tipped his head ever so slightly to the side. "Relics? Which relics?"

"The ones at the basilica of Santa Croce. They have been stolen."

"Oh no!" the baron exclaimed. "God forbid! Which ones?"

"All of them this time."

"*Santa Maria!*" He shook his head. "The cardinal and I have begged the Holy Father to hide them away, and now you see the result of him not listening! All the same, I would not choose to be proven right in such a way."

"And the guard was murdered."

Marullo's thick dark eyebrows came together, and he was briefly silent. "Was he now? I suppose... There must have been a fearful struggle."

"There was no sign whatsoever of a struggle. Most likely the thief sneaked up behind him and thrust a knife in his back."

Marullo's right hand began to play with the end of his mustache. "Regrettable. Indeed, most regrettable."

Something about the way he said it annoyed me. "It is much more than regrettable!" I exclaimed.

Marullo raised both hands before him, fingers spread, and shook them gently for emphasis. "I certainly don't mean to minimize the tragedy, Dr. Vernier. All the same, those relics are irreplaceable."

I gave a sort of snort of bitter amusement. Given half a day or so, I could easily come up with duplicates of all the missing objects, and then I could claim the relics had been miraculously restored. I could not say that aloud, but I could see clearly enough that Holmes had read my thoughts.

Marullo gave a long weary sigh. "I can only imagine how distraught his Eminence must be."

"We saw him this morning," Holmes said. "He is very disturbed, more, I think, by the murder than the theft."

"Really?"

"Yes," Holmes said.

Marullo shook his head. "I had already planned to see him later this afternoon. More reason, now, for my visit. I shall try to console him, and we must discuss what steps to take. I suppose you will be investigating the theft, Signor Holmes?"

Holmes gave him an appraising stare. "So I shall, Baron."

"Then there is hope, after all! Still, it will be difficult."

Holmes's eyes were still fixed on him. "That remains to be seen. I have my suspicions."

"I only hope it was not some wicked group of atheists or allies of the state who might wish to destroy the relics, rather than sell or ransom them. The thought that someone might willingly destroy them..." His shoulders rose dramatically. "It makes me shudder!"

"Tell me, Baron. Have you heard of the Camorra?"

Beneath the enormous mustache, the baron's mouth stiffened. "Anyone from Naples will have heard of the Camorra."

"And what exactly have you heard?"

"That its members are brigands and bandits, riffraff who thrive on extortion and threats! Why do you ask? Surely they could have had nothing to do with the theft?"

"The guard was probably stabbed with a stiletto, an assassin's weapon, and the police *commissario* said that was a favorite of the Camorra."

Marullo laughed. "Forgive me, but that seems a great leap of logic! The stiletto is not unique to the so-called *camorristi,* and anyway, I have never before heard of them stealing relics or religious objects. What purpose would it have?"

"You just spoke the word 'ransom.' That would be a logical enough reason. I suspect the Vatican would pay a fortune to have them back."

Marullo was frowning. "The *camorristi* are scoundrels, but I cannot believe them guilty of such a sacrilegious crime. Even the poorest and vilest *napoletano* has some vestige of the Catholic faith, even if it is only a sort of superstitious awe. They would fear divine retribution."

"You do seem to know something of the Camorra."

"Please, Signor Holmes—I am only speculating. Its members are far below the class of my associates. They are the very lowest of the low, the dregs of Neapolitan society!"

"So you have never mingled with any of its members?"

"Never, Signor Holmes—never! And I resent your even asking such a question! It is a breach of etiquette, to say the least. What have I possibly done to deserve such disrespect?"

The baron had grown somewhat agitated, but Holmes continued to stare at him, calm as ever. "Forgive me, Baron, but it is my business to occasionally ask unpleasant questions."

"This shows the true blight of the *camorristi* plague! Anyone from Naples is somehow automatically suspect, even one, such as myself, of noble blood and of devout faith to our mother the Roman Catholic Church. I promise you, I would not so lower—so debase—myself as to have any intercourse whatsoever with the Camorra."

Holmes nodded. "Bravo! I am glad to hear it. But do you know of anyone else from Naples, here in Rome, who might lack your scruples?"

"I do not! Again, my friends and acquaintances are of a class that does not abase itself dealing with the human vermin of the Camorra."

"I see. It is good to know that the noblesse of Italy is made up of those with such moral fortitude."

Marullo gave him a wary, appraising look. He was unsure, but I had little doubt that Holmes was being ironical.

"Well, setting aside the Camorra, Baron, do you have any idea who might have committed such a crime?"

Marullo grew very stern again. "I have little doubt who did it. It has all the marks of the Italian government! It was those same atheists and nonbelievers who marched into Rome and stole the lands and property of the Church. They will not be content until they have stolen everything from the Church, even its most precious possessions, the relics of the saints and martyrs! They have started with the Basilica of Santa Croce, but I foresee the day when the soldiers storm into Saint Peter's and strip from that holiest monument of Christendom its precious objects and relics! There is no limit to their iniquity."

"An interesting theory."

"Believe me—it is more than a theory."

"Perhaps so. If it were true, we could not expect much real help from the police."

"Even so! Do not trust this *commissario*! He is trying to throw you off by bringing the Camorra into the matter."

"Ah yes, that is a distinct possibility. Thank you for enlightening me."

"Trust no one in official Rome—*no one*."

"Certainly not. Well, this has been a most interesting and helpful conversation, Baron. There are some other leads we must pursue, so we shall leave you."

"And I must be off for the Vatican to see Cardinal Cicogno." The baron shook his head sadly. "How I pity him. But it is not his fault. The pope would not listen."

"Perhaps some good will come of this, after all," Holmes said. "Now the Holy Father will have to listen."

"Even so, Signor Holmes. Even so."

We stood, said our farewells, and then the servant let us out the front door. It was just after three, and sunlight shone on the paved stones of the narrow quiet street.

"What a fanatic," I remarked. "I think, too, that he's something of a lunatic."

Holmes had put on his top hat, and the brim cast a shadow over his eyes. He smiled faintly. "Not at all. Come along—enough of business for one day. Let us walk for a while and see a few of the sights, and then we shall return to the hotel with a good appetite."

Holmes and I arrived back at the hotel around seven o'clock. A boy was selling newspapers, and Holmes bought one. The headline was *Reliquie Sante Trovate, Poi Ancora Perdute!*: "Holy Relics Found, Then Lost Again!"

We strolled into the spacious lobby and saw a familiar figure sitting at one end of a huge overstuffed sofa. Father Blackwell sprang up from his seat, the motion somewhat akin to a jack-in-the-box bursting forth from its box. He wore the usual black soutane, the white of his round collar showing, especially in the notch at the front, just below his prominent Adam's apple and strong firm jaw. He took two steps, then stopped before us, his forearms raised and his fingers spread wide apart.

"There you are at last! Thank God you've come. I did not know how long I would have to wait. I must speak to you!"

Holmes had removed his top hat and held it and his stick in his left hand. "We are at your service, Father Blackwell."

"Monsignor Greene told me everything! I promise you—I swear by all that is sacred, in the name of almighty God—that I had nothing to do with the theft of the relics or that terrible murder! You must believe me."

Holmes blinked. "Of course I believe you."

Blackwell stared at him. "You do?"

"Certainly. You were never a suspect."

Blackwell let out a great sigh. His eyes lost focus, and he touched his forehead with his fingertips. "Thank God." He swayed ever so slightly. "Forgive me. I'm a little dizzy."

"Are you ill?" I asked.

"No. I think I just stood up too fast." He lowered his hand, then sighed again, smiling faintly. "I'm better now."

"That happens to me sometimes, too," I said.

"I was afraid..." Blackwell began. "I thought you might possibly believe that I was somehow involved."

Holmes shook his head. "The idea never even occurred to me. You are hardly the type to murder a man by thrusting a stiletto into his back."

Blackwell paled slightly. "That was how it was done?"

"Yes. You explained to us why you took the finger of Saint Thomas. Count Antonelli is dead now—and buried?" Blackwell nodded in affirmation. "Obviously you would have no further motive for stealing the relics."

"I am glad you understand that, Mr. Holmes. All the same… I cannot help but blame myself for this. Perhaps I set something in motion—I gave someone the idea."

I shrugged. "They would have thought it up, anyway."

"But if I had not stolen the relic, that guard might still be alive. I feel somehow responsible for his death."

Holmes's smile was bittersweet. "Father Blackwell, you need not take upon yourself all the sins of the world. Perhaps the two thefts are related, but it does not follow that you are responsible. In a case of cold-blooded murder like this, the perpetrator is the guilty party. You certainly did not put him up to it, and there were certainly other alternatives for him than stabbing the guard to death. This was a cold-blooded crime and, from what the *commissario* said, not the first committed by this man."

"What do you mean?"

"He has recently found other bodies most likely stabbed with a stiletto. He suspects that a *camorrista* is involved."

"A what?"

"A *camorrista*—a member of the Neapolitan Camorra. It is a criminal society akin to the Sicilian Mafia. They specialize in robbery and extortion."

"Oh, how I wish I were back home in England!" Blackwell

exclaimed. "I should never have come to Rome." Now that he was calmer, you could see the signs of exhaustion in his face, the odd set of the mouth, the weariness in his eyes.

"But then," I said, "you would have never met Count Antonelli and his daughter."

He looked at me, opened his mouth, closed it, then finally said, "Exactly." I gave him an appraising stare, but his eyes would not meet mine. "Well, I have plenty to do. I'm so far behind in my studies that I don't quite know where to begin. I'll leave you gentlemen in peace."

"Why not join us for dinner?" Holmes said.

He looked surprised. "I really have so much to do."

"When did you last have a decent meal?" I asked.

His forehead scrunched up. "I can't quite recall."

"Come along, then," I said. "Doctor's orders."

"Oh, all right. I am hungry, I suppose. And I cannot really concentrate. Too much on my mind."

Holmes nodded. "That's settled, then. We'll take you to a place Monsignor Greene recommended."

For the first time since his arrival, Blackwell actually smiled. "If Richard recommended it, it must be good. Let me just get my book, and then we can go." He turned, went over to the sofa, and picked up a thick leather-bound book. He shook his head slightly. "Saint Thomas Aquinas in the original Latin is difficult enough even when you are at your best, but today…"

Chapter Six

As our meal progressed from *antipasti*, to the *primi piatti* of pasta, to the *secondi piatti*, of meat, and as we drank our wine, Father Blackwell gradually relaxed. Always before I had seen him on edge, a prey to some fierce consuming energy, but that evening, he even showed flashes of a certain self-deprecating humor, as well as considerable charm.

Among other topics we briefly discussed our professions: consulting detective, doctor, and priest. Both Holmes and Blackwell had known from an early age what they wanted to do, but I had settled on medicine later in life. I must say, I rather envied them. Also, I did not think I possessed the natural talent for medicine that my wife Michelle did. Blackwell spoke rather longingly of his youthful faith and aspirations, in a way which suggested to me that something had changed for him. Holmes mentioned that faith could be misused and described a case I well remembered, wherein some Yorkshire country folk were willing to stand by and watch a young woman be sacrificed to their serpentine deity. Holmes had stopped it in time, and the fake high priestess behind the plot, who knew the whole thing was nonsense, was caught up and destroyed by her own scheme.

Blackwell shook his head. "In the end, I think perhaps you are a greater force for good than we priests, Mr. Holmes."

Holmes smiled. "Somehow I have never quite seen myself in that light."

"It's true, though," I said.

Holmes's smile faded. "I'm not exactly sure that fighting against evil is the same as doing good."

Blackwell sipped at his wine. "Of course it is." He thought for a moment. "There's that line from a Protestant hymn, which seems to make more and more sense to me as I grow older: 'God Moves in a Mysterious Way.' I wish I knew the rest of it. I think it's a shame that we Catholics and the Anglicans cannot share hymns."

"I was raised a Catholic too," I said. "That must be why I don't know that hymn either, although the expression is familiar."

Holmes set down his wine glass and smiled.

"'God moves in a mysterious way

His wonders to perform;

He plants His footsteps in the sea,

And rides upon the storm.'"

He stroked his chin. "I vaguely remember the second verse. Ah, yes:

"'Deep in unfathomable mines

Of never-failing skill,

He treasures up his bright designs

and works his sovereign will.'

"I can't recall the other verses. Except perhaps..." He frowned in concentration. "Only a fragment–'Judge not the Lord by feeble sense.'"

Blackwell smiled. "'Feeble sense.' I like that! All our intellectual efforts often seem feeble indeed."

I raised the wine bottle and poured the last of it equally into our glasses. "I'm not much of a believer myself, as you may have discerned, but I certainly agree with you on that, Father."

Blackwell swirled his glass, stared at the red liquid. "In the end, it's all... a mystery, a great mystery." He smiled reflexively. "Somewhat trite, that. You would think I could do better after so many years studying theology."

"Not at all." I raised my glass. "A toast! To life as a great mystery."

Holmes smiled. "Very good, Henry." He clinked my glass, and after we had all exchanged clinks, we drank.

Greene had recommended the homemade Italian cake, the *torta limone*, served at the restaurant, and we all sampled it along with some *digestivi*. By the time we had finished, Blackwell seemed truly a new man from the one we had known up until then. At last Holmes took out his watch and said we must get back to the hotel; we would be visiting Cardinal Cicogno first thing in the morning. He rose, and I did the same.

Blackwell remained seated, his blue eyes fixed on me, his expression suddenly grave. I gave him a questioning look, but he bit at his lip and stood up. Holmes insisted on paying for the meal, and soon we were out in the street. We said our goodbyes to the priest, but his expression remained grave. He kept staring at me.

I stared back. "Is something the matter, Father Blackwell?"

He hesitated, then drew in his breath resolutely. "Might I possibly speak with you, Dr. Vernier?"

"Of course."

He glanced briefly at Holmes. My cousin set his hand on my

shoulder. "I shall see you back at the hotel, Henry. Take your time." He turned and strode away.

Blackwell lowered his eyes, then raised them again. "Could we walk for a while? I am not used to eating so much."

It was a fine spring evening with a faint breeze, and many people were on the narrow street, the street lamps casting yellow light upon the cobblestones here and there. Ahead was another restaurant, the diners spilling out onto the pavement because of the fine weather, all of them talking and eating with enthusiastic Italian gusto. Many were couples, young men with their grand black mustaches, dressed in dark suits, and women with colorful scarves, dark eyes, and broad full mouths. Nighttime hid some of the squalor of Rome, and I was glad to be there, although eager to have Michelle with me. We walked along, and I glanced sideways at the priest. He was staring grimly ahead, his relaxed state at the restaurant clearly gone. I felt a curious pang of sympathy for him.

"Something is troubling you," I said.

"Yes. I wanted to talk to you about... well, about women." He flinched slightly at the word. "You see, I know hardly anything about them—except for my mother, and well, one's mother is not exactly... typical. I have no sisters. Then, too, I don't know anyone who really knows anything about women, who has actual *experience* with them—I've never known anyone like that. At the preparatory school and the seminary, it was always males only, and here in Rome... All my friends now are priests. In fact, the only married people I have really known as an adult were the count and his wife, and she died not long after I met her. That was why... You are married—you must know something." He had raised his hands in agitation.

I laughed. "Yes. *Something.* But that hardly makes me an expert. So, you've never had a sweetheart?"

"No. I always knew I was going to be a priest. It would have been... a temptation, and it would not have been fair, since marriage would not be possible."

"So never even one kiss?"

"No! That is the sure way to ruin."

A bemused smile lingered about my lips. "You had it all figured out."

"Yes, I suppose I did. But as they say, 'pride goeth before destruction, and a haughty spirit before a fall.'"

"Isn't that just a wee bit melodramatic?"

He finally seemed to relax somewhat. "Yes, I suppose it is." He was briefly silent. "Do you like being married, Dr. Vernier?"

I answered immediately. "Yes. Very much. It is the best part, the happiest part, of my existence. I think..." My voice trailed away. I did not want to offend or wound him.

"What do you think?" he asked.

"Knowing and loving a woman is the greatest joy in a man's life."

He did not speak, but I could see he was troubled.

"I'm sorry. Perhaps I shouldn't have said that. But it is the truth for me. Perhaps the truth is different for different men."

Again he bit down on his lip, fiercer than ever. "And is that joy—is it—is it...?" He drew in his breath. "Is it spiritual—a union of two souls, or is it merely... carnal?"

"It is both. Souls cannot be joined without bodies also being joined."

He gave me an incredulous look.

"It's true. So help me God."

We had turned a corner, and although his gaze was fixed straight ahead, he seemed unaware of our surroundings. His stride had grown faster and faster, and I put my hand on his arm, slowing him. "This is about you and Anna, isn't it? That's what you want to talk about?"

He came to an abrupt stop. "Yes. It's about Anna. What on earth am I going to do?" His voice shook.

"Do you love her?"

"I don't know! I don't even know what love is. No one ever taught me anything."

"Not even your mother and father? Do they not love one another?"

He drew in his breath, and I could see that fearful energy gather again in his eyes. "No, I don't think so. They only tolerate one another. Barely. He never showed any real affection for her. I did not truly realize how barren their relationship was until I was around Count and Countess Antonelli. Tomasso adored his wife, and she cared deeply for him. That was obvious enough after my first brief visit. And it was one of the reasons I so enjoyed their company."

"I see." I decided to press my question again. "And do you love Anna?"

Again he flinched. "What does it matter whether I love her? I am a priest. I can never marry—I can never pursue your union of souls and... bodies." He almost seemed to choke on the last word.

"Oh, I think it does matter. If you love her, it changes everything."

"It cannot!" he moaned. "I took a solemn oath, Dr. Vernier. I have not betrayed my vows, and will not. I cannot touch her—although, God forgive me, I have wanted to!"

"Even so, tell me if you love her."

"How should I know? As I said, no one ever taught me anything about the love between men and women."

"Not everything about life has to be taught." I shrugged. "Let me make it easier for you. The answer is obvious enough. You do love her."

He drew in his breath and stood up to his full height. "God help me, I do—I do. If only… She is so beautiful, so very beautiful. I did not understand before I met her what beauty is in a woman—how compelling, how all encompassing—what an aura it casts—more than any saint's halo. Do you…? Is your wife beautiful, Dr. Vernier?"

"Oh yes, and you have it exactly right." I smiled. "A woman's beauty is God's great gift to us men."

"Is it really?"

"Yes. For me, anyway. I must admit, I've always had an eye for women, but when you add love into the mix…" We had begun walking again. Blackwell lowered his head, then raised it again. "I'm afraid that what I'm telling you isn't exactly what you wanted to hear."

"No, it is not. But… I did want the truth."

"Well, you have it as best I know it."

We turned another corner and came to a much broader street with even more people. The breeze on our face was cool and pleasant, but thick with the complicated odors of the city, horse dung and smoke from cooking oil being predominant. Blackwell and I did not speak for a while. He was the first to break the silence.

"The count's illness brought Anna and me together. We talked so often, so intimately—we discussed everything. But now… I know what I must do, but I don't want to hurt her, not while the great wound of her father's death is still raw. Sometime soon I must stop seeing her. We must go our separate ways. I shall ask to be sent back to England where I cannot be tempted. A clean break is the best thing for us both."

I could not restrain myself. "I very much doubt that."

"I will not break my vows."

I sighed. "I appreciate you confiding in me, Father Blackwell, and I wish I could be more supportive. However, if there is one thing in life I believe in, it is love. That is the greatest of all God's gifts. I can never believe that it is somehow wrong. To the contrary—turning away from love when it is offered seems to me…" I was going to say, "seems the greatest of all sins," but I stopped myself. I licked my lips. "It seems wrong."

"I understand what you mean, Doctor, and I… I envy you. But we have separate and very different lives. We must each do what we think is right." I gave a half-hearted shrug. "But now I really must return to my lodgings and my studies, and there before us is your hotel."

We walked to the front entrance where the attendants stood nearby in their gaudy Italianate uniforms with epaulets, stripes, and plumed hats. Father Blackwell extended his hand, and I gave it a firm shake. "Thank you again, Dr. Vernier." I thought I could detect anguish in his voice. "You are a truly decent man."

"I wish I could have been more consoling."

"I wanted the truth. And you gave it to me. Good evening."

"Good evening, Father Blackwell."

He turned away, took a step, and stopped. "Might we talk again another time?"

"Any time you wish."

I watched him walk away, a tall dark figure in his black cassock. With a final sigh, I went into the hotel and took the stairs up to our suite.

Holmes was seated on the leather sofa smoking a worn pipe, a book on his lap. "What did the good father want?"

"It was as we suspected. He has it badly—he is in love with Anna."

Holmes's black eyebrows came together, two furrows appearing over his nose. "And…?"

"He thinks he must make a clean break with her. He wants to go back to England to avoid temptation. He really cares for her, but he does not want to break his vows." I sighed. "I felt sorry for him. He is quite miserable. He has led such an odd, sheltered life, and he admitted he knew nothing, really, about women or love."

Holmes's mouth twitched, a brief bittersweet smile flickering there. "I, too, pity him."

The next morning, Holmes and I arrived at the Papal Palace promptly at nine. Holmes had sent a note to Monsignor Greene the day before asking him to meet us at the cardinal's office in the morning. Two bored-looking Swiss Guards in the brash striped uniforms with their black berets stood before the doorway holding their halberds. Holmes told them who we were, that we had come to see the cardinal, and that we knew the way. They waved us through with barely a glance. Soon we were walking down the familiar marble-floored hallway, a golden frieze and elaborate arches on one side, tall windows on the other, and overhead, the angelic and saintly figures painted in vivid colors. Ahead of us a tall figure in a black soutane came around a corner. The priest's step briefly faltered, then he lowered his gaze, half nodding as he quickly strode past us. His vivid reddish-brown hair was cropped short. I didn't really pay much attention to him, continuing forward, but then I realized abruptly that Holmes was no longer at my side.

I turned and saw him about ten feet behind me frowning fiercely. He whirled round and started back in the other direction toward the priest. "Where are you going?" I asked. Cardinal Cicogno's office lay in the opposite direction. Holmes didn't answer but walked more quickly.

The priest turned toward us, then turned again and broke into a run. "After him!" Holmes shouted, as he too began to run. Rather baffled, I followed them both.

We came to the end of the corridor and the stairs. Holmes took them quickly, stumbling once and nearly falling, but catching himself just in time by gripping the ornate balustrade. The red-headed priest was running down the corridor ahead and had nearly reached the entrance. I caught up with Holmes, whose labored breath had a slight wheeze to it.

Soon we were back outside, the two Swiss Guards on either side of us quite startled. Holmes ignored them. The priest was ahead of us walking fast now, rather than running. Holmes started after him, and soon we were all off again at a sprint, headed away from the Papal Palace toward the great domed edifice of Saint Peter's! The priest was very quick, but we had started to gain on him.

Holmes was gasping for breath. Finally he staggered slightly and came to a stop. I went to him, and he clutched at my arm, his face pale, still breathing hard. "Catch him, Henry—catch him! I'll follow." There had been other times in the past when I had seen the effect of Holmes's smoking on his lungs, so I was not surprised.

I took deep breaths as I ran after the priest. The cobblestoned street was narrow, a few trees in a clump to the right, then ahead, an archway through an ancient wall of red brick. I passed under the arch, then saw a sort of forest of thick white pillars rising up to a white roof. It was the curved colonnade that surrounded Saint Peter's Square, four pillars deep at each interval. Each pillar was about eight feet wide, perched on a square base. I swept by them and came into the vast expanse of the square.

I had lost sight of the priest, but there he was, headed for the grand entrance to the basilica itself. Startled, a small flock of pigeons at once took flight in a great fluttering and flapping of wings. Nearby, a well-dressed group of tourists watched curiously. You didn't often see a priest run. Atop both the colonnade and the church rooftop, Bernini's monumental marble saints stared placidly down upon us. The cloudless sky was a bright blue.

I was off again at once, soon bounding up the many stairs to reach the monumental doorway wherein I had seen the priest disappear. I paused, briefly, to catch my breath, then went inside. I looked about, but I could not see the priest anywhere. "Damnation," I murmured. The scale of the interior was overwhelming. This was merely the portico, a sort of gigantic vestibule, an entrance area bigger than many normal churches.

There were several colossal doorways into the basilica; the fourth had one of its huge bronze doors open. I strode through into the basilica proper, blinked a few times as my eyes adjusted to the dimness, then drew in my breath in dismay. A colossal maze stood before me, all of marble and gold, with huge pillars towering far overhead, and myriad side altars, and everywhere statues and paintings of saints and martyrs! The floor itself was an intricately designed pattern in all different colors of marble, including some rose and orange hues which I would not have believed existed. People were scattered about taking in the sights, dwarfed by their surroundings. Faintly I heard the sound of voices murmuring in unison. A Mass must be in progress before some hidden altar in a distant corner.

"Oh Lord," I murmured. "This is hopeless."

I stepped forward, walked to the left, then to the right. All that happened was that my sense of standing before a vast maze was amplified. The priest had vanished, swallowed up somewhere in this cavernous maw.

I returned to the center, then started down the nave toward the distant baldacchino above the main altar, Bernini's dark bronze creation with its four ornate sinuous pillars, each about sixty feet high. I looked to either side, hoping against hope that I might see the man. I did see three different priests in black cassocks, two short stout ones and one tall thin one with black hair, but no redheads. Many tourists also wandered about, the men in dark jackets, their hats clutched in one hand, while the women in their colored dresses all had their heads covered with either scarves or hats. My steps echoed faintly, and the airy expanse above me seemed to almost hum softly, as if it were somehow alive, sentient.

Discouraged and very much aware that Saint Peter's was indeed the largest church in the world, I stopped halfway to the altar. The basilica was about twice the length of Notre-Dame, and the nave seemed to go on forever. There were a multitude of nooks and crannies where someone might hide. I was not going to find the priest.

I turned and started back. Ahead of me, coming my way, was the tall slender figure of Holmes in his black frock coat and striped trousers, his top hat under his arm. We had dressed formally for our visit to the cardinal.

We came together and halted. "This is truly hopeless," I murmured.

Holmes nodded. "Indeed it is. Let us return to the Papal Palace." He was frowning, the muscles about his mouth rigid. "We cannot waste more time here. The cardinal…"

Our words seemed somehow feeble in that great space, minute, tiny bubbles of sound drifting upward only to pop and vanish.

We walked quickly toward the same doorway through which we had entered, then headed for the nearest exit to the portico, which led out to the steps and the square. I was about to go through, but Holmes grasped my arm tightly, stopping me.

"Look," he said.

A heap of black cloth lay tucked near the doorway, upon it a mysterious bristly red lump. Holmes laughed softly, then bent over and picked up what was evidently a wig of short red hair. He dropped it, then seized the black cloth and raised it, revealing a cassock with its row of small black buttons. He folded it into a wad, took the wig, and held them clutched to his side.

"He no longer needs his disguise, so he sheds it like a snake does its skin. No doubt, the cassock was worn over regular clothes. He must have taken it off somewhere inside, then doubled back behind us. We would have a hard time recognizing him now out in the square. All the same, it was most considerate of him to leave the remnants behind for me to examine! But come—we must hurry."

We stepped out into the bright sunlight, leaving behind the monumental heaviness of the church interior, and started down the steps. "Who was that man?" I asked. "And why did you chase after him in the first place?"

"We have seen him once before, Henry, but in a different disguise. When I realized that, I knew he could be up to no good. I wanted to question him, but he ran."

"Where did we see him?"

"One night at dinner." He gave me a brief amused smile. "It was when we were with Signorina Antonelli. Remember the young man with the pompadour and the fantastical mustache who was making eyes at her? That was him."

"Good Lord—are you joking? But the mustache..."

"Was either shaved off or was fake, the latter case being most likely. It was rather preposterous, after all."

"But how could you possibly recognize him? Especially since he had on a wig."

"It is my habit to notice things which others do not. In this case, that evening at dinner, the mustache and his interest in the girl troubled me. I did not like the way he stared at her, and if the mustache were fake, I wondered why he would be hiding his face. I looked for some detail which would allow me to recognize him if we met again, and I found it. The bottom of his right ear had a red scar, as if someone had started to cut off the lobe."

I shook my head. "Only you could notice such a thing."

"When we passed him in the hallway just now, I thought he looked odd. It took me a few seconds to realize he had the same scarred ear. That's when I turned to follow him."

"What business could he possibly have had there?"

Holmes drew in his breath slowly through his nostrils, hesitated. "It is obvious enough, I fear. But I would rather not say it aloud."

We crossed the square and went under the colonnade and between the pillars, then came out on the cobblestone street leading back to the palace. Before the doorway, the same two Swiss Guards in their berets and colorful uniforms stood at attention with their halberds. The taller one stepped forward. "What is going on, Signor Holmes?" he asked in Italian.

"One of you had better come with me."

The guard nodded and followed us inside. We started down the corridor toward the stairs. Holmes looked quite grim, and I realized exactly what the fake priest's business might be. My stomach had a queasy, half-nauseous feeling of dread.

We went up the stairs, down a corridor, turned, and Holmes opened the tall door to Cicogno's rooms. His assistant, the young priest I suspected was Austrian, smiled and stood up from behind his desk. Monsignor Greene also rose from his armchair to greet us.

"Good morning, Signor Holmes," the priest said.

"Good morning, Father. Have you been here long?"

"Yes, about an hour, since a little after eight."

"And was a priest here to see the cardinal, a tall one with short red hair?"

"Yes, indeed."

Holmes glanced at Greene. "Did you see him, too, Monsignor?"

"I did indeed. He just left a few minutes ago. Quite polite—he said, '*Pax vobiscum, fratelli*,' as he departed."

Holmes made a bitter sound akin to a laugh. "'Peace be with you.' The fellow does have nerve." He drew in his breath slowly. "You had better all come with me." He walked past the desk toward the door to the office.

The priest sprang forward. "You cannot go in unannounced! The cardinal doesn't allow it. He will be upset!"

"I think not."

Holmes opened the door, and the priest followed him through. I hesitated, knowing now, for certain, what was to come. "Dear God!" the young priest cried. I stepped inside, Monsignor Greene and the Swiss Guard just behind me.

"Oh Lord," Greene murmured, even as the guard whispered, "*Gott im Himmel.*"

The cardinal was sprawled across the top of his mahogany desk, face down, white papers scattered under him, a vivid red splotching those on one side near his body. One arm was reaching forward, his long white fingers outstretched. His zucchetto had come off and lay beside him, its inner red lining showing the shine of silk. The skin on the bald crown of his head was pale and splotchy, with a few freckles. A dark stain soaked his cassock in the middle of his back, the crimson color hidden amidst the black fabric.

The young priest started forward as if to seize the cardinal, but Holmes held him back. "Don't touch him—I'm certain it is too late to be of any help. But I shall just make sure." He slipped his fingers under the cardinal's wrist, gripped it loosely, searching for a pulse. "Nothing."

Holmes stepped forward and leaned over slightly, examining the wet stain. The cardinal looked almost as if he had been somehow dropped onto the desk. His entire torso was sprawled there, his legs dangling behind him, his feet under a wooden bar between the chair legs. Holmes hesitated, then reached out with his forefinger to touch the center of the wet spot. "The same tear exactly, Henry. And no doubt the weapon was also the same—a stiletto."

"But why on earth would the Camorra meddle in Church business and murder a cardinal?" I asked. "It makes no sense."

"I agree," Monsignor Greene said. "I have never heard of such a thing. Even some ignorant peasant who was not much of a believer would consider it bad luck."

Holmes said nothing. His face was pale and very stern. At last he glanced at Greene and the other priest. "Neither of you heard anything?" They both shook their heads. "He probably showed the cardinal something, most likely those papers, then slipped behind him. He put one hand over his mouth so he could not cry out, then slipped in the blade with the other hand. The cardinal would have died almost instantly. Then he simply let the body collapse onto the desk. This man is a butcher." His voice quivered with anger.

The young priest shook his head in dismay. "This is the worst sacrilege yet—killing a priest! The relics are nothing."

Holmes folded his arms. "Tell me, Father, did Baron Marullo happen to stop by yesterday afternoon to see the cardinal?"

The priest looked puzzled. "Yes. Who told you?"

"And after his visit, could you comment on the cardinal's mood? Was he, by any chance, annoyed or angry?"

"It was odd, you know, Signor Holmes. As you probably recall from your visit yesterday, most of the day, the cardinal was very sad about the theft and the murder, but he completely changed after seeing the baron. He was furious! I have seen him angry before, but not like that, and never with the baron. They have always been the best of friends. Usually the cardinal's was a cold anger that sent shivers down your spine, but yesterday he was shouting."

"Did you happen to hear what the cardinal said?"

"Yes, as the baron was going out the door, he shouted, 'Not one *centesimo*, do you hear—not one *centesimo*!'"

Holmes and I exchanged a look. "Not a penny, as we might say," Holmes murmured. "I think we had better visit the baron, and soon. Do you want to come along, Monsignor?"

"Yes, I suppose so." He sighed deeply. "I guess Father Schmidt and the guardsman can take care of the cardinal."

The tall guardsman nodded. "I shall have to fetch the captain of the guard immediately, and the police, as well."

The young priest seemed almost in tears. "It's far too late for the last rites. May God have mercy on his soul."

Greene nodded. "Yes. The cardinal and I… we did not exactly get along, but I would never have wished such a thing upon him—*never*."

Holmes turned to the guardsman. "That supposed priest we were chasing was the assassin. He was wearing these." Holmes pointed to the wig and cassock which he had set on a nearby table. "Before we go… There is no time to waste, but I must have a quick look."

He took the cassock, looked inside it, then put his hands in the pockets. He gave a dry laugh as he produced a black rosary. "This fellow obviously has an eye for verisimilitude." He set the cassock down, picked up the red-brown wig, carefully turned and opened it, even as he stepped closer to the window and its light. "Ah." Letting the wig lie flat in his left hand, he carefully reached down with thumb and forefinger and extracted something. "A light brown hair, his actual color, Henry."

He set down the wig and the hair, thoughtfully regarding both, then reached into his jacket pocket and took out an envelope. He opened it, placed the hair inside, then sealed the flap. Back into his pocket it went. "We must be on our way, gentlemen."

Monsignor Greene gazed once more at the cardinal. "*Addio, Eminenza,*" he murmured. He lay his hand on the dead man's shoulder. "*Requiem aeternam dona eis.*"

Holmes, Greene, and I quickly returned to Saint Peter's Square and soon found a nearby cab to take us to the baron's lodgings. None of us spoke much during the ride. Both Holmes and the monsignor were grim. I felt the usual sort of dismay and anxiety which always followed the discovery of violent death.

The short, stout butler answered the door and soon led us into the baron's small sitting room cluttered with worn furniture and appalling knick-knacks.

The baron was wearing another of his elegant suits, this one of a pale gray wool with a matching waistcoat. He grinned at us, which made his grandiose waxed mustache seem somehow even larger. "Ah, three of you this time, including Monsignor Greene!" Our grave expressions registered with him. "Is something the matter?"

"Yes," Holmes said. "Cardinal Cicogno has been murdered, most likely by the same person and the same stiletto that killed the guard at Santa Croce."

Marullo opened and closed his mouth, even as the color began to bleed from his face. "Is this some joke?" he stammered.

Holmes gave his head an emphatic shake. "Hardly."

The baron's lips formed the word *Cicogno*, but hardly anything came out. He stepped back, then sank into a chair, almost gasping as he drew in his breath. "I cannot believe it. I cannot believe it." He ran his small brown hand back through his thinning black hair. He was deathly pale. "I should have never…" His brown eyes rose to us, then quickly fell, even as his mouth twitched. He sobbed once, then struggled to control his breathing. "I… I don't feel well." A sudden terror showed in his eyes.

I looked about, then noticed a decanter of brandy on the sideboard. I walked over, poured out half a glass, then took it to him. "Drink this."

His hands were shaking as he took the glass with two hands and quickly downed the contents. "Oh God help us—God help us…" His eyes were still fearful. "With a stiletto, you said?"

Holmes nodded. "Yes."

His eyes filled with tears. "Poor Carlo. He did not deserve this. It is all—" He bit off his words. "A tragedy—yes, a great tragedy." His gaze turned inward; he didn't appear to even see us.

His hands were trembling so much that I feared he might drop the glass. I reached down to take it from him and set it back on the sideboard.

Holmes glared mercilessly down at him. "It is time, Barone, for you to be frank with me. If you cooperate—if you tell the truth—just possibly, we may be able to save your life."

Terror flared anew in the baron's expression. "What are you talking about!"

"I suspect you have unleashed a force which you cannot control. That force will consume you next."

"Force—force—what are you talking about!"

"You and the cardinal were worried about the relics. You both thought they should be hidden away, but the Holy Father wouldn't listen to reason. Then one of the most precious relics, the finger of Saint Thomas, was actually stolen. When it was returned, the two of you decided that it must never happen again. The time for talking, for debate, was done. You would take matters into your own hands. You yourself would have the relics stolen, and then the cardinal would hide them away, securing them so that the Church need never have to worry about losing them again."

The baron drew in a shaky breath, clenched and unclenched his teeth. "I don't know what you are talking about."

"You would take care of the theft—or rather, one of your Neapolitan associates would see to it, one connected to the Camorra. However, the thief was not content to simply steal the relics. He casually killed a man in the process. Despite his faults, Cardinal Cicogno could not accept this. I imagine he was quite angry about the murder, and then you compounded your error, making matters far worse."

"What do you mean?"

"You asked the cardinal for money. He thought you were a man of faith, but you showed your true colors. He was outraged. 'Not one *centesimo*!' he shouted."

The baron's mouth opened wide. "How can you know that?"

"I have it right, do I not? And who is this *camorrista* you employed? Give me the truth, and I still may be able to save your miserable life."

"I..." He drew in another great shaky breath, then staggered upward and went to the sideboard. He poured another glass of brandy, then drank it down. His fists clenched and unclenched.

He was still pale but he seemed to have regained control. His eyes shifted to Holmes once more. "I really don't know what you are talking about, Signor Holmes."

Holmes gave a sharp laugh. "So that is the way it is going to be?"

The baron drew himself up, swallowing. "Always it is the same for us *napoletani*. We are all thieves, criminals, murderers, and *camorristi*! Always we are suspects. It is unjust—especially, too, since I am a devout Catholic. Every Sunday I go to Mass—I never miss a Sunday—*never*." He stared at Greene. "Monsignor, can you believe what he is saying? Surely you know better."

Greene looked sternly at him. "It makes a good deal of sense to me. As they say in English, 'The road to Hell is paved with good intentions.' However, I would have hoped a cardinal of the Church would know better."

"Exactly so, Monsignor! Cardinal Cicogno—God rest his soul!— would never be party to such a thing." He turned again to Holmes. "You do me and the cardinal a great wrong, *signore*."

Holmes shook his head. "You deserve whatever is going to happen to you. I have little patience with hypocrisy, but there is none worse than the religious kind. On one hand, you claim to be a devout and faithful Catholic, and yet you employ murdering thugs to rob the basilica."

"I did not know—" He almost bit off his words. "That is, I did no such thing."

"So perhaps you, like the cardinal, were taken by surprise. You have dangerous friends, Barone, very dangerous. The head man seems a clever devil. Besides his brute skills with the knife, he has a genuine gift for disguise. I also see flashes of a certain twisted sense of humor. Perhaps you think you can reason with him. All the same, I would never wish to put myself at his tender mercy."

The baron had grown pale again. "I don't know what you are talking about."

His repeating that same phrase was becoming quite tiresome.

"This is useless. I shall leave you to your fate." Holmes glanced at Greene and me. "Gentlemen, we are wasting our time here. Let us be off." He turned to leave.

The baron raised his hand. "Wait! You said—can you protect me?"

"I can protect you if you tell me the truth."

The baron stared at him, a muscle on the left side of his mouth twisting. "I have told you the truth." He hesitated only a second. "So help me God."

Holmes smiled faintly, even as Monsignor Greene gave his head a slight shake. "I can almost feel sorry for you, Barone. Religion can be a force for good in some people, but for others it becomes a strange, complicated web, a sort of contradictory tangle of warring impulses of good and evil. You probably did want to help the Church, but you also saw no harm in enriching yourself in the process. I suspect you consider the guard's murder regrettable, but not so much so that you will try to see justice done to the killer. Your relationship with the cardinal was self-serving, but he was your friend. Even so, you are not willing to help me catch his killer. Are you?"

Marullo stared at him silently. He opened his mouth and closed it without speaking. Anguish was apparent in his face. "Good day, then, Barone."

Monsignor Greene and I followed Holmes out of house and back onto the cobblestone street. I had half-expected the baron to try to stop us. I pulled out my watch. It was not even noon, but the morning seemed to have lasted forever.

Chapter Seven

That afternoon Holmes and I felt we needed some respite from murder and violent death, so we again went out with Monsignor Greene. We took a boat ride down the Tiber which would have been pleasant were it not for the circumstances. We had dinner in a small restaurant in the Trastevere neighborhood not far from the Vatican. By then we knew we could not go wrong with any of the monsignor's choices, but we were subdued after the events of the past two days.

As we sat sipping our *digestivi*, Monsignor Greene let out a long weary sigh. "I cannot believe that Cardinal Cicogno is really gone. He was always a difficult man, but even so... Always so angry. Anger is one of the seven deadly sins, you know, and he had it in spades. I'm afraid many of us clerics are hardly exemplary."

I smiled at him. "You, on the other hand, seem one of the least angry men I have met."

Holmes nodded. "Even so."

Greene gazed down at his plump hands resting on the table. "I doubt I can take much of the credit. It seems somewhat a matter of native disposition. I have never been one of a truculent nature. Partly it is merely being practical—of what use is anger? All it does is stir you up, muddle your thinking, and make for trouble."

One thing we did not talk about was how the case would be pursued and what might happen next. It all seemed rather hopeless to me, although I could not fathom what the Camorra might want with a bunch of relics.

Before we left, Greene asked if we might want to attend Mass with him the next morning. There was a small church, Santa Maria della Vittoria, near the train station, which had the famous Bernini statue of Saint Teresa. When he heard I had not seen the statue, Greene said I absolutely must make the visit. "Besides," he added, in French, "we must make you Catholic again."

Holmes and I both smiled. "I fear I'm something of a lost cause," I said.

"No one is ever a lost cause," Greene murmured.

The Hotel Eden was only a ten-minute walk from the church, and Greene met us in the lobby at quarter to ten, Sunday morning, so we could be there for the Mass starting on the hour. The exterior of Santa Maria might be rather plain and unimposing, but the interior made up for it. Although small compared to the monumental churches we had visited, the inside was a riot of color and ornamentation. There were more fabulous shades of marble filled with black, blue or a flecked golden-brown, and more gilt friezes all around the painted ceiling where Mary reigned supreme while sinners fell into Hell at the other end. White sculpted angels hovered everywhere on high. Pillars of every assortment abounded—round and square, small and large, while balusters and balustrades of spectacular marble stood before each of the three altars.

And there, above the altar on the left side, all of white marble, Saint Teresa herself was sprawled out upon a cloud with an angel standing over her holding a spear-like arrow. Behind the two figures, thin golden beams representing the divine light streamed down. The saint's robes formed an intricate and rather abstract pattern which hid her body and her hair; only her face, her left hand and her left foot showed.

The pews could hold at most about a hundred people, and they were only half full. We managed to sit near that left altar, and I must admit that rather than concentrating on the Mass, my eyes often wandered over to the saint, and especially that bare left foot which was the nearest part of her. As a Protestant, Holmes could sit during much of the service, but I reverted to form and sat, stood, and knelt even as the locals did. Inevitably I grew bored during Mass, so the saint was a welcome distraction.

The complicated folds of her garment were a confused tangle, compared to the slim, plain, and rather sensuous elegance of her hand and that foot. They were amazingly life-like. I was certain Bernini must have been a lady's man. Not for him those muscle-bound hulks like Michelangelo's David and Moses!

It was not quite so obvious with Saint Teresa, but late last week, Monsignor Greene had taken us through the Villa Borghese, and we had seen Bernini's statue of Daphne and Apollo. Daphne was almost completely naked, slender, and beautiful in an openly erotic way, even though tiny branches were starting to sprout from her fingers and toes as Apollo transformed her into a laurel tree. Nearby, in another of Bernini's works, Pluto had been hauling off a mostly naked damsel—Proserpine, and the fingers of his hand were clearly pressing into her bare thigh. Bernini certainly had a way with women's hands and feet. Of course, none of these marble creations could compare with the real thing–with a woman like my wife Michelle, who would be arriving the next day.

The priest had begun the *pater noster*, and I tried to pay attention. After all, the church of Santa Maria della Vittoria was hardly the place for impure thoughts! All the same, married men could not really have impure thoughts about their wives, could they? And was lusting after inanimate objects of marble also wickedness? Again, I tried to concentrate on the prayers.

I glanced over at Monsignor Greene, whose head was nodding piously, the lines in his forehead showing beneath thin sandy hair. I wondered if he had ever been troubled by such longings. If so, perhaps he had aged past them by now. However, it was clear Father Blackwell must be having sensual thoughts about Anna. Some men could live a celibate life contentedly, but I was certainly not such a person. Neither, I suspected, was Father Blackwell. Hidden away and living apart from women for many years, he had managed to hold back a part of himself, but now it would no longer be contained.

I remembered how in my early twenties I had felt a certain emptiness at the core of me, a loneliness I felt even amidst the gaiety of my male friends. It wasn't until I met Michelle and fell in love with her, that I realized what had been missing in my life. Men and women were, in a fundamental way, made for one another. I might have my doubts about God, but not about that, which was why a celibate priesthood seemed so fundamentally misguided to me. I could never, in good faith, tell Blackwell that his vocation should come first–that he should forget about Anna–or that his desire, his longing, was wicked. To the contrary, it is fleeing from love that seems wicked.

I sighed and tried again to concentrate on the Mass. Abruptly I realized Holmes was watching me, his lips forming that familiar sardonic smile. I knew he could not really read minds, but he certainly understood me. My distractibility clearly amused him. Most likely, too, he had noticed that I seemed more interested in Saint Teresa's foot than in the Mass!

Afterwards, we wandered about Rome and had lunch with the monsignor before returning to the hotel in the mid-afternoon. The attendant behind the desk gestured toward Holmes. The message in an envelope was from Commissario Manara: he wanted to see Holmes at the Questura as soon as possible.

Holmes shook his head grimly. "It is as I feared."

Manara, as well dressed and groomed as before, greeted Holmes and me with enthusiastic handshakes, then gestured to the chairs next to a small round table. His spacious cluttered office smelt of tobacco smoke, and indeed, a big ashtray of crystalline glass was filled with butts. He waited for us to sit, before he sank into a large chair with leather-covered arms and crossed his legs. From his inside jacket pocket, he produced a silver cigarette case which he opened and offered to us. "Cigarette?"

Holmes took one and said, "Thank you," while I shook my head.

Manara struck a match and lit Holmes's cigarette, then his own. His dark brown eyes had a curious expression, somehow both faintly angry and faintly playful.

"Do you know why I wanted to see you, Signor Holmes?"

Holmes exhaled smoke. "Because there has been yet another murder since that of the cardinal?"

"Oh Lord," I murmured in dismay.

"Baron Marullo?" Holmes asked.

Manara smiled, the corners of his waxed black mustache rising. "Splendid, *signore*. Again, I see your reputation is most justified."

"And I suppose it was done as before, a thrust of the same stiletto in the back."

"It certainly appears so."

"Where did it happen?"

"Would you care to venture a guess?"

Holmes stroked his chin thoughtfully. "He must have known the kind of man he was dealing with. If he had any sense, he would have locked himself in his house along with a bodyguard or two and…" His drew in on his cigarette, his voice trailing off, then he winced slightly. "But it is Sunday. And he said he never missed Mass, and after all that has happened, he would have needed… spiritual consolation." He sounded both bitter and ironic.

"Better and better!" exclaimed Manara, with an appreciative nod of his head.

Holmes tapped his cigarette into the huge ashtray. "So he was killed in a church?"

"Superb, *signore*, truly superb."

"Tell me how it happened."

Even as he inhaled from his cigarette, Manara set his free hand on the table and drummed lightly at the wood with his fingertips. A large solid gold ring was on one finger. "As was his custom, this morning he went to the Basilica del Sacro Cuore di Gesu. He had one of his men come along, a brawny one who could act as bodyguard, but the fellow went outside for a smoke while…" His hand made a fist and struck the table once.

"This is a nice touch, indeed. The baron was going to confession! He had apparently knelt on one side of the wooden confessional at the back of the church and was waiting his turn with the priest, when his man briefly stepped outside. When the servant returned, he found the baron slumped against the wall of the confessional. He went to shake his arm, and the body sprawled out upon the floor. The Mass was about to begin, and this caused general consternation. A nearby policeman was called in, and soon the news reached the Questura. I had told them to contact me if there were any more killings like that of the guard and the cardinal where a stiletto was the presumed weapon." He shook his head. "Three murders in three days. The fellow keeps himself busy, Signor Holmes! He also seems to have a special fondness for sacrilege. When will this end, I wonder?"

Holmes was frowning. "I suppose somehow the baron thought he would be safe in a church, that it was a sacred place. Obstinacy, stupidity—call it what you will. Surely he should have known his man well enough to understand that the location would not hold him back in the least."

"He must have felt a need for confession," I said.

"All the same," Holmes said, "it was foolhardy. Were there any witnesses to the murderer?"

"There was an old woman praying in a nearby pew. She heard a muffled noise and saw a tall young man leaning over on that side of the confessional. She thought he was only talking to the other man inside. However, all she really noticed of the tall man was his mustache."

Holmes gave a bark of a laugh.

"She said it was an incredible sight, slightly reddish, gigantic and quite extraordinary."

Holmes glanced at me. "I think we have seen that particular mustache."

"Indeed?" Manara said, drawing on his cigarette.

Holmes told him about our dinner and the young man watching Anna Antonelli.

"But why on earth would he have been at the restaurant?" Manara asked.

"The *signorina* was, I think, so to speak, an innocent bystander who caught his attention. I suspect he was there to see Sherlock Holmes, to gauge his opponent, the man whom the Vatican would pit against him."

Manara crushed out the small remnant of his cigarette in the ashtray. "The Swiss Guard told us that the man who killed the cardinal had no mustache."

"It is the same man—I would wager anything on it. The mustache always seemed a rather obvious fake."

Again, Manara shook his head. "This man is like no *camorrista* I have ever dealt with! They do not wear disguises. They do not kill priests or commit murder in the church. They do not steal relics. They are not so clever—they are simple-minded brutes. And yet that stiletto... The technique of the killings is typical of their assassins."

"There does seem to be a certain youthful audacity at work here. Perhaps it is his first major undertaking, although he must have picked up his skills with a blade earlier."

Manara ran his fingers back through his hair, gave his head a shake, then took another cigarette and lit it. "I pray to God he will stop! My superiors are not happy at all, Signor Holmes. Killing a cardinal... It was in all the newspapers this morning. Do you think our tall friend has come to the end of his killing spree?"

Holmes nodded. "Yes. It was as I told the baron: I think the baron and the cardinal decided to steal the relics."

Manara stared in disbelief. "Steal the relics?—but Cicogno was their guardian."

"They wanted to steal them in order to hide them away for safekeeping, not, initially, for personal gain. Cicogno left the details up to the baron, who enlisted the aid of the Camorra. However, both the *camorrista* and the baron thought there might be some profits to be made in the theft. You said the baron had gambling debts. He asked the cardinal for money, after the fact, and the cardinal was furious. He was already upset about the guard being murdered. I don't think the baron foresaw that either. Anyway, no money was forthcoming from either the cardinal or the baron, and either man might have admitted to the authorities or the pope what they had done, so the *camorrista* simply got rid of both men."

Manara scowled. "I don't think we will ever see those relics again. He will find some religious fools willing to pay through the nose, although it may take some time and some searching. You cannot simply advertise such merchandise."

Holmes put his fingertips together. "There is another possibility."

Manara tipped his head slightly. "Yes?"

"The Catholic Church may have lost certain of its territories, but it still has great wealth."

Manara again struck the table with his fist. "Ah, bravo, *signore*! *Eccellente.* He will try to ransom the jewels! Even for those who might be skeptical of the sacred nature of these relics..." He gave us a slightly amused, conspiratorial look. "However, the Church cannot be skeptical. They will pay to have them returned."

"The Holy Father told us they were priceless, but our thief will come up with some hefty price, I am sure. In the meantime... If we were in London, I would have my sources to consult with about various criminals, but here in Rome, I am at a loss. Do you have any informers in the Camorra?"

"A few, but none higher up. However, I did receive an interesting telegram this morning from one of my counterparts in Naples. A certain Antonio Gallo, a head of one of the most prominent *camorrista* families, left for Rome on a train this morning. He comes to Rome often, so the timing may be just a coincidence. All the same…"

Holmes had lit a second cigarette. "Can you have him watched?"

"Yes, I already thought of that. I have put one of my men on it."

I frowned. "Is this Gallo the head of the whole Camorra?"

Manara shook his head. "No, the Camorra does not have a single leader. It is a loose amalgam of families, each with their own sphere of influence. Occasionally they war with one another. The Sicilian Mafia is a much more centralized organization."

"Could Gallo be behind the theft?" I asked.

Manara drew on his cigarette, leaned forward to tap off the ash, then sank back in his chair. "I very much doubt it. Again, our tall friend is not acting like any *camorrista* I have ever known."

A policeman thrust his head through the doorway. "*Commissario?*" he murmured.

"Ah," Manara said, stubbing out his cigarette. "Do you have any other questions for me, *signori*? I have other business which needs my attention."

Holmes shook his head and took a last draw on his cigarette. "No, Commissario. I hope you will keep me informed of any further developments. Here in Rome, I am at your mercy."

Manara smiled faintly. "And I hope you will do the same for me, Signor Holmes! The Vatican likes to keep their secrets, but we must work together to find the killer."

We shook hands with him and stepped outside. "*Arrivederci,*" Manara said, then ushered the waiting policeman into his office.

* * *

The next day, Monday morning shortly after eight o'clock, Holmes and I went into the hotel restaurant for breakfast. Seated at a table in the corner was Monsignor Greene with a newspaper before him. He glanced up at us and smiled briefly, but his blue eyes remained troubled. Holmes and I sat at his table.

"This is an unexpected pleasure," Holmes said.

Greene's smile was long gone. "The Holy Father wants to see you. As soon as possible, but of course, you needn't skip your breakfast." He gestured toward the newspaper. "The baron's murder has made the front page. The article emphasizes its sacrilegious nature."

Holmes and I had merely coffee and a pastry each, then took a carriage with the monsignor across Rome to the Vatican. As we went past the Swiss Guards into a gaudy baroque hallway, I realized how ominous the Papal Palace had become. Nothing particularly good ever seemed to happen here!

We were ushered into the pope's study, and he rose from his desk to greet us. He wore the usual white cassock and white zucchetto and nervously thumbed at the pectoral cross at his breast, his wide mouth drawn into a grim straight line. Holmes and I both bowed, then shook his hand, while Monsignor Greene kissed the papal ring.

Again, he gestured toward some simple armchairs, even as he went to the more throne-like one. First, however, he picked up a piece of paper from the desk. "Seat yourselves, *messieurs*." As before, he spoke to us in French.

Still holding the paper, he turned toward Holmes. "I have not had the chance to truly thank you for your many efforts on our behalf, Monsieur Holmes. They tell me you nearly captured Cardinal Cicogno's assassin on Saturday."

Holmes smiled ironically. "I'm afraid the credit there must go mainly to Henry. He came far closer than I to outrunning him. Unfortunately, our prey hid himself in Saint Peter's."

The pope's face stiffened. "To think he would profane so sacred a place with the cardinal's blood still on his hands. God's justice may be delayed, but it will fall upon him at last for so grave an offense. The state of the Church here in Rome is precarious, as you know, but these recent events... Some diabolical force is loosed amongst us, a beast with no conscience who kills without hesitation."

Holmes looked equally grim. "I'm afraid that does indeed seem to be the case."

"Sacrilege after sacrilege—there seems no end to it. Our most sacred churches have become mere slaughterhouses for this monster. And now... Have a look at this." He handed the paper to Holmes. Monsignor Greene and I leaned over to read in florid Italian:

Dearest Holy Father,

I have the honor of having borrowed certain holy relics from Santa Croce in Gerusalemme. Be assured they are in good hands. I am taking excellent care of them and honoring them with the utmost respect! Should you wish their return, I must request that you pay a certain sum, a trivial one, given their incalculable value. I require twenty-five jewels, each of at least five carats in weight. I shall let you choose between rubies, emeralds, and diamonds, although of course my preference would be for diamonds. I am certain this payment will be only a small drop from that ocean of the Church's boundless treasures. These jewels are to be delivered to me by Mr. Sherlock Holmes, at a time and place I shall specify to him in another day or two. If you fail to cooperate, it will unfortunately be necessary for me to consign the precious relics to a roaring fire. I am certain we all wish to avoid such a catastrophe. Need I warn you the police are to be kept out of this business? Surely not! Expect to hear from me soon with further details.

Your most humble and obedient servant, a certain Rafaello

I shook my head in disbelief. "He really is insufferably arrogant. Your prediction to the *commissario* was certainly exactly on target."

Holmes returned the paper to the pope. "Well, we have a name: Rafaello."

Greene hesitated. "He is surely no angel, this Rafael."

The pope frowned. "He is a devil instead. I hope, Monsieur Holmes, that you are willing to remain in Rome and assist us in this matter."

Holmes nodded. "Of course, your Holiness. I shall stay as long as it takes. I, too, wish to see the end of this business."

"Very good. You have our most sincere thanks." He smiled ever so faintly. "I could not expect better from a devout member of the Church."

"I take it you plan on paying the ransom," Holmes said.

"We have little choice, Monsieur Holmes. We cannot sit by and let this creature destroy the most precious relics of our faith. It grieves me to pay him, but the jewels would be a small price for even one of these relics."

Holmes's gray eyes met mine briefly. I suspected he was thinking the same thing as I: these so-called relics weren't worth "a *centesimo*," especially compared to a man's life.

The pope sighed. "On the very Saturday he was killed, Cardinal Cicogno had arranged to meet with me in the afternoon. Now I shall never know for sure what he wanted to tell me." His dark brown eyes stared severely at Holmes. "Have you any idea, Monsieur Holmes?"

"Perhaps. Do you have any... suspicions of your own?"

"Suspicions. An interesting word, that." Briefly the pope put the palms of his two hands together, almost as if in prayer. "Cardinal Cicogno was a man of great faith and intelligence, but he lacked a certain... charity." He and Monsignor Greene exchanged a knowing look. "He also had great energy and religious zeal, which could sometimes be carried too far. He cared greatly for the relics, so much so that they became an obsession for him. For a long time, hardly a month would go by without his begging me to hide away those particular ones at Santa Croce under lock and key, and when I refused, he would storm out. I finally forbade him to raise the subject with me again. He did not understand, but I did so more out of concern for the state of his soul, than for the relics themselves. He never considered..."

The pope sighed and lowered his hands. "Relics are curious things. There are many, many relics of the true cross. Realistically, one understands that not all of them can possibly be genuine. Regardless, they still assist the faithful. They provide moments of awe and reverence. They can help make the fact of the crucifixion more real, more tangible; thus they allow us to share in the suffering and death of our Lord Jesus Christ. And therefore, ultimately, perhaps the whole question of their genuineness is of little real importance—unless one starts buying and selling relics, or trading them like other historical knick-knacks! However, one thing is obvious: if the relics are locked up and hidden away, they can no longer be of any real use to the faithful. That is why I always refused Carlo's request."

I stared thoughtfully at the small old man with the white hair over his ears and the dark eyes. Perhaps I had grown too cynical about things. I had not expected such understanding from him.

"You asked me about suspicions, Monsieur Holmes," the pope said. "Do you think the cardinal had something to do with the disappearance of the relics?"

"I do, your Holiness. I believe he and the baron decided to take matters in their own hands. The baron had connections with the Camorra and he had them steal the jewels."

The pope sighed. "What an abomination."

Holmes raised his hand. "The cardinal did not expect murder to be part of the bargain. He was greatly shaken and upset by the killing of the guard. There was a falling out between him and the baron. However, in the end, the *camorrista* involved wanted to be paid. He also didn't want anyone to remain alive who could give details to the police and the authorities. You know the rest."

The pope shook his head. "It is enough to make me wish to lock up those relics once and for all. Perhaps that is the answer—better than their becoming objects of greed and agents of death."

"No, your Holiness," I said. "What you said earlier was true. They are no use to anyone hidden away, but there at Santa Croce, they can help the believers."

"Well, we shall see, Dr. Vernier. It is all rather moot at this point, since we no longer have the relics. All the same, we shall pay for their return."

I noticed Monsignor Greene staring at me. Suddenly he smiled. He seemed quite pleased with me.

Michelle's train was over an hour late. When we finally found each other on the platform, we shared a brief passionate kiss. The two of us were not given to public displays of affection, although in private it was quite another matter.

She touched my cheek with her fingertips. "How I've missed you."

"And I you. I have not adapted the customs of the clerical natives: I was not cut out for monastic existence."

"Nor was I." She ran her fingers down my cheek to my jaw. "As well you know."

Although the hotel was not far from the train station, we took a cab with her luggage stowed in the back. Once seated inside, she gave me a mischievous smile. "How many corpses this time?" As I began to relate all that had happened, her smile soon faded. "Oh Henry, in the future we must promise never to joke about such things again! The reality of these terrible deaths is hardly amusing."

The bellhop accompanied us up to our rooms carrying her bags. Once we were alone, the kissing recommenced. One thing led to another, and soon we were in bed together, our clothing strewn all about the floor. With a certain twinkle in his eye, Holmes had assured me at lunch that he would be gone all afternoon. I had suspected he was remembering the time when I vehemently explained to him that it was not only wealthy gentlemen and their mistresses who indulged in amatory acts in the afternoon, but respectable married couples as well.

Afterwards we lay together for a long time, my hand clasping hers, and I related in more detail everything that had happened. I told her all about Father Blackwell and Anna Antonelli.

"Poor girl," she murmured. "To lose both her father and her mother at such a young age! And then... You do think she is in love with Father Blackwell?"

"I would wager odds on it."

She let out a long sigh. "It seems cruel. Marriage is a hard thing to ask someone to renounce forever."

"I agree."

She gave my hand a squeeze. "I didn't exactly realize how difficult until I met you, my darling."

After a long while, we finally rose and dressed for dinner. Monsignor Greene had arranged for a grand meal at a favorite restaurant close by; we were all to be there, including Anna and Father Blackwell. However, Greene had mentioned at lunch that the priest had written, making his excuses and saying he was simply too busy to come. Monsignor Greene had not elaborated, but his expression made it clear to me that he understood something of Blackwell's feelings for the girl.

I did up the small buttons at the back of Michelle's blue dress, then raised her long red hair to kiss the white nape of her neck. She turned, and we shared a final kiss. She tapped my cheek lightly. "Yes, celibacy would truly have been wasted on you."

"And on you as well," I replied.

She turned away, took some swipes with a brush at her hair, then gathered it up, curling it in back and forming a chignon which she soon had pinned in place. I watched silently, pleased merely with the sight of her.

We went downstairs around six. It was much too early for dinner, so the hotel restaurant was deserted. However, we sat at the usual corner table and ordered coffee to revive us. Sipping the strong dark brew in small white cups, we talked more about all that had happened. She was curious about the relics and laughed at my obvious disgust toward that fragment of bone which was supposed to be Saint Thomas's finger.

Finally, we strolled together through the narrow, cobbled streets of Rome to the restaurant. Because of the continued pleasant April weather, a few tables had been set out in the front, and customers were already at work on plates of spaghetti or meat courses, their glasses filled with red wine. We went inside and found Anna Antonelli waiting near the main counter.

She smiled at me, then nodded toward Michelle, as I introduced them to each other. Michelle hesitated, then reached out to grasp the girl's arm. "I am so sorry about your father."

Anna's eyes immediately filled with tears. "Oh, thank you."

The two women were quite a study in contrasts. Michelle was taller by a good six inches, her skin pale with a few freckles, eyes a vivid blue, and hair distinctively red. She was well-built, robust, and curvaceous. Anna was so slight and slender, waif-like, skin tinted olive despite her light brown hair, eyes large with dark brown pupils, her hands small and delicate. Michelle wore an electric-blue silk dress with the "leg of mutton" sleeves ballooning out from the shoulders, while Anna had on a black dress, the traditional color required for mourning. However, both women had a certain animation, a power of spirit, which showed through despite their disparity.

While the introduction was finishing, Monsignor Greene and Holmes came through the door. The monsignor stared curiously at Michelle; clearly she was not what he had expected. "So, dear lady, you must be the Dr. Doudet-Vernier about whom we have heard so much!"

"This is Monsignor Richard Greene," I said, then glanced at Holmes. "And I believe you already know this reprobate with the lean and hungry look."

Holmes was not generally comfortable touching women, but Michelle was an old friend indeed. His hand rested briefly on her shoulder. "I am glad to see you. Now at last, perhaps someone can keep Henry on his toes."

Monsignor Greene turned to speak with the proprietor, a lean man in a black suit with a huge black and gray mustache compensating for his bald head. "Our table is ready," Greene said.

Anna frowned slightly. "I wonder where Father Blackwell is. It's not like him to be late."

"I'm afraid he's not coming," Greene said. "He sent his excuses. He is very busy catching up with everything."

Anna bit briefly at her lower lip, her disappointment obvious. "It seems so long since I have seen him, but I suppose it isn't, not really."

We followed the owner to a rectangular table at the back with six place settings laid out. Michelle and I sat on one side, the other three, on the other. Monsignor Greene picked up the menu and spoke in a voice heavy with mock gravity. "My friends, I hope you will vouchsafe me the great trust of ordering for us all! I swear that I will not disappoint you."

We all nodded, and Holmes said, "We are in your very good hands, Monsignor."

Greene turned to the owner and launched into a lengthy discussion of the menu in some Italian dialect I couldn't exactly follow. Each man had a grave expression, and there were frequent nods and hand gestures. Soon after the owner left, a waiter appeared with a bottle of wine which he opened and poured into our glasses. He set down the bottle, then picked up the plate and utensils for the unused place setting.

Greene raised his glass. "Let me propose a toast. Although we have not—"

Holmes touched his arm. "Someone appears to have changed his mind."

Indeed, Father Blackwell was making his way through the tables and soon stood before us a tall figure in the usual soutane, his black hair ruffled. He smiled, and then his gaze fell upon Michelle. He seemed somehow surprised. I introduced the two of them. Michelle gave me a quick glance, her eyes faintly amused, probably, I suspected because she found him so strikingly handsome. Anna gave him a radiant smile.

Father Blackwell took the empty spot next to Michelle, and the waiter soon returned with the place setting he had just removed. Monsignor Greene poured wine into Blackwell's glass, then raised his glass again. "As I was about to say, although we have not been long acquainted, already I have the warmest feelings for Mr. Holmes and Dr. Vernier. To us all, then—newfound friends, indeed!"

There was much clinking of glasses, and then we all sipped the cold white wine, a vintage from near Venice. Monsignor Greene decreed that there was to be absolutely no discussion of the missing relics, murders, or gloomy subjects; this was to be a joyous occasion. Anna asked Michelle if she was indeed a physician, and that quickly became their topic of conversation. Blackwell listened with a puzzled, slightly skeptical expression on his face.

The waiter soon appeared with a spectacular platter of antipasti: various thin reddish slices of salami and dried sausages, an assortment of cheeses, and in the center, a dish of green and black spiced olives glistening with oil, on one side, and on the other, quartered artichoke hearts. I realized how hungry I was and took various samples, all of which soon proved to be delicious.

Monsignor Greene smiled at me. "There are those who believe that resurrected bodies in Heaven will have no need of food, but I have always thought there must be feasts there as well. Perhaps in doctrinal matters I am influenced more by my stomach than Saint Thomas Aquinas. All the same, a good meal with good companions has always seemed to me one of the great joys in life."

"I agree with you, Monsignor," I said. "How can Heaven be Heaven if the great pleasures of life to do not continue on there?"

Michelle's lips compressed ever so slightly in amusement, and I knew she had caught my meaning.

Father Blackwell gave Greene a puzzled look. "Are you being facetious about Heaven?"

"Only half facetious. The afterlife is a great mystery, but it is exactly as Dr. Vernier said: what gives us joy here must somehow have its counterpart there."

"That seems to rather trivialize the afterlife," Blackwell said. "It also makes far too much of our brief corporeal existence here on Earth. We were not put here to have a good time, but to earn salvation."

Michelle smiled at him. "Can one not have a good time earning salvation? Must it be all pain, sacrifice and denial?"

Blackwell's face had grown quite stern. "Those are requisite for salvation."

"Yes, they are, but are not joy and love necessary as well?"

Blackwell's gaze strayed toward Anna. "Yes—but it is love of God and the joy of our faith that are most important."

"But surely," Michelle said, "it is through human love that we learn to love God. One is not possible without the other."

Blackwell frowned in earnest. "So are Monsignor Greene and I, therefore, incapable of loving God?"

Michelle gave him a puzzled look. "I did not say that at all. Surely, in your case, you must have loved your parents, and there is also love between friends. It needn't be between a man and a woman, although—" she smiled "—that one is my particular favorite."

"Perhaps religion and politics should be taboo as well," Monsignor Greene suggested. "Although, I promise you, Edward, it will be all bread and water for me for several days after our English guests depart! I assure you, too, that it is only the strict duties of hospitality which explain our recent explorations of the best restaurants in Rome."

Blackwell smiled. "I absolve you of all fault, Monsignor."

Holmes shook his head. "Perhaps it is due to my profession, which deals with the concrete, with hard facts and evidence, but I have always found elaborate debates upon theological matters tedious. They are far too abstract and ethereal for my tastes."

Anna suddenly smiled. "That reminds me of when I was in school in England with the sisters. My year with Sister Mary Anne, we spent much of our time discussing more and more complicated theoretical situations concerning ethical questions. Frequently this involved desert islands!" She laughed. "I remember—" She stopped, a flush appearing at her cheek even as the corners of her mouth rose and fell.

"I always loved considering such dilemmas!" Michelle exclaimed. "Tell us about this particular one."

She shrugged. "Oh, it is all too obvious I suppose." She was still blushing.

"What is it?" Michelle asked.

"Well, there was one, which a classmate devised. If a man and a woman are stranded on an island after a shipwreck, only the two of them, and they fall in love, and there is no priest available, can they… can they… be married, so to speak?"

"That is an easy one," Michelle said. "Of course they can—they can marry themselves."

Blackwell appeared startled. "Do you really think so? Only a priest can perform the sacrament of marriage."

"But there is no priest, so the answer is obvious."

Greene sipped at his wine. "I agree. The answer is obvious enough in this case."

Blackwell gave a shrug. "I suppose so."

Anna glanced at him. "Sister Mary Anne thought so, too."

Holmes shook his head. "See—this is exactly what I meant. A man and a woman shipwrecked together on a desert island! How absurd. Next thing you know, another man will be shipwrecked as well, and then the complications will truly begin."

Anna nodded. "As a matter of fact, my friend Catherine did suggest that possibility."

I smiled. "Unless the man is a priest. Then everything is neatly resolved."

Michelle groaned. "Leave it to you to come up with that possibility!"

Soon the waiter and our host arrived bearing plates of spaghetti in a red sauce and set them before us. Small flecks of red pepper and bits of pancetta stood out on the glistening strands. From a bowl of grated cheese, Monsignor Greene took a spoonful to sprinkle over his portion, then said, "*Buon appetito!*"

We had a long leisurely meal, and the food was amongst the best we had eaten in Rome. Anna had many questions about Michelle being a doctor, and Father Blackwell chimed in now and then. I could tell that he was one of those men who questioned whether medicine was a fitting profession for a woman, but Michelle's ready responses and her obvious competence seemed to bring him round. Holmes and Greene talked about the art of detection, and I confessed that I did not share my cousin's extraordinary abilities.

Blackwell and Anna also talked about their families and their youth, and the contrast was obvious. Her affection for her parents, the warmth of the relationship and in her home, was clear in her every word, as well as her enthusiasm. Blackwell was somehow subdued; it was almost as if he was describing someone else's family. He hardly spoke of his father at all, and when he spoke of his mother, it was to explain her opinion on the Church and her great desire for him to enter the priesthood.

Anna seemed to be doing well, but finally her voice faltered, even as her eyes filled with tears. Obviously talking about her parents had made her realize again the full depth of her loss. All conversation at the table briefly halted; we could hear the talk and laughter of the people in the big dining area. "I miss them so," she managed to say.

"You will always have those memories," Michelle said. "And that sort of love never fades away."

Blackwell stared at Anna, a sort of dull misery showing in his eyes. "It was a very difficult time. But I hope... I tried my best to help you, but I should have... I should have been able to do *more*."

Anna shook her head. "You did all that you could, and I could never have managed without your help. I can never repay you for all you did—*never*."

"You owe me nothing," he said.

Monsignor Greene sighed. "Dr. Doudet-Vernier is right. That sort of love never really goes away. My mother and father have been gone over twenty years, but I still miss them."

After we had finished the excellent roast lamb, we were served a chocolate torte for dessert. Michelle and Anna were still talking.

Obviously they had hit it off well. Father Blackwell seemed content just to watch the two of them, his gaze shifting from one to the other. I suspected he was taking the rare opportunity to enjoy two different manifestations of female beauty. After lingering a while over *digestivi*–some of which came from the largest bottle I had ever seen, perhaps gallon-sized and containing a pungent brown liquid–we rose at last to depart.

We stepped out into the cool night air and went past the tables set out in front of the restaurant. The quiet was a relief after the noise and chatter of the interior. Father Blackwell excused himself, saying he must do some work at last. He said his goodbyes to Michelle and Anna.

"I'm so glad you came, after all!" the girl exclaimed.

"So am I." He smiled, but the expression wavered and faded away. "I shall talk to you soon."

He and Monsignor Greene departed, but Anna asked if she might accompany us back to the hotel. Holmes and I were soon in the lead, the two women deep in conversation behind us.

Holmes drew in his breath. "A truly memorable meal, Henry. Our stay in Rome would not be half so pleasurable without the good monsignor's company."

"He is a genuinely kind and decent man, and... not quite so fanatical in his faith as his younger compatriot."

Holmes smiled faintly. "You must not take Father Blackwell quite so much at face value. I suspect that what he says and what he truly thinks may not always be exactly the same."

When we went into the hotel lobby, Anna was still with us. The two women obviously wanted to continue their conversation. Holmes and I were about to leave when Anna suddenly raised her hand. "Mr. Holmes?" He turned to look at her.

"Perhaps it is nothing, but somehow... somehow I thought it best I should tell you. I am unsure... I..."

"My dear young lady, by all means—what is troubling you?"

"Do you remember that young man with the extraordinary mustache we saw in the restaurant last time? The one who kept staring at me? Well, I saw him today again. In fact, he came up to me in the street, bowed and left me with an envelope. I did not want to open it, but I needed to know. It was a... poem, one expressing most inappropriate and unexpected sentiments."

Holmes looked grave indeed. "*Signorina*, it is most fortunate you told me. This troubles me greatly. That man is, I fear, very dangerous. Perhaps... it might be best if you left Rome for a while."

"Oh, I cannot go—not now! I..." She caught her lower lip between her teeth.

"Well, think it over. In the meantime, do not go anywhere unaccompanied, and if you see that man again—beware. Don't speak to him. Ignore him and let me know at once. And if a policeman should be at hand, tell him that man is wanted by Commissario Manara, and should be arrested immediately."

She nodded. "So I shall."

Holmes gave his head a brusque shake, then turned away. Michelle took my arm. "I shall be up in a while, Henry." She and Anna were soon seated at a large sofa, and the girl had pulled off her gloves and held her two small, finely shaped hands before her, fingers outspread.

Holmes and I went to our suite on the top floor.

"This business troubles me greatly, Henry."

"Do you really think the scoundrel is interested in Anna?"

"Who knows? He is a wild card indeed. I am going to turn in. Until tomorrow."

I sat on the sofa in the sitting room and read for a while, then glanced at my watch. It had been over an hour since I had left Michelle. Weary, I decided to briefly close my eyes.

Much later, the sound of a key in the door awakened me. Michelle came through the doorway and smiled at me. "Asleep already?"

"Dozing, anyway. After all, it was a busy afternoon." I looked again at my watch. "Goodness, the two of you must have talked for well over two hours."

Michelle's brow furrowed with concern. "Indeed we did. Poor girl." She sat down beside me, then took my hand in hers. "By the way, you were right about Father Blackwell—he is a very handsome man, indeed! But not so good-looking as my husband." She gave my hand a squeeze. "And it is as you suspected. Anna is utterly and hopelessly in love with him. At one point she tried to tell me how sinful and wicked that was." Her voice grew very stern: "But I would not hear of it! I told her that that kind of love in and of itself can never be wicked, that it is what one does with it which…" She sighed. "Oh, Henry, unlike you, I still consider myself a Catholic, but I cannot bring myself to wish them to remain apart! It seems such a waste. They so obviously love one another, and she would be good for him, I think. Why must all these popes and bishops be so stubborn? Why shouldn't Catholic priests be able to marry like the Anglican ones and other Protestants can? It makes no sense."

"You certainly don't need to convince me of that."

"I don't know really what to tell her. She thinks she should avoid him, but just now… She needs him so much."

"He thought the same thing, that he should not see her again. But he doesn't want to hurt her."

"Neither of them wants to hurt the other! Oh, it is all so absurd. I cannot believe God would have brought them together just to make them both miserable."

Chapter Eight

I woke up around eight the next morning. Michelle, no doubt exhausted from the long train voyage and her first day in Rome, was still fast asleep. I dressed and went to our sitting room, arriving even as a door swung open and Holmes appeared. He suggested we take a brief walk and breakfast somewhere other than at the hotel.

Soon we were strolling along the pavement, carriages passing us by, the horses clopping on the cobblestones. I glanced at Holmes. I could not see his brow beneath the black top hat, but something about the set of his mouth made me think he was frowning. His gray-blue eyes turned briefly toward me. I was about to ask him what was wrong, when a voice behind us said, "*Signori–scusate, per favor–scusate.*"

Holmes hesitated, then turned. I also looked behind us. A tall man in a black bowler had raised his gloved hands. His dark gray suit was well-cut and expensive, and the chain of his watch made a glittering arc between a button of his waistcoat and its pocket.

Directly behind him were two much shorter, sordid-looking fellows in worn woolen jackets and trousers of varied shades of brown, each with a battered version of the same hat as the man who had addressed us. All of them had almost stereotypical faces of southern Italy: olive skin, dark eyes, full ruddy lips, and of course, great bushy black mustaches. Their leader had a youthful face, but the creases at his eyes and hints of white in his mustache, as well as a thick fleshy neck, made me think he was probably about forty years old.

"Signor Holmes, we must speak with you." He spoke Italian with a strong regional accent.

Holmes folded his arms. "I think not."

"Please, we mean you no harm. My name is Giuseppe Gallo. It is important."

"Good day, *signore.*"

The man sighed. "I must insist." He half turned to speak to the men behind him. "Show him." The two men opened their jackets. Each had a cartridge belt, and the handles of two revolvers thrust out from their trousers. "We do not want unpleasantness, believe me. I promise you we mean no harm. You will find it most interesting. It concerns the missing relics."

"Ah." Holmes unfolded his arms and lowered his hands. "Does it now? Very well, I shall come along, but you needn't detain my cousin. Let him return to the hotel."

"As you wish, *signore.*"

"I'm not going anywhere but with you!" I exclaimed.

The man nodded. "He will be safe, I promise, Signor Holmes. It is not far, and we shall not keep you long."

Holmes shrugged. "Lead the way, then."

We turned the corner into a very narrow street. Gallo walked beside us, while the two other men were behind. My hands felt slightly sweaty, the back of my neck cold–I was thinking about the revolvers and wondering how far we could trust these men.

"Have you enjoyed the very fine weather, *signori*?" Gallo spoke with the utmost sincerity.

"We have indeed," Holmes said.

There were no further attempts at conversation after that. After about ten minutes, we turned again into a narrow alley where one would hardly be able to get a carriage through. A worn brick building had a sign that said BAR CAPRI. Gallo opened the door for us. Inside it was quite dim. A few men sat drinking coffee at small round tables, and behind the wooden counter was a big man with a mustache wearing an apron. He nodded. Gallo led us through a hallway into a room at the back.

Inside, seated at the end of a long rectangular table was an older man, and nearby stood two other men virtually identical to the ones accompanying us, including those same worn woolen jackets with the telltale bulges of revolver handles. The older man slid back his chair and stood.

As far as Italians went, he was a giant, well over six feet tall, broad and portly too, with a great rounded second chin showing above his spotless white collar. His hairline began a way back along his massive gleaming forehead, and his dark shiny hair was combed back in a somewhat futile effort to cover a bald spot. The semicircles of his eyelids were half-hidden under sagging skin, and his black eyebrows and mustache were shot with gray. His suit was similar in cut to the younger man's–made with a lustrous fabric of dark blue wool–but much larger, the jacket enormous to compensate for his great belly. He extended a rather small, graceful hand for such a giant.

"*Buon giorno, signori. Sono Antonio Gallo. Beviamo un po'. Va bene?*" He had an accent similar to the other man's but much stronger. He gestured toward a decanter on the table, then began to pour into some rather dirty-looking glasses. Their cleanliness was probably the least of our problems. He came around the table and handed both Holmes and me a glass, then took the other two, giving one to the younger Gallo.

I stared in disbelief at the clear liquid. It certainly could not be water! "We haven't even had breakfast," I murmured.

"When in Rome…" Holmes murmured softly.

The big man raised his glass. "*Salute, signori!*" He downed the contents in a single gulp.

Holmes waited only long enough to say, "*Alla vostra,*" then swallowed his down.

I decided it was better not to reflect, and I simply raised my glass and gulped down the contents. It left a fiery trail down my esophagus, making my eyes fill with tears even as I gasped for air. "What was that?" I stammered.

Holmes was smiling fiercely. "Grappa."

I shook my head. "I think I prefer coffee first thing in the morning."

Antonio lumbered back to his large chair at the table end, then sank down even as he gestured to the other chairs with his hand. "Sit, sit." Holmes and I sat at one side of the table, Giuseppe on the other. "*Sono napoletano.* I no speak Italian well, Signor Holmes, but we try. These relics—and *il barone, il cardinale*—terrible, terrible. How did it come to this? The baron was my friend, and the church… *Camorristi* do not kill priests, they do not steal blessed relics. *Qual'orrore!*" He glanced at the younger man; the family resemblance was clear enough in their dark eyes, their noses, their mouths. "Tell them, Beppo. Tell them about Rafaello."

Giuseppe's mouth curled upward on one side, his eyes suddenly dangerous. "It is about my brother, *signori*–my stepbrother, Rafaello."

"Ah," Holmes nodded. "He is the one who has killed three men and stolen the relics."

"*Esatto!*" Antonio exclaimed.

Giuseppe had set both hands on the table, probably to indicate his good intentions and that he was not going to pull a knife on us. "Rafaello is fifteen years younger than me, the result of... an indiscretion of my father, with a certain Contessa Teresa Pozzolo. He was raised with his mother's family, but when she died about five years ago, he was taken under my most generous father's wing. He was given every advantage and acknowledged as a second son–I have only sisters, you see. He was always a wild young man, given to extravagance and outrageous behavior. He liked gambling and women. He is..." Giuseppe drew in his breath, obviously struggling to remain calm.

"There is no denying his intelligence; he speaks many languages, including English. He and his mother spent time in England, and he went to boarding school there. She had a house in Milan where they lived. There her disgrace was not so well known." A rather smug look had appeared on his face. "Recently he and Baron Marullo became friends. Both men liked the cards, but the luck was always with Rafaello. The baron was a very religious man, and he was worried about the precious relics in Rome. He knew my father was a Camorra *capo*, and he broached with us the idea of having us take the relics so he and the cardinal could lock them away. He said it would be a way to redeem our souls, and that there would, no doubt, be some payment for our good deed."

"My father–" he glanced at Antonio "–always thought this a rather foolish idea, but it seemed to delight Rafaello. Rafaello said he would deal with the baron and handle everything. My father was most indulgent, and left things to my brother's good judgment—a grave mistake, *signori*. Rafaello took the relics at the baron's bequest, then asked to be paid for his services. The baron had assured him the cardinal would pay, but the cardinal was outraged by the murder of the guard. The cardinal's death was meant as a warning, and Rafaello gave the baron twenty-four hours to come up with a certain large sum of money. When it was not forthcoming, he killed the baron as well. But this you all know, I suppose."

Holmes nodded. "Most of it, I do, but how did you discover all these details?"

Antonio gestured with both hands raised. "A letter, *signore*. A letter."

"My brother wrote to tell us everything he had done and assured us that he was in control of everything, and that the Church would pay a king's ransom to have the relics back. *Stupido, stupido*. My father does not want our family honor and that of the Camorra Napoletana stained by such outrageous deeds. He sent my brother a letter expressing his displeasure and telling him to return the relics at once, then to come back to Naples."

Holmes had both elbows on the table, and he placed his fingertips together. "Obviously Rafaello had other ideas."

"Yes. And now he has disappeared. He and his servant are gone from their usual lodgings. We have been searching Rome for him—and the relics—without success. When we find the relics, rest assured, we shall return them to the church. We are not, after all, pagans."

Antonio gave a fierce nod. "Not pagans, no!"

"And Rafaello will be... disciplined."

"You must leave him to me," Antonio said.

Holmes lowered his hands and sat back in the chair. "What makes you think you can find him?"

"We shall find him, never fear," Giuseppe said.

"He is quite clever, I'll grant him that. He also has a fondness for disguises." Holmes smiled ever so faintly. "I'm not sure even his own brother would recognize him in some of them."

Giuseppe's expression was grim. "Oh, I shall recognize him."

"Where exactly did Rafaello pick up his skills with a stiletto?"

Father and son froze briefly, exchanging a glance. "I taught him," Giuseppe said. "I, and one of my best men. He had all the useless skills of a gentlemen, including fencing, but none of those necessary to survive on the streets of Naples. We taught him what he needed to know." It was clear that Giuseppe despised his stepbrother.

"He has a gift with the blade," Antonio said, rather proudly. He hesitated, then smiled. "And with the ladies."

"I have noticed that," Holmes said.

"Unfortunately, he does not always limit himself to unmarried women." Giuseppe was clearly annoyed. "And the stiletto—a primitive barbaric weapon, in the end! I prefer a revolver myself. Rafaello has sought out every opportunity to demonstrate his abilities with a knife, and his opponents are never left merely wounded. He has a gift for killing."

Holmes was frowning ever so slightly. "How did he get that scar on his ear?"

Father and son exchanged another look, the old man's expression severe. "An accident," Giuseppe said. "He moved when he should have held still. He is lucky not to have lost an ear."

"It is hard to imagine how someone could have received so small and precise a cut in a knife fight. One would expect, rather, a broad slash of some sort."

Giuseppe shook his head impatiently. "No matter. We have told you all you need to know about Rafaello. What is important is that you leave him to us. There are many of us, and we have our allies in Rome. We shall soon find the relics and return them to you to give to the Vatican."

"He has threatened to burn them if he isn't paid a fortune in jewels."

Antonio had a look of horror. "He could no do this!"

Giuseppe said nothing, but it was clear he did not share his father's conviction. "This is family business, Signor Holmes, and we shall take care of it. You must not interfere. Do you understand?"

Holmes smiled faintly. "We both have our methods. In this case, I am far from home. You are much likelier to be able to find Rafaello than I. If you do find him first, obviously his fate is up to you. However, if I find him... He has murdered three men in cold blood. He must suffer the consequences. I shall turn him over to the Roman police."

Antonio shook his head forcefully. "No, no."

"You must give him to us," Giuseppe said. "He will not go unpunished."

Antonio's eyes were faintly pained. "We make him understand."

If I were Rafaello I would not want to be left to my brother's tender mercies, but his father was another matter. He obviously was fond of his bastard son. However, I suspected Rafaello could run rings around both his father and his brother. Likely, neither of them had quite his audacity or intelligence.

Holmes shrugged. "I can promise nothing, *signori*. If you want to deal with him in your own way, then you must find him first."

Giuseppe's eyes grew very cold, his mouth stiffening. "If we lock you away, you will certainly not find him first."

Antonio raised his right hand and shook his head. "No need." He looked imploringly at Holmes and me in turn. "You understand now, *si*? We help you, *si*? We all want relics back. We find Rafaello and get them back."

Holmes smiled faintly. "That would certainly simplify matters and make the Holy Father happy."

"Good, good. We are friends now. We drink again, and then you go." He took the bottle and began to pour into our glasses.

"None for me," I said. Holmes gave me a reproachful look, but I was spared. Even after a meal in the evening I had never liked grappa; it tasted like some nasty industrial solvent.

Again Antonio's big hand clutched the glass, then raised it high as he downed the contents in a single swallow. Giuseppe and Holmes did the same. As his long slender fingers set the glass back on the table, Holmes did give a slight shudder, and he smiled at me.

Antonio stood first, and we did the same. Giuseppe had a faintly wary look, his dark eyes still cold. Antonio came round the table and shook hands with us again. "*Piacere, piacere*," he said—*a pleasure*.

We went back down the hall and through the bar to the street, Giuseppe and his two men behind us. Out in the alley a cool breeze stirred a few papers discarded on the stained stones. "My father does not want trouble with you," Giuseppe said. "Neither do I. But you must give us Rafaello if you find him."

Holmes met his glare and shrugged ever so slightly. "We shall see."

I grabbed his arm just above the elbow. "Certainly," I said to Giuseppe, then to my cousin, "Let's go."

"*Arrivederci*," Holmes said to the men.

Giuseppe nodded, his look still threatening, but he did not try to stop us as we quickly strode down the alley. We came out onto the much wider street with carriage traffic and the bustle of pedestrians.

"Thank God," I murmured. "I wasn't sure, for a moment there, if they were going to let us go."

"A challenging, if interesting start to our day, Henry! It has given me something of an appetite."

"My stomach is still churning—and that grappa—on an empty stomach!"

"I must admit I could have done without the grappa. Obviously, however, it was part of a certain ritual, so it could not be refused."

"Why don't we return to the hotel and eat there? Perhaps Michelle is awake by now and can join us."

Holmes nodded, and we started walking. An icy wave surged up my spine, making my shoulders rise in a brief shudder. "This Rafaello does sound like a very devil."

"Yes, indeed. A bastard son, no doubt raised as a gentleman, then turned *camorrista*. I suspect he is more cold-blooded even than his half-brother."

"There seems no love lost between the two."

"No, indeed, Henry." He smiled faintly. "The eldest son should inherit his father's kingdom, but in this case... I think the younger son may wish to usurp his place."

"Do you think they will find him?"

"No, I think not. Their odds are far better than for the police, but our Rafaello is a wily one."

"So what now? How, then, do we find him?"

"We do not. We wait for him to contact me, as he has said he will." We turned the corner and ahead of us was the sign of the hotel. "Why not take a break from the case today, Henry, and spend time with Michelle? I have some business to attend to, and I wanted to speak again with Commissario Manara."

"The note said not to involve the police."

"I shall not tell him everything. However, some of what the Gallos revealed should interest him. Then, too, the sheer manpower of the police can sometimes be useful."

"A day alone with Michelle does sound very agreeable. Although I only hope..." My voice trailed away.

"What do you hope?"

"I am almost afraid to speak it aloud—I only hope we are done with murders for a while."

Holmes smiled ever so slightly. "Today, I dare say, we may be safe."

When we stepped into the lobby, a familiar figure in a black soutane rose and stood before us. Father Blackwell's handsome face looked worn and haggard, and his black hair was even more unkempt than usual. Blackwell opened his mouth, then closed it. He glanced at my cousin, then his blue eyes remained fixed on me in a kind of mute appeal.

I sighed and touched Holmes's shoulder. "Tell Michelle I should be back soon." I turned to Father Blackwell. "Come along." I started back toward the big double doors, and he followed. "You haven't eaten, have you?"

"No, but I'm not hungry."

"Well, I'm starving, and you should eat something as well."

Just down the street was a small Italian bar, the type that served coffee and rolls in the morning. I ordered two cups of espresso and two *cornetti*, the rather inferior Italian version of the French croissant. Father Blackwell and I took our plates to a table next to the big plate-glass window with a view of the street. I took a huge bite of my *cornetto*, then sipped at the strong black coffee. Blackwell took a swallow of his. He hadn't shaved, and the shadow of his beard was darker than usual alongside the pale skin of his cheek. In the morning light I could see what a clear deep blue color his eyes were.

"You wanted to talk to me?" I asked.

"Yes." He slowly drew in his breath. "It's as I said, there is no one else who could begin to understand, no one who has ever... known a woman."

I smiled faintly. "Well, I'm hardly any sort of expert."

His expression grew grave. "I understand now why your marriage is so important to you. Your wife is both beautiful and intelligent."

"She is indeed, but then... so is Anna."

He closed his eyes tightly, in a sort of grimace. "I know what I must do, but I lack the courage."

"And what is that?"

"As I told you before—give her up—never see her again."

I took another swallow of coffee. "That will be hard on you both."

"It must be done."

I sighed. "I shall never understand, you know. If you love each other..."

"If you cannot understand—who will?" He drew in a breath, giving his head a shake. "I have... such thoughts. Such sinful thoughts."

I repressed a smile. "That comes with the territory."

He looked genuinely puzzled. "Does it really?"

"Eat some of your *cornetto*. Yes, it does. I told you before, love isn't just a spiritual thing." I was staring at him, but he would not meet my gaze. "Have you never had such thoughts before?"

"Not like this. While her father was ill, that occupied us both, but now... she has... my full attention."

I hesitated a long while. "Are you absolutely certain that you want to remain a priest?"

His jaw stiffened. "I have made my final vows. There is no going back."

"But did you really comprehend what you were giving up when you made those vows?"

His brow furrowed. "No, I suppose not. But that doesn't matter."

I sighed again. "As I said, I shall never understand."

"But you do understand—you know what I feel—this—this longing—this hunger for her."

I smiled faintly. "Yes, I suppose I do."

"I have always wanted to be a priest, to serve others, to serve God, but here in Rome... It is nothing but theological abstractions and angels dancing on the head of the pin! None of it is real, none of it matters. Setting Anna aside, that is why I really must leave Rome. I need to get back to a parish where I can see real people, where I can help them live well and die well. I'm so weary of Latin and Italian and other tongues." He gave a sharp laugh. "Perhaps I just want to speak English to someone again!" He tore rather savagely at his *cornetto*.

We were both quiet for a while. We sipped our coffee and stared out the window. An old couple, very formally dressed, passed by, arm in arm, the tiny bent man with a cane in his left hand. They weren't speaking, but were completely at ease with one another, sharing a familiarity beyond words. At last Blackwell spoke.

"I suppose if cannot make you understand that I must leave her, then you surely cannot approve of my decision."

I took the last swallow of my coffee, then set down the cup. "I'm afraid not."

He turned away from the old couple and looked at me. In the light his eyes glistened faintly. "But can you at least forgive me?"

"Oh Father Blackwell, of course I can. But can you forgive yourself?"

He smiled bitterly. "No, perhaps not." He drew in his breath. "But eventually..."

"I do agree that it is time for you to leave Rome. You don't want to stay here thirty years like Monsignor Greene. All the same…"

"All the same?"

"Well, as you certainly know, my preference would be that you took Anna with you."

"But then I could no longer be a priest."

"No, I suppose not."

"Although…" He was staring off into the distance out into the street. "The sacrament of Holy Orders leaves a mark on the soul, a mark that can never be removed. Even if a man abandons the priesthood he is still, in God's eyes, a priest."

I smiled faintly.

"What is it?" he asked.

"That sounds like those theological abstractions you were talking about. Surely now… Well, you do seem to realize that love of a woman is not an abstraction; it is as concrete and as real as the woman herself."

His gaze shifted to the distance again. "When I first met her, her vivacity and her charm appealed to me, but it was only over time that I realized how beautiful she was. Now I cannot imagine how I ever failed to see it."

I gave a long sigh. "You really do love her."

"*Yes.* But today I must leave her. I can put this off no longer. It is a torture to us both. She will understand. She is a good Catholic. Perhaps… she is young, rich, and beautiful. She will surely find someone else." Slowly his mouth rose upward on one side. "But you cannot understand such a choice?"

I shook my head. "No. But I can… I can respect you, even if I do not understand."

He gulped down the last of his coffee and set down the cup. "Then that will have to do!" He stood up abruptly.

I rose, and we shook hands. His palm felt faintly moist, but his grip was fierce. He gave a quick nod, then turned and strode out the door and swept past the window at a fearful pace.

"Oh Lord," I murmured softly.

I found Holmes and Michelle savoring coffee in our favorite corner table at the hotel restaurant. Still rather ravenous, I ordered a second breakfast for myself. I told them briefly about my conversation with the priest.

Michelle shook her head. "Life is difficult enough—why must people torture themselves?!"

After I had eaten, Holmes departed, and Michelle and I set out to explore Rome together. She had only been there once before as a girl, so we visited some of the most popular spots: the Colosseum, the scattered ruins of the Forum, the Trevi Fountain, the Pantheon, and the nearby church of San Luigi dei Francesi. This church was dedicated to the French and Saint Louis, a thirteenth-century king of France, and at one altar were some spectacular paintings with striking chiaroscuro of Saint Matthew's life by the Italian painter Caravaggio.

As we wandered about, I felt myself gradually relaxing, and I realized how much I had missed Michelle. She wore a blue hat with a big floppy brim to protect her fair skin from the sun. Often, she would give me a certain knowing glance, even as she smiled, and we would squeeze one another's hand. Among our topics of conversation were Father Blackwell and Anna; we both felt badly for them.

We were to join Holmes for dinner around eight, and we didn't get back to the hotel until seven. The lobby had tall painted vases with gigantic ferns, a fantastical carpet from the Arabian Nights, and large overstuffed chairs and sofas. Seated at the end of one of the sofas was Anna, her thin white face contrasting with the black of her mourning dress and hat, and the black leather of the sofa. When she saw us, she stood, then clenched her gloved hands tightly. Her eyelids were red and puffy, and her face seemed somehow thinner than usual. She managed a smile, which was more alarming than reassuring.

Michelle approached her slowly. "Oh my dear, are you all right?"

A swallow made its way along her slender throat. "It is finished." Obviously, she found it difficult to speak.

Michelle raised her arms, and then the two of them embraced each other fiercely. Michelle was all in blue, and as before, I was struck by the contrast between the two women. They soon stepped apart. Anna's jaw was thrust forward slightly, her teeth clenched. I could see that she was determined not to cry.

"Would you like to tell me about it?" Michelle asked.

"Perhaps," Anna managed to say.

Michelle gave her hand a squeeze, then turned to me. "If I'm not back by dinnertime, don't wait for me."

"We can eat in the hotel restaurant," I said. "The food isn't bad, and that way you will know where to find us."

Michelle nodded. "Very well." She touched Anna gently on the shoulder. "Come along, dear."

They were halfway across the room when a sudden memory made me stride after them. "Michelle." She turned to face me. "Be careful. Remember what Holmes said about the tall man with the mustache who was so interested in Signorina Antonelli. Don't go far, stick to the main streets, and if anyone suspicious seems interested in you, come back at once."

She nodded. "So I shall."

I sighed, then looked about. A well-dressed, dark-haired man with the matching ubiquitous black mustache of Rome, lowered his eyes again to the newspaper on his lap. He, along with the few others seated there in the lobby, had been witness to that brief drama.

I took the stairs up to our suite. Holmes was seated by the window, his pipe held in one slender hand, the fingers of the other drumming lightly at the large chair arm. I told him about Michelle and Anna.

He gave his head a shake. "Father Blackwell certainly did not waste any time. Perhaps, in the end, it is for the best."

"You will never convince me of that."

Holmes smiled affectionately. "Ah, Henry! You are a hopeless romantic indeed."

"I suppose that's true."

"Let's descend and have an *aperitivo* in the restaurant. Perhaps the ladies will eventually join us."

"I rather doubt it."

We had to walk through the lobby to get to the restaurant. At one point, Holmes's step faltered. He stopped at the doorway, then surveyed the room behind us, his expression grave.

"Is something the matter?" I asked.

"No. Not really."

We followed the waiter into the dining room, and he took us to our favorite table. A virgin white tablecloth was spread out, and the place settings were of fine china and silverware with handles of an elaborate design. Holmes sat at the back where he could survey the entire room, which, indeed, he quickly did. I sat at his side and glanced around myself. It was early by Italian standards, and only two couples were seated at tables over near the windows.

"Might I order for you, Henry? Let us try to be like the natives this evening." He turned to the waiter. "*Due vermouth rossi, per favore.*"

We discussed our activities of the day and sipped our pungent, pale red drinks, somehow both bitter and sweet at the same time. Holmes seemed curiously distracted, often glancing toward the entrance to the dining hall. Another couple came in, both the man and woman stout and Germanic-looking—indeed, a few guttural consonants soon verified their nationality—and then a tall man with a black mustache, the one who had been sitting in the lobby earlier. The cut and fabric of his black suit marked him as the master, and the much shorter man in drab brown at his side, as his servant. The servant also had a black mustache, of course, and his cheeks were pockmarked.

Holmes slowly eased out his breath and sipped again at his drink. "This is really quite good. The Italians invented red vermouth, you know, the French the dryer white variety."

"It is agreeable," I said, "but I would not want to drink it every night."

"Nor I."

His gray-blue eyes had a curious sort of simmering anger, of ferocity. "Are you sure nothing is the matter?" I asked.

His smile had the same intensity. "Not at all. Things are progressing nicely." He was staring past me, and he raised his hand in greeting.

I turned and saw the young man with the black mustache smile and raise his hand in response.

"Do we know him?" I asked.

"More or less. That would be Rafaello."

I choked briefly on my drink. "Good Lord—are you serious?"

"I would hardly joke about such a thing." His hand still raised, he flexed his cupped fingers twice toward himself.

Rafaello stood up, straightened his jacket, brushed once at some bit of dust on the left sleeve, then slowly sauntered over. He bowed ever so slightly to Holmes and me. He had a long straight nose and full, rather sensuous lips beneath the mustache, which must be a fake, along with that pompadour of curly black hair. Looking at his right ear, I could see the thick red seam of the scar running up where the lobe attached to his skull.

"Well, as they say in all the tales of adventure, Mr. Holmes—we meet at last! I cannot tell you what a great pleasure this is. I have read all of Dr. Watson's books about your adventures—in English, of course." Holmes started to frown, but Rafaello raised his hand. "However, I know they must be mostly fictional! They hardly do you justice. And surely Dr. Vernier here is superior in every way to Watson!" He spoke English with no accent at all.

"Do I know you?" I stammered angrily.

"Oh, we have not been formally introduced, but since you had that, no doubt, pleasant visit this morning with my stepbrother and father, I'm sure they must have told you all about me. All the same..." He put his hand over his belly and bowed very formally. "Signor Rafaello Pozzolo, at your service. Might I join you for a drink?"

"Certainly," Holmes said.

Rafaello pulled out a chair, sat, then waved at the waiter, who strode over. "I'll have what these gentlemen are having." The waiter nodded. Rafaello sat well back from the table and crossed his legs, showing off a well-crafted shoe of fine cordovan leather. "A pity the ladies could not join us!" He gave me a leering sort of smile. "Your wife is quite spectacular, Dr. Vernier! Statuesque, as they say. She looks like a 'handful!' Personally, though, I prefer more petite beauties, like the exquisite Signorina Antonelli."

"Don't you dare talk about them!" I exclaimed.

Holmes gave him a severe look. "Henry is right. You needn't speak of them, especially in that manner."

"Well, you don't need to get all huffy about it! I meant what I said as a compliment, Vernier. By the way, since this is just, so to speak, a friendly chat, it shouldn't be necessary to mention that there should be no thoughts of pouncing upon me and taking me into custody, or any silly thing of that sort. My man Luca there"—his servant, who had remained at their table was watching us closely—"has a revolver under his jacket, and he is an excellent shot."

Holmes nodded. "Understood."

Rafaello was smiling broadly at Holmes. "I still cannot actually believe that I am seated face to face with the famous Sherlock Holmes! I really do admire you, you know. And the opportunity to actually match wits with you... How could I resist it!"

Holmes did not return his smile. "Thus far I have seen little evidence of 'wits.' It has been nothing but brute, murderous violence with a stiletto."

"But my disguises—those have been a nice touch, have they not? You of all people should appreciate the effort I put into them."

Holmes stared at him without speaking.

"I thought I made a rather good priest. I fooled the Swiss Guards, an actual priest and a monsignor and the cardinal himself. And that phantasmagorical mustache of mine! It takes almost an hour to construct, but I dare say the results are worth it. I use two or three different shades of hair." He raised his fingers, tweaked them before his face. "This one is nothing in comparison, but it suffices. By the way—" he gave a bark of a laugh—"You will find this hard to believe, but I swear it is true! When I was young, about fifteen, I actually wanted to become a priest! I was quite sincere about it. I had been an altar boy, and I was very devout. For a brief period of time, my grandfather—my mother's father, a count—actually approved of me. However, it soon became obvious that I was not cut out for that sort of life."

Holmes sipped his drink, then set down the glass. "Trouble with a young lady, I suppose."

Rafaello laughed. "*Touché!* A hit, a palpable hit! I see you understand me, Mr. Holmes."

"Oh yes, I'm afraid I do. If I am to deliver the jewels to you, I must make one demand of my own."

"The jewels—oh yes, I had almost forgotten them. No hurry. Perhaps in a day or two. As I said in the note, I shall be in touch."

"Once you have them, you are to stop annoying Signorina Antonelli. You are not to see her ever again." His voice was stern.

"Oh, come now—it's probably the most excitement she's ever had in her life! A dashing rogue pursuing her? What girl could hope for more?"

I shook my head. "You are impossible."

"All the same," Holmes said, "it is a condition of my acting on your behalf."

"Oh, very well. Once I have the jewels, I shall, Alberich-like, renounce forever the love of the lovely *signorina*." Briefly he showed his perfect white teeth.

"What are you talking about?" I asked. "Alberich-like—whatever does that mean?"

Holmes glanced at me. "Alberich is the dwarf in Wagner's *Das Rheingold* who renounces love forever to get the Rhine gold."

Rafaello clapped his hands together, making the German couple stare at us. "Bravo, Mr. Holmes! Bravo! You are a Wagnerite! I always knew the one thing in the stories that must be true was your love of music—and the violin—tell me you have the violin—the Stradivarius!"

Holmes nodded. "I do."

"Excellent! I too am a lover of music, especially grand opera, although I cannot truly choose between Verdi and Wagner. Each is unsurpassed and original. You have, no doubt, made the pilgrimage to Bayreuth for *The Ring*?"

Holmes nodded again. "I have."

"I too, as a mere youth in the company of my mother! Unforgettable—simply unforgettable." His gaze shifted from Holmes to me, and he smiled. "Don't worry, Dr. Vernier. I assure you I am quite sane."

"Permit me to have my doubts," I said. "And there is always the fact that you have murdered three men in cold blood."

He shrugged. "Oh, rather more than that, I'm afraid. People who get in my way have a bad habit of ending up dead. But we mustn't dig up past skeletons."

Holmes had his gaze fixed on Rafaello. "Is that why you killed Cascone?"

"Cascone? Whoever is that?"

"The man guarding the relics at the church."

"Oh, him! Yes, I was just being thorough. Such a monstrous big brute! No use taking any chances. But we're getting distracted. What was I saying? Oh yes, once I have the jewels, I shall set aside my great passion and not trouble Signorina Antonelli anymore." The waiter set a glass of red vermouth before him. "*Grazie mille.*" He raised the glass. "Cheers!" He took a swallow. "Did you have an agreeable chat this morning with my father and stepbrother?"

"It was most informative," Holmes said.

"I hope they were not too hard on me. My father is a man of... substance, but he is somewhat lacking in imagination. That is even more true of Giuseppe. He hasn't an ounce of it, and he dares not make the tiniest move without my father's consent. I offer to make them a small fortune with these relics, and certain foolish scruples combined with religious superstition hold them back! Some Frenchman once said '*l'audace, toujours l'audace*,' and that has always been my motto." He sipped again at his vermouth.

"Tell me," Holmes said, "did you always plan on killing the baron?"

He shrugged. "Oh, not exactly, although the odds were against him. I wasn't exactly surprised that the cardinal was outraged. I knew Marullo had no money himself, but I did give him twenty-four hours to raise what should have been a trivial sum for a man like him. The cardinal was meant as a warning. And when Marullo failed..." He shrugged again.

I glared at him. "You murdered him. You murdered another man in a church."

"Surely an educated man like yourself, Dr. Vernier, doesn't really believe it makes a difference *where* you kill someone? He's just as dead, regardless."

"Was it really necessary to kill the cardinal?" Holmes asked.

"Better safe than sorry! Again, I was just being, so to speak, thorough. I wanted my identity to remain unknown, and it would have been, had not my father taken you into his confidence. What a disappointment." His mocking expression faded. "But then I could never exactly count on my father." He smiled again. "All the same, it has given me the opportunity to meet with you, Mr. Holmes—and, dare I say it—to match wits!" He laughed. "Tell me, Mr. Holmes, do you play chess?"

"I do."

"Of course you do! If only we might have a game together, but... no, I think not. Perhaps another time when this business is completely done with. You see, after all, the jewels aren't really the point. It's only the game that matters! And now that you sit before the board... Tell you what, I shall give you a sporting chance—very British, that!—good sport that I am, *hear, hear, old boy, pip, pip*!" He had assumed a very bad mock-British accent. "I'll give you a hint. Yesterday I hid the relics in the obvious place."

Holmes's brow furrowed, his head turning ever so slightly. His gray eyes were thoughtful, but he did not speak.

Rafaello held the stem of the glass delicately between thumb and two fingers, took another swallow. "That's all you'll get! I suppose now I had best be running along. The ladies may show up, and I might say something again which would infuriate the good doctor and cause our little visit to end with bad feelings."

"Indeed you might!" I said angrily.

Holmes sighed. "It's far too late to try to remonstrate with you and persuade you to return the relics. You have murdered three men, and for that you must pay. Given your upbringing, I suppose it's little wonder you turned out as you have."

Rafaello's good humor vanished. "There was nothing wrong with my upbringing! My mother was a true saint!"

"Perhaps, but she was always under a cloud with her family. I doubt they could ever forgive her indiscretion."

Rafaello smiled bitterly. "'Indiscretion.' Very good, Mr. Holmes. I suppose character analysis is also in your line of work."

"And now you must prove yourself to your father."

Rafaello laughed in earnest, then downed the last of his vermouth. "You are wrong there—I must prove myself *better* than my father. And my brother, as well, I suppose. As I told you, they lack imagination. They could have never managed this business with the relics. And now, rather than submit to further examination of my troubled psyche, I shall be on my way."

He stood up and gave a very formal bow, hand again just above his waist. Holmes and I did not get up. A faint smile flickered briefly over Holmes's lips. "The drink is on me, sir."

"Ah, thank you! Until we meet again, then, which should be soon—a day or two, at most—and then you will bring me jewels in exchange for the relics. I have a clever location in mind! But do try not to come up with any of your usual little tricks or ingenious schemes. In keeping with the gaming metaphor, I hold all the cards. Again, Mr. Holmes, it has been a great pleasure and honor to meet you. And you, Dr. Vernier..." He raised one eyebrow, glancing at Holmes. "What do you see in his company?"

"He has a certain fundamental integrity you could never understand."

"Ah, I shouldn't have given you an opening! Good evening, gentlemen." He grinned. "Give my regards to the ladies!"

He turned and strode back toward his table. His servant rose and followed the tall figure all in black out the doorway. The waiter watched them go, obviously surprised at their departure.

Holmes and I looked at one another. "Good Lord," I murmured at last.

"Rather hard to get a word in edgewise, was it not?"

Chapter Nine

Holmes and I dined alone, then went up to our suite. The fancy clock on the sideboard had just chimed nine when the door opened and Michelle entered. She removed her hat, then pulled off her gloves. "I'm sorry I couldn't join you for dinner. Anna needed some company. She kept telling me everything was for the best, and I didn't have the heart to contradict her. Perhaps she is right, after all. Did I miss anything?"

Holmes and I exchanged a glance. "We met Rafaello," I said.

Her eyes widened, even as she clenched her fists. "What?"

We told her about the meeting. Holmes scowled. "He plays the buffoon, but I don't think I have ever met a more consummate and dangerous villain."

"That 'hint' he gave you—can you make any sense of it?" I asked.

"Oh, I have some ideas, but I thought I would settle in with my pipe and mull things over." He rose. "There is a most comfortable chair in my room, and I know great clouds of tobacco smoke do not agree with you. Goodnight to you both." He closed the door behind him.

With a sigh, Michelle joined me on the sofa, and I put my arm around her and drew her close. She set her hand on my leg and squeezed. "Oh, Henry, it all seems so foolish. What is the good of religion if it just makes people miserable?"

"I am sure you are not the first to wonder about that."

"I feel... discouraged. What could I really say to her? One's first true heartbreak always hurts the most."

I squeezed her shoulders. "The words didn't really matter. She just needed someone as good and kind as you to be there. It was your presence that mattered."

"Oh, Henry, you are sweet."

We sat for a long while listening to the loud tick of the clock. Even with the door closed, the odor of pipe smoke gradually began to coalesce around us. When we finally stood up, I glanced at the door, and at the bottom, a sort of wispy billowy strip of cloud had seeped out.

In the morning, we came back into the sitting room just before eight. The tobacco odor was very strong, the room ever so faintly hazy. I shook my head. "I know I am going to regret this." I walked across the room, hesitated, then turned the knob and opened the door.

A great reeking haze clouded the interior, but I saw Holmes seated in a large wing chair near the bed, slumped sideways, his long thin face resting against one side, his eyes closed. Asleep and, no doubt, exhausted, he seemed oddly vulnerable. He had on his favorite worn purple dressing gown, and the pipe sat on a nearby table next to an ashtray. I closed the door softly so as not to wake him.

"That is a truly foul shag he was smoking, the kind he uses when he is contemplating some problem. I suppose since he uses so much, he is trying to be frugal, but surely he could afford better."

Michelle smiled. "Since he is thinking so hard, it must not matter."

"Come, let us have some breakfast, and let him sleep."

However, only about twenty minutes later, Holmes strode into the dining room and came to our table. He looked none the worse for wear, although his face appeared even thinner than usual.

I waited until we had all eaten before I asked, "What is the plan for the day? Have you made any sense of Rafaello's words?"

"I have some ideas about that, which I shall pursue in the company of Monsignor Greene. He told me he would be in his office at the Vatican during the day, should I need him. I would like your company as well, Henry, but Michelle–" he nodded in her direction, smiling "–must take precedence."

She laughed. "I yield him up gladly!" She set her hand on my wrist. "Not that I am not always happy to be at his side. All the same, I told Anna I would try to see her again today. Perhaps I can take her on some outing and divert her from her sorrows."

Holmes's expression grew stern. "If you do go anywhere, be very careful. In fact, it would be better if you and she did not go out. Rafaello's interest in her worries me greatly."

I frowned. "He did say he was going to renounce love like what's-his-name?–the dwarf in the opera?"

"Alberich. But Signor Pozzolo absolutely cannot be trusted. In fact, Michelle, you might try to encourage the *signorina* to leave Rome for a while."

Michelle was frowning. "Perhaps I should just take her back to England with me."

"But you just got here!" I said.

Again she squeezed my wrist. "With this dreadful case, you barely have time for me as it is, and the poor girl has no one to look after her. She needs our help badly."

I sighed. "I suppose you are right. I mustn't be selfish."

Holmes still appeared stern. "My hope is that things, one way or another, will soon be resolved, but I would feel much better if I knew Signorina Antonelli was out of harm's way."

Michelle nodded. "I'll see if I cannot persuade her."

We all soon set out upon our appointed tasks. Holmes and I took a cab first to Santa Croce in Gerusalemme. We stepped out into the square before the church, and Holmes paid the driver and asked him to wait. He turned to me. "This is a very long shot indeed—much too obvious." He smiled. "Too obviously obvious."

We entered the basilica and strode down the nave's elaborately patterned floor, then went down the sloping hallway to the chapel of Saint Helena. With the relics gone, it was deserted. The door to the case had new glass, but the shelves were empty. Holmes and I proceeded to examine every nook and cranny of the chapel, but we found nothing.

Holmes gave a curt nod. "As I said—too obvious."

We went back to the church and started down the nave, just before the doors swung open, and the slender, bald-headed figure of Monsignor Nardone appeared, wearing his black soutane with the violet sash. He smiled at us, raised his hand, then started forward. "Signor Holmes—a pleasure!" He kept his voice low because we were in the church.

"Monsignor, I was just about to seek you out. I have a favor to ask. There is a possibility—albeit a remote one—that the missing relics are hidden somewhere in the basilica. Could you conduct a thorough search and let me know if you find anything? Time is of the essence."

"Good heavens! Hidden in the church? What a blessing that would be! I shall see to it, Signor Holmes. I shall enlist the help of the good brothers from the monastery next door. With their help it should take only an hour or two."

"Excellent, Monsignor! If you do find anything, send a message immediately to the Vatican and to my hotel."

The monsignor's smile faltered. "And if we find nothing?"

"Still send a message to my hotel. And now, *arrivederci, Monsignore.*"

We got back into the cab and crossed Rome to the Vatican. Soon we were again wandering the ornate Papal Palace. I could not help but recall the recent time when we passed Rafaello, who had just murdered Cardinal Cicogno. Holmes rapped on the door to Monsignor Greene's office.

Greene appeared genuinely pleased to see us, a broad smile on his plump florid face above that narrow white band of the Roman collar. His office was in its usual disarray, books and papers strewn across his desk, with more volumes piled on a nearby table. "Come in, come in, gentlemen!"

We sat down in some comfortable armchairs, and Holmes told him about Rafaello's visit. Creases appeared in the pink, lightly freckled skin above his bushy reddish-brown eyebrows, and his eyes were troubled. "But can you possibly believe anything he says, especially this so-called hint?"

"To him it is all, as he said, an elaborate sort of intellectual game. He wants to 'match wits' with Sherlock Holmes. I do not think he would 'cheat' quite so openly."

"And this logical place?"

"Henry and I had a good look around the chapel at Santa Croce, and Monsignor Nardone is conducting a search of the basilica. However, as I told Henry, that is perhaps 'too obviously obvious.' We must consider other logical places. The Vatican must have many of its treasures—and relics—stored away somewhere nearby."

Greene tapped lightly at a bare spot on his desk. "There are the Vatican archives, of course, but they have mostly documents, shelves after shelves of them, and then there is the Vatican museum. There are nearly as many treasures in storage as there are on display. In either case, it would take days to conduct any sort of thorough search of the vast storage areas."

Holmes nodded. "I know. There is only one real hope."

Greene and I exchanged a puzzled look. "And what is that?"

Holmes smiled. "That one of the custodians has a sharp eye and a thorough knowledge of his domain."

The monsignor led us through the maze of ornate hallways and down a floor. We came out into a great cobbled square, completely framed by four- and five-story buildings with tall arched windows. In the very middle, a fountain spewed water that sparkled in the Italian sunlight.

"This is the Cortile del Belvedere." Greene pointed to the far, narrower side in the distance. "The archives are just there at the opposite end, and the library is also off the square."

We crossed the *cortile* and came to a tall wooden door with distinct panels. Greene opened it for us, and we went into a small dimly lit room with glass display cases along one side. Two men in black suits with black mustaches sat behind large desks. One of them stood up and came over to us.

"Can I help you, *signori*?"

Holmes nodded. "*Si, per favore.* Tell me, are deliveries to the archives made here?"

"No, that would be in the back where Giovanni is in charge, next to the Cortile della Pigna."

"Could you take us there? We need to speak to him."

We went first through a dusty room with ancient, monumental

tables where a few men, mostly priests, sat peering at ancient-looking documents by the light of lamps, then down another formal hallway. Again, I had the sense of being in a maze with highly decorated walls. We eventually came out in a room with two big arched windows and another desk. A short, stout man stood up. He was wearing a brown woolen waistcoat and trousers, and his shirt sleeves were rolled up, revealing brawny, hairy forearms. Monsignor Greene introduced us and said we were looking for the missing relics on behalf of the Holy Father.

"Tell me, *signore*," Holmes said, "did you have any deliveries the day before yesterday?" It was now Wednesday morning, so that would have been Monday, and we had met Rafaello yesterday evening, on Tuesday.

"There are always deliveries, *signore*."

"This would likely have been in a large wooden crate, brought by two men, one tall and slender, probably dressed as a priest, and his companion, a shorter man."

I was briefly puzzled, then realized he must be referring to Rafaello in his clerical disguise and his servant.

Giovanni shook his head. "There were two or three deliveries, none of them very large, and nothing brought by a tall man."

Holmes sighed, then shrugged. "*Grazie mille, signore.*" He turned to us. "Let's try the museums next."

We went out the door and crossed another square, this one slightly smaller, with four large rectangles of thick, brilliant green grass. At the far end was another ornate building with a formal entranceway, and before it was an odd sculpture of what must be an upside-down pine cone, in worn greenish-black bronze, taller than a man. On either side were much smaller, sculpted bronze peacocks.

We went inside to find another desk and two more men in black suits. Greene asked them if the storage for the museum was in the building. One of them shook his head and told us it was in a warehouse about a ten-minute walk away, just outside the Vatican boundaries. He gave us an address and led us through another labyrinth of high-ceilinged rooms filled with bronze or marble statues of every size—busts, torsos, naked bodies, or flowing marble robes—and more paintings of saints, angels, warriors, and the like in bright colors.

We soon stepped outside and went through one of the archways in the ancient wall round the Vatican. The day was a pleasant one, a faint breeze on our faces, only a few clouds overhead, and this was a quiet corner of Rome, only a few men and women about, all of them modestly dressed, and nary a soutane or Roman collar to be seen. A horse pulling a lone carriage clopped down the street.

"Don't you get tired of all those ancient palaces and all that ornamentation?" I asked Monsignor Greene. "It all seems..." I hesitated.

Greene smiled. "Pompous? Overblown? Hardly in keeping with the tenets of a poor carpenter who died on the cross?"

I laughed. "Exactly so."

"Well, I have been here so long I hardly notice it anymore, but my initial reaction was probably much like yours. I was, after all, only a country boy from rural England."

"There are some fine sculptures in the museums," Holmes said, "but it is somewhat like the Louvre where the sheer volume of art overwhelms. The effect is like having too great a feast spread before one, a surfeit of delights." He raised his stick. "Ah, I suspect that must be the warehouse just there."

Across the street was an old building of red brick, a poor cousin indeed of those edifices round the Vatican *cortile.* The big main door had peeling gray paint all around the doorframe. Holmes opened the door and let us enter first. Here was another large wooden desk inside a large room, but it was almost lost amidst all the clutter: every wall had wooden shelves going all the way to the ceiling, stacked with dusty parcels, wooden boxes, ornate goblets, a glittering golden monstrance (alone and very much out of place), a marble bust of an emperor with a crack down his forehead, a sword in its scabbard, a wooden jewel box, and on, and on.

The surface of the desk could not be seen beneath the layer of papers. Behind it sat a rotund, balding priest in a worn black soutane with its row of tiny buttons (the third one down undone) and white Roman collar round his vast second chin. He held a big cigar in his right hand, and the room reeked of it. I realized I had never seen a priest smoke before.

"*Signori, buongiorno.*" He did not stand up.

Greene again introduced us and said we were acting on behalf of the Holy Father in search of missing relics.

"I am Father Giorgio, *signori*, master of this bricked domain and its splendors. How can I help you?"

"Tell me, Father, did you have any deliveries on Monday?"

"Certainly. Mondays are always busiest. Three or four, as I recall."

"Any large wooden crates?"

"Yes, of course."

"And was any one of them brought in by a tall priest and a smaller lay person?"

Father Giorgio had a broad hand with massive fingers; he knocked cigar ash off into a glass ashtray. "Yes, I think so. As I recall... he would not stop talking."

Holmes stood up taller, a glint in his eyes, black pupils swollen in the dimly lit room. "That is our man!"

"Let me see." He turned to a stack of papers on his desk, then leafed through them, finally raising one sheet. "Yes, it was this one, I'm sure. He had a crate of ancient, blessed chalices from the Holy Land, and he wanted a receipt, Father..." He gazed on the paper. "Father Angelo Nero."

Holmes gave a sharp laugh, glanced at Greene and me. "Angelo Nero—Black Angel. Very good! Did you notice if the priest had a scar on his right ear?"

Father Giorgio laughed. "I don't make a habit of staring at people's ears."

"We must have a look at that crate. Do you know where it might be?"

"Not off hand." He gave a weary sigh, drew in on his cigar, then knocked off more ash. "Let's have a look." Getting out of the chair seemed to require a Herculean effort.

He lumbered forward, and we followed him to a door and stepped through the portal into a vast cave. Massive wooden beams and an occasional skylight loomed overhead; the warehouse was filled with rows and rows and rows of tall shelves stacked with boxes and crates as well every conceivable religious or artistic object imaginable.

"Good Heavens," I murmured in dismay.

Father Giorgio smiled at us. "It's out here somewhere."

Holmes's dark eyebrows had come together. "Have you no filing system?"

"No. I have something better than that." He looked around, then shouted, "Antonio! Antonio! *Vieni qui!*" He took another draw on his half-smoked cigar.

At the end of a row a thin man in a worn brown suit appeared and strode quickly toward us. His eyes had an odd gleam in them, a strange fiery intensity, and his mouth curved upward oddly on one side. His Adam's apple was huge, his neck scrawny, and he had wild brown hair with a great cowlick shot with gray drooping over his left temple. He raised his thin bony hand in almost a salute. "*Si, padre padrone, si.*"

"These gentlemen want to look at that crate the tall priest brought in on Monday."

Carlo nodded. "Yes. Chalices from the Holy Land. Row GH, second shelf up."

"Very good," Father Giorgio said. "Show us."

Antonio wheeled about dramatically and shot off at a rapid pace. Holmes was right behind him, I next, with the two heavier priests in the rear. We followed an odd sort of zigzag path amidst the towering shelves stuffed with various contents, which rose on either side of us. As we walked, shafts of sunlight intermittently lit up Antonio and Holmes's backs and a square of the concrete floor, then the two were swallowed in shadow.

I shook my head, murmured, "And I thought the Papal Palace was a maze."

Holmes looked over his shoulder, smiling. "Perhaps the Minotaur lies somewhere at the heart of this labyrinth."

We turned another corner, went about twenty feet, and Antonio stopped so abruptly that Holmes almost ran into him. "Here, that's the one," Antonio said, pointing to a wooden crate perhaps five feet long and two feet wide resting on the second wooden shelf a couple feet off the ground. A smaller wooden crate was on the floor, and on the shelf above were some dusty golden chalices, and various gold and silver reliquaries which looked to be empty.

Holmes gave me another smile, his delight obvious enough. "Let's have a look. Help me with this, Henry."

Antonio joined in our effort, and we had the crate lowered to the floor by the time the two priests caught up to us. Holmes raised his hand toward Antonio. "Might I borrow your crowbar?" It was hooked onto a leather tool belt round his waist. Antonio pulled it out and handed it to Holmes, who eagerly began prying up one of the cross pieces. We all crowded round in anticipation. I helped Holmes raise one of the boards. Inside, dirty beige cotton wool and crumpled newspapers hid the contents.

Holmes reached inside, felt about, then using both hands, he strained to withdraw some massive object wrapped in a blanket. He knelt to set it on the floor, then quickly unrolled the blanket, revealing a tall ornate golden cross atop a heavy square base, two small, sculpted silver angels with golden spears on either side of the base. I drew in my breath sharply, then smiled.

"*Dio mio*," Father Giorgio muttered with the cigar still in his mouth.

"The fragment of the true cross!" Monsignor Greene exclaimed in English. "By George, you've done it, Holmes! Very good indeed. So Rafaello was actually telling the truth. We won't have to pay him those jewels, after all."

"Don't count your chickens before they hatch," Holmes said. "And indeed, we have hardly counted all our chicks yet. I suspect…"

He pulled out another, much smaller, object wrapped in a torn square of blanket. This was the mostly silver reliquary with a sculpted, circular ring of thorns, and in the center, the two, supposed actual thorns. Next came the reliquaries with the rectangular *titulum*, a fragment of the sign nailed to the cross, then the one containing the nail, and finally a dome-like one with a cross on top. Each glittered of smoothly polished gold and silver.

"Which one is that?" I murmured, not recognizing the final one.

"That has the fragment of the scourging pillar," Greene said, "and possibly a piece from the crib of Jesus, too."

I shook my head but said nothing. *Crib of Jesus, indeed!* I thought.

Holmes rooted about in the wool and newspapers but found nothing more. "That, I believe, is it."

"Bravo, Holmes!" Greene exclaimed. "You have indeed done it!"

Holmes smiled at him, as he slowly rose to his feet. "Your arithmetic is off, Monsignor. We are missing one."

"Are we?" I asked. "Which one?"

Holmes shook his head. "Henry, Henry—which relic were we looking for in the first place?"

I drew in my breath, aware suddenly of the missing one. "Saint Thomas's finger. That ghastly gray piece of bone."

"Exactly."

"And you are sure it is not there?"

"I am, which makes perfect sense. Rafaello was willing to give up some of the relics as part of the game, but not everything, and Saint Thomas's finger is still worth a ransom in jewels."

Monsignor Greene was scowling. "It seems as if he should at least reduce the price!"

Holmes laughed, genuinely amused. "Ah, Monsignor! But you forget—as the Holy Father told us, they are all priceless." He turned to Father Giorgio who had been watching in amazement and occasionally taking a draw on his cigar. "You are sure this was the only thing that the priest brought?"

Giorgio only turned to Antonio and squinted slightly. Antonio's Adam's apple bobbed slightly as he swallowed. "Si, *signore*—this is all."

Holmes nodded. "Well, that is the bulk of them, anyway, even if each one is invaluable. We had best pack these back up. They will eventually need to go back to Santa Croce, Father Giorgio, but not just now."

Monsignor Greene's smile had returned. "Well, we've certainly earned a good lunch today!"

We soon left the warehouse, and the monsignor took us to a small nearby restaurant. He recommended the spinach and ricotta ravioli. "They are perhaps the best in Rome," he assured us. First, however, the waiter brought us a plate with various salami and cheeses, along with a basket of bread with a thick, crispy crust and a bottle of Apulia wine.

Monsignor Greene poured wine into each of our glasses, then raised his for a toast. "Well, we have five of the six relics back, so we have gone full circle and returned to the same point where we were when we first met. All the same, with Holmes on the case, there can be no doubt as to the ultimate outcome. Your health, gentlemen."

We clicked glasses and drank. I spoke first. "Regardless of the ultimate outcome, what happens next?"

Holmes turned his glass ever so slightly, letting the light illuminate the dark red liquid. "I fear I am not so confident as to the end result. To use Rafaello's metaphor, we have made our move and captured a few pawns. The next move now is his: we wait for another note from Signor Pozzolo, which should not be long in coming."

I was aware of a faint scowl pulling at my face. "And then we just hand over the jewels?"

Holmes shrugged. "I am not, as I have repeatedly said, a miracle worker." He smiled at the monsignor. "Again, miracles are more in your line of business than mine. However…" His gray eyes had a grave expression. "We shall see. I do not like to give up without a struggle. Nevertheless, I think it is time I took possession of the ransom jewels, so as to have them ready."

Greene nodded. "Very well. They have been prepared for you. We can fetch them after lunch. But are you sure you want to carry them about Rome?"

"I have a hidden pocket in my frock coat. They should be secure enough there for a brief time."

Greene took a bite of bread and some yellow cheese. His eyes shifted to mine. "What is your wife doing today, Dr. Vernier?"

"She is with Anna." I hesitated, unsure how much to say.

"Ah. Father Blackwell came to see me yesterday. I suspect he and Anna are equally miserable." Greene shook his head. "It's enough to make me wish... If I had not introduced him to the Antonelli family, none of this would have ever happened. All the same, I don't know how she would ever have made it through her father's final illness without Edward at her side."

I opened my mouth once, closed it, then repeated both actions. He smiled faintly at me. "What is on your mind, Doctor?"

"They seem made for one another."

Greene set down his bread, raised his plump right hand and briefly massaged his temples. He looked out the window, then at me. "I know. God help me, I know. Frequently one is tempted to do things which are clearly wicked. But this kind of temptation..."

"What did you say to him?"

"What he needed to hear: that he was a priest who had taken his final vows, and as such, romantic love and marriage are forever out of the question."

Holmes was watching him closely. "Do you truly believe that, Monsignor?"

His expression grew even more pained. "Don't ask me that

question, Holmes. I... I care too much for them both. Encouraging false hopes would be cruel."

Holmes's smile was faintly bitter. "Life plays curious tricks on us. It mocks our certainties, our vows, our assumptions." He shrugged. "It keeps us humble, I suppose."

Greene gave a fierce nod. "Amen to that! And now, let us give our meal the full attention it deserves. Pondering imponderables makes for indigestion."

Holmes laughed. "Well put! I don't know how Henry and I would have ever gotten by here in Rome without you. Truly you have been like Virgil to Dante, his guide to the celestial realm, the Paradiso of Roman cuisine!"

Greene smiled broadly. "Thank you very much. However, there is a flaw in your description."

Holmes frowned briefly, then smiled again. "Ah yes, Virgil was Dante's guide in Hell and Purgatory, but Beatrice took over for Heaven."

"Very good, Holmes!" He was still smiling. "I fear, however, that I have little in common with Beatrice."

After we had eaten, we lingered over our small cups of dark strong Italian coffee, then left for the Papal Palace. Greene led us hither and yonder, finally ending up at a small office on the second floor, where yet another Vatican bureaucrat, a thin man with neatly combed hair, in a dark suit, sat behind a spotless desk. He rose, greeted us, then led us to the big black safe in the corner. In large letters across the front was written FACCHELLI.

"Ah," Holmes said, "the same Milanese manufacturer who made Monsignor Nardone's impressive padlock at Santa Croce."

I stared at him. "How do you remember such things?"

"It is a talent, which, like any other, can be cultivated."

The clerk carefully turned the dial twice in each direction, finding the requisite numbers, then used the big metal handle to open the massive steel door. From the top shelf he took a small tan leather pouch and handed it to Monsignor Greene.

"Shall we have a look?" Greene said.

Holmes raised his slender hand. "Let's put them on the desk. We don't want any falling on the floor."

"Good idea," Greene said.

We all went to the desk, and the monsignor loosened the strings, then poured out the contents.

"My heavens," the clerk murmured.

I shook my head. "They are beautiful."

"Indeed they are," Holmes said. He began to separate them; there were eight red rubies, eight green emeralds and nine diamonds, each gem perhaps three-quarters of an inch across, their facets sparkling under the light of the nearby lamp.

"They must be worth hundreds of pounds," I said.

Holmes picked up a ruby, held it closer to the light and turned it slowly. "More likely thousands—far more than a consulting detective, a monsignor, or a physician would earn in several lifetimes. I must admit to a certain fondness for rubies."

"And all for a piece of small gray bone," I murmured.

Holmes glanced at me. He did not speak, but his mouth formed a familiar sardonic smile. "Few things have intrinsic value, Henry: it is always about what one is willing to pay." He opened the pouch, then put the jewels back in. "Well, all twenty-five are here. I suspect Rafaello will want to count them."

He reached inside his black frock coat with his right hand, moved his fingers about, no doubt opening up the hidden pocket, then placed the bag inside. He patted his chest. "Safely stowed."

He nodded politely at the clerk, "*Grazie, signore,*" then turned to Greene. "We must be on our way, Monsignor. Thank you for your assistance this morning, and for another superb meal."

Greene seemed strangely subdued. "I hope… I hope that monster does not get to keep those jewels."

Holmes shrugged. "What will be, will be."

Holmes and I spent the afternoon wandering about Rome. We made a stop at Santa Croce to give Monsignor Nardone the good news about the found relics, and he was clearly delighted. He said he would continue to pray for the recovery of Saint Thomas's finger. We returned to the hotel around six.

Seated on the big leather sofa near a tall palm in a three-foot high Chinese vase, were Michelle and Anna. They rose to greet us. As before, Michelle's height and robust frame, imposing in a green silk, made Anna appear waif-like. The black of Anna's mourning garb also added to her melancholy appearance. She did not appear distraught like she had been last time, but a certain restraint, a certain sadness, showed in her brown eyes and the set of her lips.

"There you are at last," Michelle said. "What came of your search?"

We told them of the recovery of the relics. Michelle set a gloved hand on Holmes's arm. "Oh very good, Sherlock!"

He shrugged. "Unfortunately I am certain it will not reduce the ransom required."

Michelle frowned. "Well, it hardly seems fair that you would have to pay the same amount for one relic as for six!"

I laughed. "You and Monsignor Greene think alike! I'm afraid fairness has nothing to do with it, not for this scoundrel Rafaello."

Holmes was staring gravely at Anna. "Did you and Dr. Doudet-Vernier discuss your leaving Rome?"

"Yes."

"And what did you decide?"

"That I shall accompany her back to England the day after tomorrow." Anna raised her shoulders in a slight shrug. "It no longer much matters where I stay. All the same, it is very kind of you to invite me, Dr. Doudet-Vernier." She glanced at me, her smile rather sad. "And you, too, Dr. Vernier. Your kindness is much appreciated, especially now."

"It is our pleasure," I said, but I felt a pang of disappointment. I had known this was likely, and it did indeed make sense. All the same, I had wanted so badly to spend some time alone with Michelle in Rome.

Holmes's brow was furrowed. "Could you not leave tomorrow?"

Michelle shook her head. "Come now, traveling does take a certain amount of preparation, Sherlock! Besides, while she is packing tomorrow, that should allow me some time with Henry."

Holmes still looked severe. "We shall see."

Again Michelle touched Holmes lightly on the arm. "I promise you we shall leave bright and early on Friday morning. You can officially see us off on the train."

Holmes's eyes were fixed on Anna, but she was not really looking at any of us. That sense of energy, of vitality, I had seen in her before was spent. I wished with all my heart that somehow she were going to England as Edward Blackwell's wife.

"Thank you for obliging me in this matter, Signorina Antonelli," Holmes said. "The sooner you are out of harm's way, the better."

Chapter Ten

That evening, a smoky haze again billowed out from under the door to Holmes's room, but by morning, it had mostly dissipated, so we knew he must not have stayed up too late. Indeed, he was waiting for us there in the sitting room, dressed in a suit of a heavy gray tweed. His lean cheeks appeared freshly shaven, and the brownish clot of a small nick was on his right jawbone.

We went down for breakfast together and persuaded him to join us for a trek to the Pantheon and the Trevi Fountain. He was reluctant to come because he expected a message from Rafaello, but we told him it could surely wait two or three hours.

The spell of fine weather was finally broken: a mass of gray cloud covered the sky, and smatterings of rain came and went. As a result, there were fewer people staring at the rushing waters and sculpted white marble figures of the fountain. When it started raining in earnest, we went into the Pantheon and were soon gazing up at that round ancient dome with its central oculus or "eye," open to the sky above Rome for so many centuries. A fine sheet of rain slowly drifted down through the shaft of light coming from the opening and formed a wet circle on the marble floor. Michelle and I were fascinated by the ancient structure, but Holmes was clearly preoccupied. Under the rim of his black bowler, his eyes gazed absently into space, oblivious to our surroundings. We had lunch together, then at Holmes's insistence, returned to the hotel shortly after one.

We had just stepped into the lobby when Father Blackwell sprang up from the leather sofa and strode toward us. Behind him was the white-haired butler of the Antonellis in a dark blue morning coat and purple velvet waistcoat.

"Thank God you've come!" Blackwell exclaimed. "Anna has gone missing! I'm afraid—oh I'm afraid..." He choked off his words. His face was pale and haggard, and he hadn't shaved that morning. His black hair was even more disheveled than usual, his black cassock wrinkled, as if he had slept in it once again.

I grabbed his arm. "Calm yourself and tell us what has happened."

He reached into his pocket and drew out a battered folded paper. "This came for her—but I know nothing about it!"

Holmes took the paper and opened it. The large letters were printed in black ink: *Come to Santa Croce at ten this morning. I must see you. Edward Blackwell.*

"I swear I didn't send it!" Blackwell said.

"Of course you didn't," Holmes said. "Blast it! It's obvious enough who did—Signor Rafaello Pozzolo. How did you get this note?"

The old butler raised his white-gloved hands. "She left it with the coachman when she went into the church. She told him if she did not come out in thirty minutes, he should come in to check on her. He did as she said, but there was no sign of her. She was gone, and he is certain she did not leave from the front doors."

Holmes shook his head. "She was suspicious—but not suspicious enough. She must have known it might be a trick, but she had to make sure. She had to find out what you wanted to see her about, Father Blackwell."

"What does he want from her?" Blackwell went paler still. "What if... if he wants to... hurt her?"

Again I squeezed his arm. "You must not assume the very worst."

Holmes inhaled slowly through his nostrils. "I have my suspicions what this may be about. In fact..." He turned toward the wooden counter, and a man in a black jacket raised his hand and beckoned toward him. "One moment please, and we may have our answer."

He strode toward the counter, and the attendant gave him a white envelope, which he quickly opened. He scanned it quickly, then gave his head a fierce shake and came back to us. "Have a look," he said.

I took the paper and read, Michelle peering over my right shoulder, Blackwell over my left.

My dear Holmes,

By now I expect you have found the five relics in the warehouse of the Vatican museum. Hardly much of a challenge for someone of your abilities, but an opportunity to display your skills, all the same! By the time you read this, a rather obvious ruse will have delivered Signorina Antonelli into my hands, and I shall have the delight of her company for a brief time. Given my amatory sentiments for this worthy young woman, I certainly would not want to harm her! However, her well-being rests entirely in your hands. Upon payment to me of the jewels, I shall release her. Should there be any subterfuge or, worse yet, any involvement of the police, I would no longer be able to guarantee her safety. Since I do greatly admire her, I hope you will not force any unpleasantness upon me!

As far as I am concerned, our game is finished. You shall have the last relic and Signorina Antonelli, and I shall have my jewels. You can turn them over to me on holy ground teeming with holy bones, especially holy skulls, femurs, and pelvises! Surely you must understand. Meet me amidst the skulls and come unarmed. Be there tomorrow morning at ten. Bring along Dr. Vernier if you wish, but absolutely no one else. Do not forget that Signorina Antonelli's life is in your hands! Again, once I have the jewels I shall turn her over to you.

Warmest regards,
Your humble servant,
Rafaello Pozzolo

I frowned fiercely. "Holy place teeming with holy bones? What on earth is he talking about?"

Holmes stared at Father Blackwell. "There is only one possible place in Rome that can be—the Crypt of the Capuchins."

Blackwell scowled. "That must be it. It is as with Santa Croce—actual soil from the Holy Land was brought to the crypt."

"But what does it mean holy bones, skulls, and pelvises?" I asked.

"The Capuchin friars are buried there for a time," Holmes said, "then exhumed, and their bones have been used to create a variety of bizarre and phantasmagorical displays. There is a chamber dedicated to skulls, another to pelvises, and so on."

Michelle shook her head. "How amazingly gruesome."

Holmes smiled ever so slightly. "It is absolutely unforgettable, but it is not a place for those of a sensitive or imaginative nature."

The butler wrung his white-gloved hands. "*Poverina, poverina.* You will take care of her, Signor Holmes?"

"I certainly shall."

Blackwell had clenched his fists and half-raised his arms. "I blame myself for this."

I shook my head, even as a sort of snorting laugh escaped me. "Of course you do! Why not? You seem determined to take the blame for all the misfortunes of the world!" He gave me a pained look, and I was sorry for my outburst. "Come now—it absolutely is not your fault that Rafaello abducted her. Although I wonder…" I turned to the butler. "Did the coachman say whether the church was empty?"

"No, it was not empty. There were a few people praying, but she was not to be seen."

"I wonder how he managed to abscond with her without a struggle."

Holmes shrugged faintly. "Probably a variation of how he tricked her into coming there in the first place: he told her he had Father Blackwell captive, and she must come with him if she wanted to ever see him alive again. In that case, they would have simply left from a side exit."

"Then it was all because of me," Blackwell groaned.

"No, no!" I said. "It will not help to torment yourself."

Michelle looked very grave. "Sherlock, do you think this Pozzolo can be trusted? Will he keep her safe and turn her over to you in return for the ransom?"

Holmes's brows came together. "I think so. His main interest is the jewels. His supposed affections for the lady are merely a poor sort of jest. He would have no reason to keep her once he has his prize. All the same, there is no telling with someone as capricious as he."

Blackwell's eyes lost focus, regained it, then once again lost focus, and he staggered slightly. I grabbed his arm and felt his body sway, his legs briefly buckling. "What's wrong?" I asked.

"I feel dizzy."

"Come sit down." I guided him over to the sofa, and he sagged down into the corner. "Have you eaten today?"

He had put his elbow up on the sofa arm and seemed relieved to be seated. "No. I have been fasting, and then once Francesco found me, I could think only of her."

I resisted the urge to say *imbecile.* "Little wonder you are dizzy. You cannot help anyone in a weakened state."

The others had all followed us to the sofa. Michelle and the butler appeared greatly concerned, while Holmes's face showed sympathy with a certain wry edge. Blackwell gazed up at him.

"Mr. Holmes, I would do anything to save her–anything to redeem her–I would gladly give my life." He drew in his breath. "I would give my very soul."

"I doubt that will be necessary," Holmes said.

One corner of Blackwell's mouth rose. "You mock me. I suppose I deserve it. All the same, is there anything I might do? Any way at all I might assist you?"

Holmes examined him, his brow creasing, as he seemed to mull this over. At last he gave a slight shrug. "Perhaps. But it is as Henry said: you are no use to anyone in your current condition."

He drew in his breath slowly. "I suppose I am somewhat hungry. I can eat. I *will* eat." He looked at the butler. "Francesco, you might as well return to the house. Reassure the other servants as best you can. We must all hope for the best—we must pray for the best. If all goes well, tomorrow your mistress should return to you."

He nodded. "Yes, Father, and thank you again for your help. When I saw that note…"

"You were right to come to me, even if I did not write it."

The old man headed for the main entrance. Holmes turned to Michelle and me. "Let me have a brief word alone with Father Blackwell, and then, Henry, perhaps you could see that he eats a good meal."

I gave him a curious look. "What are you up to?" I could see he wasn't going to tell me. "Very well. As soon as you are finished with him, I shall take him to lunch." I glanced at Michelle. "You don't mind if…"

She smiled. "Not at all! I have spent so much time with Anna. I completely understand."

The two of us walked over nearer the counter. Holmes had sat on the sofa and was speaking intently to Father Blackwell. The priest appeared very stern.

I reached over to grasp Michelle's hand and gave it a squeeze. "Well, our romantic trip to Rome has certainly turned out little better than the usual state of affairs back home."

She gave me a reproachful look. "Those two certainly need our help."

"Oh, I'm only joking. Blackwell is a decent enough fellow, although so frightfully and terribly serious. And this Pozzolo... He is certainly a dangerous man. Holmes may not be a miracle worker, but I hope he comes up with some way to put him behind bars."

"I just want Anna to be safe."

Holmes and Blackwell were still talking, an aura of fierce intensity about them both. "Somehow," I said, "I suspect he is not going to simply turn over the jewels to Pozzolo and be done with him."

Michelle smiled. "I hope not!"

Blackwell gave a final nod, and then Holmes stood up and came over to us. "I have some business to attend to. I hope to see you around seven or eight, and then we can go to dinner together."

"I'll see to Blackwell," I said.

I gave Michelle's hand a parting squeeze, then walked toward the sofa. Blackwell took a deep breath, preparing himself. I extended my hand, helping him to his feet. "Careful."

"I feel better now. Much better." And indeed, some color had come back into his face.

We stepped outside. The rain had abated, but the cold breeze was a reminder that winter was not long past. The fresh air and the walk seemed to revive Blackwell even more. His face was almost ruddy, and that look of desperation was gone, replaced by a weary sort of calm. I wondered again what Holmes might have said to him.

We went into the small restaurant which was mostly empty, and the proprietor, short and stocky, with the usual grand dark mustache, wearing a white shirt and black apron, greeted us warmly and led us to a table. Blackwell glanced briefly at the menu, then ordered *penne all'arrabbiata*, macaroni in "angry" sauce, so called because it was made with fiery chili peppers. With some encouragement on my part, he also ordered as a second plate, the veal *osso buco* which I knew was excellent.

After all the excitement, I also thought a glass of red wine might do us both some good. The owner poured from a big glass container with straw woven round the bottom. The color was so dark it verged on purple, and it had a strong tannic taste. It might not be the equal of a good Bordeaux, but it was more than tolerable.

I raised my glass. "Your health, Father Blackwell."

He raised his. "And yours."

We both sipped. "You must take better care of yourself."

"I shall try. I must fortify myself."

"Fortify yourself?"

He nodded, but would not elaborate. Soon a plate of steaming pasta was placed before him. He began to eat, slowly at first, but the food seemed to revive his appetite. His clear blue eyes glanced at me. "I was hungry, after all." We didn't really talk much until he had finished and pushed his colorful ceramic bowl to the side.

"Have you decided, after all, to go back to England?"

"I have. I discussed the matter with my superiors. They wanted me to finish my studies, but I couldn't see the point. I cannot seem to concentrate, and I wanted to avoid… as they say, the near occasion of sin." His smile was faintly ironic, as if he understood how ludicrously formulaic that sounded.

I sighed softly. "'The near occasion of sin.' I remember that phrase well. So is that how you think of Anna Antonelli? As the near occasion of sin?"

He swallowed once, then sipped his wine. "She is… a temptation."

I smiled faintly. "That is the glory of women. They are temptations." I vaguely remember a time as an adolescent boy when the universe teemed with snares and temptations, great pits waiting to swallow me up and send me down to Hell. Existence was little more than an obstacle course, one challenge after another thrust before me. It was not a good way to look at life. Perhaps Blackwell had outgrown that stage, but now, confronted with the supreme "temptation," he was reverting back to his youth.

"Have you ever thought," I asked, "that you might have it all wrong? That perhaps the temptation is not Anna, but instead the celibate priesthood?"

"You cannot be serious," he said.

I shrugged. "Perhaps I am. After all, is it not a sort of pride that makes a man think he can forever renounce the love, both carnal and spiritual, of a woman? And, as a part of that love, the simple companionship of marriage, the friendship that comes with it. After all, didn't God make men and women for one another?"

"I have dedicated my life to God. I made my vows."

"But you grew up amongst only boys and men, in male society exclusively. You did not really understand what you were giving up."

He sighed. "I suppose not."

"If you had it to do over—if you were free—would you make such vows again?"

"I don't know."

"Be honest. I think you do know."

He set his big hands flat on the table on either side of the empty plate. "I suppose not. But what's done is done, and I do want to be a priest... *I do.*"

I felt as if I were kicking someone when they were down. He was truly caught up in an impossible dilemma. I recalled suddenly the marble statue of Laocoon and his sons in the Vatican museum. Blackwell's vows and his religion were like those snakes wrapped about the heroic figure who struggled in hopeless agony against their fatal embrace. Laocoon could not save himself, but Blackwell?

I sipped the wine. "All the same, think about what I said: that, in the end, the priesthood may be the temptation, and not Anna. Remember when we were talking with Holmes about that Protestant hymn? 'God moves in a mysterious way his wonders to perform.' And what was the rest? Something about 'bright designs.'" I smiled. "Anna Antonelli is truly a bright design! Like Michelle." Blackwell looked so stricken that I reached over to squeeze his forearm. "I don't mean to torment you. You are a good and decent man, and that will be true whatever you decide. One thing I am convinced of—this is not a matter of black and white, of cosmic good versus cosmic evil. Whatever you choose will be for the best—stupid as that sounds."

He stared curiously at me. "Do you truly believe that?"

"I do."

The waiter set down a plate with the veal slab of *osso buco*, the round bone in its center, chopped tomatoes, onions, and parsley on top of it.

"That looks delicious," I said. "Enough philosophizing! Eat and enjoy your meal."

"It does look good." He took up his knife and fork, but his eyes were fixed on me. "I shall think about what you have said—but only *after* Anna is free and back among us. Until then, saving her from that villain must be our main concern."

I nodded. "Amen to that!"

Michelle and I were sitting together on the sofa drinking brandy. The china clock on the sideboard showed half-past seven, and Holmes had still not returned from his afternoon outing. A rap sounded on the door, then a second, louder one.

I stood up. "I wonder if Sherlock forgot his key."

I walked over and opened the door. Before me stood one of the hotel employees from the front desk in his black suit, and beside him was a stooped old man wearing the worn, outlandish clothing of a tramp. His bowler hat and his brown woolen jacket were too big for him, even though the sleeves on the jacket were too short. A pot belly showed under a hideous black-checked waistcoat, and he wore black and gray striped trousers, knees shiny with wear. Only his shoes were respectable. In one hand he held a cane; with the other he clasped the two wooden handles of a big, battered cloth bag.

He nodded repeatedly, saying, "*Dottore, dottore, buona sera, buona sera.*" Because he was stooping, I couldn't see his eyes under the brim of the hat, only a great bristling white mustache which hid his mouth and curly white hair curling about his ears, half covering them.

I took half a step back. "What is this?" I asked.

The hotel man shook his head. "I'm sorry, Dr. Vernier, but he insisted on seeing you. He stumbled into the main lobby, and when I went to hustle him out onto the street, he insisted he knew the famous Sherlock Holmes and his companion, a very good friend, Dr. Henry Vernier."

"*Si, si!*" The old man raised the hand with a cane, revealing a woolen glove with open fingers like the kind a clerk might wear. "*Dottore Vernier, il mio vecchio amico! Come stai, Dottore? Stai bene?*" He spoke Italian with a quavering husky voice, and his clothes smelled: a weird mixture of dirt, tobacco, probably wine—but above all, garlic. I had never met an Italian who reeked so strongly of it.

"I've never seen this man in my life," I said.

"I thought so. Come along now. Don't make me call the police."

"*No, Dottore, per favore! Siamo amici, grandi amici! E sua moglie, Michela—lei deve conoscermi!*"

I scowled. "Michela?" Abruptly I realized Michela was the Italian equivalent of Michelle. "How do you know her name?–and how dare you call her Michela?"

"*Si, si, la bella Michela, la dottoressa.*"

"Who on earth has he been talking to? He knows more about us than he possibly could."

"*No, Dottore–siamo amici, veri amici!*"

"Maybe I should keep him here until Holmes returns."

The old man nodded enthusiastically. "*Si, si, anche il mio amico– Ohmz, Ohmz!*"

The hotel man gave me a troubled look. "Are you certain you wouldn't like me to simply throw him out onto the street?"

I frowned, staring at the old man in his ridiculous clothes. Still, Holmes knew many a beggar back in London, and he did employ them and street urchins on occasion. Michelle had come up behind me. "Oh, Henry, he seems harmless enough. If Sherlock doesn't know him, we can always give him a few coins and send him away."

"*Si, si, bella donna, bella Michela, bella dottoressa!*"

"He can stay for now," I said.

The hotel man shrugged. "As you wish. Should you need any help, come to the front desk at once."

"Very well."

With a final hesitant look, the hotel man withdrew and closed the door. The old man dropped both his bag and his cane, clasping his hands before him in gratitude and shaking them for emphasis. "*Grazie, grazie mille!*"

Suddenly he staggered forward and, before I could retreat, he embraced me. The garlic smell was overwhelming, and he felt surprisingly muscular. He stepped back, paused only an instant, and then before I could stop him, he embraced Michelle as well! Rather than being offended, she only laughed, genuinely amused.

"*E allora...*" The old man gave a great sigh, then hobbled over to the sideboard. He took a glass, then carefully poured out brandy from the crystal decanter.

Michelle and I shared a look of disbelief. "Now this is really going too far." I started toward him. "I think you've already had more than enough to drink!"

The old man took off his hat, revealing a mop of curly white hair. He smiled at me, his gray eyes amused. "I think not, Henry." He took a big swallow of brandy.

I gave an exasperated sigh. "Oh Lord, I should have known!"

Michelle laughed and clapped her hands together. "Bravo, Sherlock—bravo!"

"It was the Italian that threw me off," I said, "that and what you were doing with your voice. And if I could have seen your eyes..."

Holmes held the glass in one hand, gave a grand sweeping flourish with the other. "Come now, Henry. I thought this was indeed one of my better disguises."

"Yes, I think so, too. How much garlic did you actually consume?"

"I rubbed two cloves about the jacket fabric, then thrust the remnants into the front pockets. I considered actually eating some raw, but that seemed to be carrying verisimilitude too far, even for me."

"Where did you get those clothes?" Michelle asked.

"There was a second-hand shop in the Roman ghetto, but the coat I bought from an actual tramp. There is no better way to disguise oneself as a beggar than to purchase the actual clothing off the beggar's back."

"But why are you dressed that way in the first place?" I said.

"Because I had important business, and I was tired of being followed about by that arrogant puppy, Pozzolo, and his lackeys!"

"Pozzolo has been following you? But... I haven't seen..."

"Oh, he is fairly good at it. He does have a certain flair for disguise. Still, that scarred ear is hard to hide, and obviously, it is no simple matter to conceal one's identity from Sherlock Holmes, especially not when I have my guard up. As I expected, he was soon on my trail when I left the hotel. I managed to lose him easily enough, and then I purchased the necessary elements for my disguise. My final stop was a famed Roman costume shop where I purchased this—" he pulled off the white wig, revealing his slicked-back black hair "—and a few other things." He raised the wig in emphasis. "No one makes wigs like the Italians do. The clerk at the store let me use one of their changing rooms to create my mustache and put on my disguise. He was most impressed when I reappeared, and he said he would not have believed it was the same man if he had not seen me go into the back. But let me get rid of this coat as well!"

He took off the jacket, then held it out at arm's length. "Phew! It does stink. Straight into the rubbish bin with this. I'll be back in a moment." He left for a few seconds and soon returned, minus the pot belly, which must have been a cushion. He looked rather comical with his very dark hair and huge white mustache.

"But if you had already lost him, why did you need to disguise yourself?" I asked.

"Because I wanted to visit a location I suspected—and rightly so—that he would have staked out. I didn't want him to know I was there."

I frowned. "What location?"

The corners of his mouth rose into the mustache, and I knew he would not answer.

"Must you always be so blasted mysterious!"

"What you don't know won't hurt you, Henry. And you must realize that you have a very transparent face—your emotions are always writ large upon it."

Michelle looked faintly puzzled. "What did you do with your other clothes?"

He pointed at the cloth bag. "Oh, they are all stowed there, and none the worse for wear. The bag came from the second-hand store, and despite its age, is obviously well-made. I think I shall keep it as a souvenir of this affair. And now, let me just change back into something more flattering, and then we can be off to dinner."

He reached for the bag, but Michelle raised her hand. "Wait, Sherlock." She glanced at me, her face stiffening, then back to Holmes. "Is there any way, any possible way, that I might accompany you to the crypt tomorrow? Perhaps I too could come along in disguise. I so much want to be there to help Anna."

I was not surprised, but I was annoyed. "Oh, Michelle—you are impossible! You know you absolutely cannot come."

She would not look at me, but kept her eyes fixed on Holmes. "Please, Sherlock."

"Henry is right, Michelle. Forgetting the personal danger to yourself, you might also be risking the girl's life as well. Pozzolo is a very dangerous man. He has murdered three men in cold blood just in the last week. He must be treated with the utmost caution. That is why I take him at his word and have not involved the police. The relics matter little to me, but I could not forgive myself if anything happened to Anna Antonelli. No, you must remain behind—in fact, I must have your promise that you will remain behind."

A flush appeared on her cheeks. "Don't you trust me?"

"*I* don't trust you in this matter," I exclaimed. "Give us your word you will come nowhere near the Crypt of the Capuchins tomorrow."

Now she looked angry. "You don't trust me either!"

"Let us just say a little extra assurance in this matter would please me!"

She folded her arms and glared at us both.

"Please, Michelle," Holmes said.

"Oh, very well. I promise."

I stared at her, waved my hand twice.

"I promise I will not go anywhere near the blasted Crypt of the Capuchins."

Holmes nodded. "Thank you. Besides, even though I know you are not squeamish, it is a rather disturbing place." His eyes shifted to me, and I was certain that he was thinking *I know who is squeamish.*

I smiled grimly. "I'm not looking forward to our visit."

Chapter Eleven

❧

The church of Santa Maria della Concezione dei Cappuccini and its crypt were only about a ten-minute walk from the Hotel Eden. Before we left, I gave Michelle a farewell kiss. Her red hair was piled atop her head, a slight flush on her cheeks, and her blue eyes stern. She looked both fearful and angry. I gave her a feeble smile, trying not to reveal any of my own nervousness. I was very much aware that Rafaello Pozzolo was a wild card, truly unpredictable, and a known killer.

Holmes and I wore dark country suits of a rough wool and bowler hats. "The crypt is a not a place for one's best attire," he had said. "Dust and dirt abound. After all, several chambers have floors of that hard-packed soil from the Holy Land."

We came down the Via Veneto, one of Rome's newest streets, the young plane trees, planted on either side just starting to leaf out. The church was to our left. Holmes had explained that it was once part of a larger, flourishing Capuchin convent, but that only a portion still remained, and the number of monks had also diminished.

Immersed in my thoughts—and my fears—I was hardly listening when Holmes exclaimed, "Ah! Look who is coming."

Before us was a tall figure in a well-tailored gray suit and black bowler. His complexion was olive-skinned, his face slightly worn with a thick neck, and he had a magnificent black mustache, his lips full, sensual, and dark red-brown.

"Gallo," I murmured, "Giuseppe Gallo. Rafaello's stepbrother. What is he doing here?"

"I suspect he also received an invitation."

"I don't like this—what are they up to?"

"Don't assume the worst, Henry. I doubt Gallo is in league with his stepbrother. Remember, they seemed to hate each other."

Gallo's step faltered as he saw us, his face suddenly stern, but then he smiled. He reached the steps up to the church first and waited for us. He touched the brim of his hat with his gloved hand, even as he nodded in greeting. "*Buon giorno, Signor Holmes, Dottore.* How are you, this fine day?"

"Very good, thank you," Holmes said. "I expect we are here on a similar business."

"Even so, *signori*, something to do with a relic. No doubt you have brought along the ransom. That scoundrel Rafaello said it would be profitable for the family. I was to come alone." His face showed a certain hauteur mixed with a restrained anger. "I don't much care to take orders from him, but I shall see what he has to say."

Holmes stared closely at him, a faint smile fixed upon his lips. "And you were not—shall we say—the least bit uneasy about coming alone?"

Gallo smiled back. "I did not exactly come alone. I brought a friend."

We were completely by ourselves, no one else nearby. "What friend?" I asked.

Gallo unbuttoned his jacket, swept back the left side to reveal the pearl handle of a revolver thrust into his waistband. "A friend with six chambers, each of them loaded."

Holmes nodded. "Ah yes, as I recall, you prefer the revolver to the stiletto."

Gallo gave him a look of disdain. "We are no longer in the Middle Ages, Signor Holmes, and my father and I are not mere assassins. Shall we go in, gentlemen?"

Before us, two sets of stairs went upward in opposite directions, then turned midway and met again before the doors of the church. We went up the stairs to the right and came to a doorway at the crypt level, down a floor from the church proper. Above the door was a representation of an olive branch in green and white marble as well as the word *Coemeterium.* Tacked to the wooden door itself was a paper with a notice scrawled in Italian stating that the crypt was closed until noon.

"What can that mean?" I said.

Holmes shrugged. "Obviously Pozzolo wants no other visitors than ourselves." He pulled open the door. "After you."

I drew in my breath and tried to steel myself. I knew I was not going to enjoy the grotesque displays. I went through first, and Gallo and Holmes followed. We were at the end of a long stone corridor, with a few windows along the outer wall letting in feeble light. Near the door was a small table.

A lone man stood up, regarding us warily. He was short and wore the brown robes and rope cincture of a Capuchin monk, but with his sullen, roguish face, he was not very convincing in that role. His black mustache was real enough, but the patchy beard was obviously fake. Pockmarks showed on his cheeks, and even I could recognize him as Pozzolo's servant Luca, the one who had been with him that evening at the restaurant. His right hand slipped into the pocket of his robe, where a large bulge suggested something was hidden, but Gallo was faster still. He had his revolver out in an instant, the blue-black steel barrel leveled at the other man.

"Take your hand out of your pocket very slowly, Luca." Gallo's voice was dangerously quiet. The man obeyed. "Now take the revolver out, again very slowly, grasping it only by the barrel, not the handle. Slowly... slowly... keep it down." Again Luca obeyed. His revolver had a shorter barrel. Gallo took it away with his left hand, put it in his jacket pocket, then thrust his own revolver back into place under his waistband. "Very good, Luca—you have some brains, after all. Don't try to pull a blade on me, either. You might as well remain here and continue to act as sentry. We don't want anyone interfering with our business."

"Your master must have told you that he is expecting us," Holmes said. "He must be in the Crypt of the Skulls."

Luca nodded without speaking. His dark brown eyes were angry.

Holmes took the lead down the corridor. I drew in my breath, then followed resolutely, even though my stomach fluttered slightly. The air was musty, heavy, with a nasty sort of odor, a mix of decay, dust, and age.

The first crypt had an ornate black wrought-iron fence across the opening, the gate ajar. A large painting of Christ raising Lazarus from the dead on the far wall was lit up by candles, but the painting was not what caught your eye: on either side were broad, square columns made up of vague, heaped shapes, only dimly lit—bones, bones of every variety; the skulls at the top forming an arch over the painting were obvious enough; but also the rounded ends of femurs and humeri, as well as the broad curved ilium bones of the pelvis and the smaller, separate vertebrae of the spine. None of them were white, instead pale shades of gray, brown, or yellow. More bones formed elaborate circles and strange blossoming star shapes on the arching ceiling overhead.

Cement platforms about two feet high went along the side walls, which were also stacked with bones, more of the same, but femurs set lengthwise against those walls formed two long open arches, and lying within each arch was the skeletal form of a dead monk in his brown habit, hooded head raised up slightly, in repose upon its pillow of bone. I didn't want to look too closely at those heads: I suspected some mummified flesh remained on the jaws and skulls, and truly, the odor was far stronger and more putrid than in the entryway above.

"Good Lord," I murmured.

"This first one is the Crypt of the Resurrection," Holmes said. He glanced at Gallo, who seemed nonplussed. "Have you been here before, Signor Gallo?"

"No, this is my first visit. Most impressive."

I prepared for the worst as we went on, but the next chamber had no bones at all. Candles lit up the marble altar with a painting of some saints above it. There were a few wooden pews, and a monk in a chair who had been bound and gagged. His hood was down, the bald pate of his tonsure showing, and his eyes gave us an imploring look, even as he made muffled noises.

"This is the Mass Chapel," Holmes said, "and that must be the actual attendant for the crypts. Your pardon, Brother, but we cannot release you just yet. I promise, however, that we shall soon set you free."

We went on to the third crypt, which was obviously the Crypt of the Skulls—obvious because of the stacks of round skulls heaped on either side of three standing skeletons in their brown monk's robes, and because there were Rafaello Pozzolo and Anna Antonelli at our appointed meeting place. She gave a cry when she saw us and started forward, but Pozzolo grabbed her arm. "Not just yet, *signorina*. Be patient a little longer."

The black curving iron gate to the burial part of the chamber was open. Standing within, were Anna in her black mourning garb and Pozzolo wearing a gray-haired wig and, once again, a black cassock, but this time with a violet sash. The chamber was about twenty feet square, and the pair stood in the center upon the dark soil amidst a smattering of standing crosses. Each of these was about a foot and a half tall, markers of the graves of monks still buried in the sacred soil. As in the earlier crypt, the side walls had raised platforms stacked with bones; and on each side femurs formed a long arch wherein the remains of a robed monk lay in repose, a wooden cross resting on the worn brown cloth covering his hollow chest. Thus there were five spectral monks in all. Next to Pozzolo on the ground was the reliquary, a leafy golden pattern forming an oval round the metal holding the piece of bone supposedly from Saint Thomas's finger.

Anna gave a cry of surprise, her chin jerking upward, even as Pozzolo pulled her closer. "Pardon me, *signorina*, but this is a knifepoint you feel at your back. However, I trust none of these gentlemen would be crude enough to force me to thrust it into you, especially our two English friends, Holmes and the good doctor."

His gaze shifted to his brother, and he switched to Italian. "*Ciao, fratello mio. Come stai?*" Giuseppe didn't bother to reply. His jacket was open, and I knew he could have his revolver out in an instant, if need be.

"Are you unarmed?" he asked Holmes, who nodded. "Your word on it?" He smirked. "As an English gentleman."

"You have my word that Henry and I are unarmed."

"Excellent! Now show me the jewels." Holmes drew the pouch from his inside jacket pocket. "Pour them out into your hand." Holmes did so, but their color and sparkle was subdued in the dim room. "I shouldn't need to ask this, but I shall, all the same. Are there twenty-five of them?"

"Yes."

"Excellent. You may put them back into the bag. Now set the bag down near the reliquary. Good, good."

He let go of Anna, and she immediately ran toward us. I opened up my arms. She ran into them, and we embraced. "I was so afraid—he said he had Father Blackwell—that he would kill him."

"That was a lie. Father Blackwell is at liberty and perfectly fine."

"Oh, thank God!" We let go of one another, but she gripped my right arm. "This place—this dreadful place—it's like some ghastly nightmare."

I gave a brusque nod. "It is indeed."

Holmes had set down the jewels near the reliquary. He backed slowly away. Rafaello slipped the knife back inside his cassock and snatched them up.

Holmes smiled. "You seem to enjoy masquerading as a priest, Signor Pozzolo."

He grinned. "As I told you, in my youth I thought I might have a vocation. I gave myself a promotion this time." He gestured toward the bright sash. "I am a monsignor."

"And the gray hairs to go with it, I see," Holmes said.

"They are a nice touch, I think. They give me a certain authority." He turned to his brother and switched to Italian. "You see, Giuseppe. I said this would be a profitable business. You cannot be as superstitious as our father—nor can you be so stupid as to refuse a fortune like this when it is offered to you!" He raised the jewels and shook them for emphasis. "Help me convince Father. I shall split the take with you."

Giuseppe stared warily at him. "You would actually give me half?"

"I would, dear brother."

Gallo pondered this briefly, then in a single fluid motion pulled out his revolver and fired it at his brother. Pozzolo cried out and clutched at his chest, dropping the jewels, then fell to his knees and toppled forward face down. Anna gave a cry of dismay, and I exclaimed, "Good Lord!" Only Holmes remained calm and unaffected.

"You killed him," I said.

Gallo shrugged. "Why settle for only half? Perhaps now he will finally be still!" He thrust the revolver back inside his trousers, then went forward. Pozzolo had fallen in a row between the crosses, and Gallo walked over. "Yes, talking, talking, always talking." He bent, then grabbed his stepbrother by the shoulder and heaved him over.

There was a sudden blur of motion from Pozzolo. Gallo gave a startled cry of surprise, then his legs gave way, and he collapsed onto Pozzolo, who pushed him aside, the heavy body snapping off one of the crosses in the process. The handle of a stiletto was sticking out from Gallo's chest, and his wide eyes were filled with surprise and pain. Pozzolo slowly got to his feet, then leaned down to pull out the blade, wiping it briefly on his brother's jacket.

"You've gotten rather heavy with age, Giuseppe," he said.

I strode forward, went down on one knee, and felt for a pulse in Gallo's throat. "Dear God—you killed him." Even in death Gallo still looked surprised. I closed his eyes and stood up slowly. "You have killed yet another man."

Holmes was watching impassively. Anna had put her hand over her mouth in dismay. Pozzolo glanced at her, at Holmes, then rushed forward, seized her by the arm and again drew her to him.

She gave a sharp cry. "Don't worry, dear, I shan't stick you unless these two gentlemen do something very stupid."

I stared at him in disbelief. "You murdered your own brother."

"Come, come, Dr. Vernier. Turnabout is fair play—you saw what he did. He meant to kill me."

I frowned. "Why didn't he kill you? He could not have missed."

Pozzolo kept one hand round Anna's arm, even as the other fumbled at his cassock. He took out a thick oval metal tray, possibly silver, with a dent in the middle, and dropped it on the ground. "Rather uncomfortable, that, but it certainly served its purpose. Giuseppe and his revolvers! How he loved them. And he always aimed for the heart. That was the way to bring a man down. Aim for the heart. I, however, am a traditionalist. You cannot beat the stiletto. An old weapon, but a reliable one with real advantages, the main one being its silence. No loud bangs, no stinking smoke. Yes, the old ways are best." He smiled sarcastically at Holmes. "You've been rather quiet, sir."

"It's always hard to get a word in edgewise around you, Signor Pozzolo."

He laughed. "Bravo, *signore*! I suppose I deserved that."

"Let Signorina Antonelli go free now. You have your jewels. Take them and leave."

"Well, you see, I am not one hundred percent convinced that the police are not waiting outside for me."

"You told us to come alone, and we did so. There is no one waiting for you outside. You have my word. Release her at once."

"Let's just say I like to be on the safe side. Anna, pick up the jewels—but slowly, and don't try anything foolish. It would break my heart if I had to stab you." She bent over and picked up the pouch. He took it with his knife hand and put it into the pocket of his cassock. "You stay here, gentlemen. Once we get outside, I'll let her go."

Anna gave us a pained look. "Please..."

Holmes stood between him and the gate. "I'm afraid I don't believe you. She serves as a sort of insurance policy, and perhaps you really are attracted to her in your own twisted way."

"I'll admit to that!" Pozzolo laughed sharply. "She has beauty and spirit. But can't you understand that you have no choice? Do I have to thrust my blade through her arm to convince you I mean what I say?"

"Oh, don't!" Anna exclaimed.

"I won't, unless these two gentlemen are complete fools."

Holmes sighed softly. "Did you really ever dream of being a priest, *signore*?"

Pozzolo looked faintly puzzled. "Yes, I did. In my younger days. I was quite impressionable. Incense, chanting, candlelight, holy water, the dim interior of great cathedrals—all of it appealed to me."

"And yet you delight now in sacrilege."

"I suppose I have swung to the opposite extreme."

"You killed a cardinal, and you murdered two other men in churches, and now your own stepbrother, here, in what you mockingly called a holy place. Look around. Look at those skulls stacked alongside those three dead brothers, and look at those other two lying calmly in their niches. They were holy men, but you... You profane this ground with your actions, with your presence, with your very breath."

Pozzolo did not answer at once, and his smile seemed mere reflex now. The silence of the place was heavy about us, and I felt the presence of all those bones. A few candles flickered here and there, illuminating and wavering the various subtle shades, no two bones the same pale brown or gray or yellow. All were in the process of decay—all stank faintly. So many skulls stacked upon each other, surrounding those three robed figures, piled up higher than a man, forming an arch overhead, and those sockets of the eyes, those nose holes, were black shadow, and none of the skulls had mandibles, although a few teeth showed in the upper jaw.

Holmes had said there were the remains of some three or four thousand monks in the crypts. They might have been holy men once, but their bones... They were only bones, after all: the spirit—and the wholeness, the marvelous unity of the human body—was completely gone. What remained was only a ghastly caricature. Those three standing monks, specter-like, in the tattered robes and cowls, their wrists no doubt wired together so they appeared to be holding crosses, were more scarecrows than men, as were the other two lying in repose.

It was all too much: too many bones all separate, all torn apart—too much shadow and darkness—too many dreadful smells—too much death. Impossible, here, to believe in resurrection, that someday these bones would reunite to again form men. Something colder even than Pozzolo's dagger stabbed at my heart. I was afraid, and not just of Pozzolo. I wanted badly to take Anna and get out of this dreadful underworld into the sunlight and the clean fresh air of day.

"You have a certain way with words," Pozzolo said, at last, to Holmes.

Holmes's mouth had the merest ghost of a smile. "You told me you were a lover of opera, *signore*. You must know Mozart's *Don Giovanni*."

He nodded. "Of course. It is a favorite."

"And do you recall what happens to him at the end?"

"How could anyone forget! The statue of the *commendatore* he murdered comes for him, and he is dragged down to Hell by demons."

"One wonders if these monks, outraged by your sacrilege, might not do the same—if all these bones might rise up to drag you down to Hell."

Pozzolo's laugh was rather hollow.

"*See, see.*" Holmes gestured toward the skeletal monk in the niche to his right, a figure which lay almost completely in shadow. Again, something very cold seemed to thrust its way through my heart. *Impossible–impossible!* My imagination must be playing tricks on me. The skeletal hand could not have moved, but then both arms straightened, even as the legs swung round. Under the hood was blackness and the grinning mandible of a jawbone, and the hands were mere bone. Anna screamed in horror, and Pozzolo let his hands drop and stepped back away from her, half-staggering toward the gate. For once his face was void of all mockery. I felt half paralyzed, but even in my terror I lunged for Anna and drew her toward me.

Holmes rushed Pozzolo and seized the wrist holding the knife, even as the monk lunged forward to grasp his other wrist. The monk was quite tall, and obviously solid–clearly no mere skeleton under the tattered dark wool.

"Henry–help us!" Holmes cried.

I rushed to them. Pozzolo had recovered, and he fought with the fury of a devil, but there were three of us against him. Holmes managed to force him to drop the stiletto, but he still swung about, thrust this way and that, trying to break free. My foot crashed against something, sending it flying, and then I bumped into Gallo's corpse and nearly fell over backwards. Anna had shrunk back against the gate. Briefly I saw Luca's scowling face outside beyond the bars–gone again, almost at once. The monk's hood had fallen back, the jaw bone had come free on one side, revealing an actual jaw still covered with flesh. It was a living man with his face all in black, makeup, no doubt–Blackwell–it was Father Blackwell.

Pozzolo managed to free one hand. He turned and seized the nearest skeletal standing monk by the wrist and tried to hurl him out at us. The monk toppled, came apart, the bones of his arm and hand coming to pieces and scattering. Blackwell backed up, lost his balance, and fell backwards. One of the crosses made a splintering sound as it broke. Blackwell was up again almost at once, but Holmes and I, instinctively, each had hold of one of Pozzolo's wrists, and we had spread apart, stretching his arms outward so he could not get away from us. "Damn it!" he snarled.

Holmes drew in his breath. "Father Blackwell, would you take his wrist? Have a care now."

Pozzolo tried pretending to give up, then struggled again, but we were ready for him. Holmes took out a pair of manacles from his coat pocket.

"Handcuffs!" Pozzolo exclaimed. "That's hardly fair."

"Take him over by the iron railing there," Holmes said, "but carefully, carefully."

We did so, and it was hard to keep hold of him. Holmes got the handcuffs on one wrist, and then we managed to get his other hand down, so that he could lock up the other wrist. We also had him up against the railing, and his hands were secured behind his back between one of the thick iron bars. Blackwell and I stepped back and caught our breath. It had been quite a struggle.

Pozzolo understood that he could do nothing now, and he gazed at us, frowning. His gray-haired wig was slightly askew. "Hardly very sporting, three against one."

Holmes was breathing hard, almost panting. I wished that he smoked less. "You had the advantage of the knife," he said.

Pozzolo shrugged. "Even so…"

Blackwell and Anna were staring at one another. She rushed over, and they embraced. "He told me he had you prisoner," she said, "that he would kill you if I didn't do as he said."

"Lies," Blackwell said, "only lies." He hesitated, then released her.

"All's fair in love and war," Pozzolo said.

I looked round the room. Three of the crosses were down and splintered, and the one monk's skeleton was all in pieces now, his robe grotesquely flat like a lumpy brown stain on the floor. The reliquary must have been what I had kicked. It lay on its side near the monk's cowl, and I could tell from the shape of the cowl that the skull must be in pieces. Gallo's body lay on its back.

Holmes walked slowly toward the reliquary and the tattered brown remnants of the habit. Across from the crypt was a window in the corridor which let some feeble light into the chamber, enough that we cast faint shadows onto the earth. Two tall brass candle holders stood in the two far corners, each with four candles, their flames flickering.

Holmes shook his head at a fallen monk. "Poor fellow. Perhaps they can reconstruct him, wire something back together. Or perhaps they can just exhume another skeleton from the earth. All the same, it could have been much worse. We might have crashed into a column of the skulls and brought the whole heap down."

Pozzolo laughed. "Now that would have been spectacular!"

I walked toward Holmes. "I don't like the look of the reliquary. I'm afraid I gave it quite a kick, possibly more than once. I was rather irritated the second time."

Holmes picked it up. "Oh no," he murmured.

"What is it?" I asked.

I was next to him, and he turned it round toward me. The sculpted wreath of silver was intact, but the glass in the center had shattered, the finger-shaped piece of gold that held the gray bone gone.

"Oh no, indeed!" I said. "After all we have been through…"

Holmes went over and took one of the candles from the holder, then he squatted down and looked about.

Father Blackwell and Anna came over. She was grasping his arm tightly. "What is it?" Blackwell asked.

"The reliquary broke," I said. "The finger of the saint—it's gone."

An odd sort of sound, not quite a laugh burst from Anna, and she covered her mouth with her hand.

"Ah." Holmes raised a small cylinder of grooved gold. "Here's the missing metal piece of the reliquary, but... it's empty, and..."

He lowered the candle. The monk's hand must have come apart just there where Holmes had found the missing piece, because there were several small pieces of finger and hand bones, any of which might have come from the reliquary.

"Those bones may have fallen from my disguise." Blackwell raised his arm. He had on a black cloth glove, a skeletal hand fastened to the back probably with pieces of thread. Three of the fingertips were missing. "The bones came completely apart on my left hand." He raised the other hand, and there were no bones left at all.

Holmes was still squatting, the candle held in his left hand. He set down the gold cylinder and stroked his jaw briefly with the long slender fingers of the other hand. "So one of these bones is from the reliquary, and the others are from some nameless Capuchins."

Pozzolo laughed. "It serves you right for trying to cheat me! If you had just let me go, you wouldn't be in this pickle."

"We could collect all those fingerbones and take them back to the Vatican. Perhaps there might be some way to..." Blackwell paused, then shook his head. "No, it seems hopeless."

Holmes looked up at the priest. "Do you believe in miracles, Father?"

Blackwell hesitated only an instant. "Yes."

"Then perhaps it is not too much to hope for a miracle in this case: God should guide my hand." He drew in his breath, then reached down and picked up one of the bones. He stood up and smiled. "This will do." He held it by his own thumb and forefinger, turning the bone slightly to catch the light. "It actually looks as I remember. But they are all very much alike." He put the candle back into its holder, then slipped the gray fragment of bone into the opening at one end of the gold cylinder and put the cylinder into his pocket. "No doubt they can repair the reliquary and put that back in."

Father Blackwell was staring at him, his brow creased, his eyes troubled. "I do not know if I can condone this."

"Have you an alternative?" Holmes said.

I grasped Blackwell's arm. "The pope himself almost said that it does not really matter whether the relics are real or not. They only serve as a concrete manifestation of a saint or martyr which helps make the person real to the faithful. That is what is important, not whether they are truly what they are supposed to be."

Holmes nodded. "Well put, Henry."

"Yes," Anna said. "After all, that bone which was there before…" She sighed. "It certainly did not give us our miracle."

"I cannot believe this!" Pozzolo said. "Perhaps I shall give the game away. I shall tell!"

"No one will believe anything you say," Holmes said.

"Well, I suppose there is that. Also… I guess you've won the game, after all–this one, anyway. However, I looked forward to our next match."

Holmes gave him a cold stare. "There will be no next match. There may not be capital punishment in Italy, but your crimes should keep you behind bars for the rest of your life."

Pozzolo laughed. "Do you think any prison can hold Rafaello Pozzolo! I could make my way out eventually on my own, but I shall have my father as my ally."

"After you killed his son!" I exclaimed.

"Oh, he will forgive me for that. After all, I am the only son left to him, and he will want an heir. Then, too, he would always choose the stronger one over the weaker. Yes, Signor Holmes—there will be another match someday, I promise you!"

Holmes shook his head. "If there is, you will lose again."

"We shall see, we shall see."

Holmes turned to me. "Henry, would you find the police and ask them to contact Commissario Manara immediately? Tell them we have the assassin and to come here in force. I won't take any chances with Signor Pozzolo. I shall remain here and keep him company."

Pozzolo gave a slight bow. "You flatter me!"

"Can we come too?" Anna's voice had a quaver. "Oh please, can we get outside? I cannot bear another minute in this horrible place!"

Holmes raised his hand. "Forgive me, *signorina*—I have been inconsiderate. By all means, go outside. There is no reason on earth for you to remain here. That goes for you, too, Father Blackwell."

The priest gave a brusque nod. "I'm more than ready to leave. It was a very long night."

"Good Lord!" I exclaimed. "You weren't actually down here all night long?"

"Not here in this crypt, but in the next one over, the Mass chapel. I slept on the floor, or rather tried to sleep. As I said, it was a very long night, the floor was hard, and I had much on my mind. However, I did lie over there in that archway for what seemed like forever. What time is it, anyway?"

Holmes took out his watch, turned it toward the candles. "Quarter of eleven."

"I must have been there nearly four hours."

"Good heavens," I murmured, shaking my head. "How could you bear it? I don't think I could do it."

"It was not agreeable. I did it because I had to." His eyes shifted toward Anna.

"So you came here yesterday?"

"Father Blackwell and I met here in the afternoon," Holmes said, "and arranged everything. We hid until the crypts were closed, then came out and set to work. We moved the skeleton lying in the arch. I told him that he would need to lie there until I gave him the signal. He could probably tell when it was coming, but at the word 'see' he was to move, slowly at first, in a wraith-like way, and then more quickly, to help me overpower Signor Pozzolo."

Blackwell laughed. "I did not recognize Mr. Holmes in his own disguise yesterday until he spoke in his usual voice."

"I brought along the necessary accoutrements," Homes continued, "the black gloves, the black makeup—by the way, no need for that any longer, Father. Best get it off before you go outside. You can use my handkerchief."

Blackwell hesitated. "Won't it ruin the fabric?"

"Don't worry. This was not a costly one, and I have several more."

Blackwell wiped the wadded cloth across his cheek, and a pale flesh-colored stripe appeared against the black. "It will be a relief to have this off."

"Did you find that brown habit he is wearing as well?" I asked Holmes.

He shook his head. "No. I left that to him. It was not the type of thing that one finds in a typical second-hand shop."

"I found it myself." Blackwell had most of the makeup off. "At school I made friends with a monk of about my height, and yesterday, I asked if he had an old worn robe he could spare.

Speaking of which..." He let the handkerchief fall, then undid the rope tied around his waist, and used both hands to wrench off the cowl with its two long flaps of cloth. Next he pulled the long robes themselves over his head and let them fall as well. He was wearing black trousers and a black shirt, not the usual cassock. "*Pah*–they stink so! Everything smells like bones. I cannot wait to take a bath." His shoulders rose in an involuntary shiver. "I hope it all washes out."

"I brought with me a needle and black thread," Holmes said. "I stitched that jaw bone to the cowl, and those skeleton hands to the gloves."

"Surely you didn't wear those all night long?" I said.

Blackwell made a sharp short laugh. "No, they would have fallen to pieces. I put the makeup, the cowl, and the gloves on early this morning. I was in place when the caretaker arrived and came through to light the candles."

Anna visibly shuddered. "It was bad enough being here for only an hour, but to lie there with all those bones practically in your face... If they collapsed and fell on you..."

"That thought crossed my mind," Blackwell said.

"You know, you did not really frighten me." Pozzolo's voice had a stubborn note. "I was merely surprised."

"Well," I said, "he certainly scared the living daylights out of me!"

Again Anna shuddered. "And me."

I gave Holmes a severe look. "Was that really necessary?"

"I needed you to react normally, Henry. And I could not risk you giving knowing glances at the monk lying in that arch."

"Are you certain you want to stay down here with Pozzolo? It is probably safe enough to leave him cuffed like that."

Holmes's mouth formed a bittersweet smile. "I shall stay until the police come. These bones do not frighten me, Henry. I feel only a certain sadness. In the end, however, these remnants are only dim empty shadows of the monks. Their originals have gone elsewhere long ago—unlike poor Gallo, lying there. I doubt he had any idea when he awoke this morning that he would be dead before noon."

Anna was starting to shiver. "Now can we please go outside?" she pleaded.

Holmes nodded. "You certainly may, *signorina*! I am sorry you were frightened, but at least now we have this villain in hand." His expression changed. "He will not trouble you again."

Pozzolo shrugged in mock sorrow. "I have cherished our time together, *signorina*. I know you will always have a special fondness for me in your heart of hearts."

She stared at him, then shook her head. "You are unbelievable—you are vile." She turned and strode through the open gateway. Blackwell and I followed.

"Flattery will get you nowhere!" Pozzolo cried.

Anna almost ran down the corridor. We went by the Mass chapel. I turned and saw the monk still bound to the chair. I grabbed Blackwell's wrist. "Can you help me get that poor fellow untied?"

He nodded, and with the two of us working at the knots, we soon had him unbound and the gag off him. " *Grazie, grazie, signori*," he said. "What has happened? I heard a gunshot, I think. Who would fire a pistol in a place such as this!"

"The man in the Crypt of Skulls can explain everything to you," I said.

Blackwell had already swept away, obviously eager to get outside and, I suspected, to Anna. I followed. There was no sign of Luca. Seeing how the game was going, he must have fled.

The sunlight was almost a shock, warm on my face, and so bright, I blinked several times. The sky overhead was a clear brilliant blue, and the air, too, was wondrously clean and fresh. Lazarus must have felt this way when he came forth from his tomb. It was good to leave behind the kingdom of the dead.

Anna stood near the doorway, her face turned away, her tiny hand raised in an attempt to hide her emotions. She was weeping softly. Blackwell stood over her, so much taller and massive compared to the small, slight woman. Both were dressed all in black. He still had a few smears of black makeup on his face, and you could tell he had not shaved in a day or two.

"Anna?" he murmured.

I touched her arm gently. "It's all right now. You are safe. It's finished."

Her breath caught briefly in her throat, but she did not stop crying.

Blackwell nodded. "He's right. You are safe now."

She turned round briefly, opened her mouth, then turned away again. Blackwell set his big hand on her shoulder. "Please, Anna. Don't cry." He tried to turn her, and she came round and pressed her face against his chest.

"I was… I was so afraid."

Blackwell hesitated, then touched her hair and let his hand slip down to her back. "Of course you were. But he didn't hurt you. Even a monster like him could not hurt you."

"You don't understand. He told me his men had taken you prisoner, but I thought he was lying–I thought he had already murdered you, like all those others–thrust that horrible knife of his into your back."

"That was a lie," he said. "He never came near me."

She drew back and raised her eyes to him. "I was afraid I would never see you again!" She bit at her lip. "And that terrible, terrible place—all those bones! I shall see piles of skulls staring at me in my dreams. And my mother and father—soon they will be nothing but bones, too—and you and me and everyone else!"

Blackwell stroked her back. "No, no. It's like Mr. Holmes said. Those bones are only empty shadows. The vital part of the monks—their souls—have gone somewhere else. And your mother and father: they are in paradise together."

She stared up at him. "Oh, are they really?"

"Yes, yes—if I believe anything, I must believe that. The great love between them, the love they shared, surely that cannot simply end. I believe that with all my heart."

She smiled briefly, but then her face contorted again.

"What is it?" he asked.

"It's true, all the same—soon I shall not see you again. You, too, will be lost to me."

"No, no, as long as I live, I swear…"

She touched his face with her hand. "I know… I know you must not—you cannot—love me…"

"Don't say that."

"But promise me that you won't leave me all alone—not now—not yet, promise me… Oh how I love you. I love you so very much." She caressed his cheek gently with her fingers, and they stared at one another.

I took a step back. No doubt, they had forgotten that I was even there. Their eyes were locked, neither of them faltering. She rose up on her toes, and slowly, ever so slowly she turned her head and their lips touched. I smiled, then went quietly and swiftly down the steps to search for a policeman.

Chapter Twelve

☙

Under the brim of her blue hat, Michelle was frowning ever so slightly. It showed in the creases at the outside of her eyes, in the way her reddish-brown eyebrows came together over the slightly turned up nose, in the tension of her mouth. The Roman sun of April had already increased the slight dusting of freckles on her cheeks and brought some color to her usual London pallor.

Before us stood the tall wooden relics case in the chapel of Saint Helena at the church of Santa Croce in Gerusalemme, and all six of the reliquaries had been returned to their rightful places behind the thick glass. The one with the fragment of the true cross on the second shelf was two or three times taller than the other five, and much more elaborately decorated; its two tiny golden angels with their long thin spears standing guard on either side of its massive rectangular base.

And of course, up on the top shelf, on the left side, was our old friend, the relic of Saint Thomas, that golden slotted finger with gray bone inside, encased in glass and surrounded by a sort of woven floral halo of silver. There were only six people in

Rome who knew that particular fragment of bone might not be the original occupant of the reliquary, and three of us—Holmes, Michelle, and I—stood before the case. On either side of the display was a guard, big men with black mustaches and black suits. The chapel pews were almost full, the notoriety of the returned relics having attracted many pious visitors and curious spectators.

Michelle sighed. "I consider myself a Catholic, albeit not a very traditional one, but I'm afraid I shall never understand the appeal of these sorts of relics. To begin with, the objects themselves are such plain, simple things—nails, thorns, fragments of wood or bone—and to put them in such gaudy ridiculous containers of gold and silver which completely overpower their contents..."

She had spoken softly because we were in a church, and Holmes replied in kind. "The contrast is one way of emphasizing their great value."

"Or inflating it," I said.

Holmes gave a faint shrug. "Perhaps."

Michelle shook her head. "No, for me, I would look for the sacred, the holy, elsewhere—in the natural world, the glories of the alpine mountains or the sinking sun out over the ocean." Her eyes shifted to me, her full lips curving briefly upward. "Or in the faces of those I love. All living things, especially the higher mammals like cats or dogs or men, have more to wonder at in the animation of their eyes than any of these lifeless objects."

I gave her hand a squeeze. "I completely agree. And I find it, too, in the beauty of a woman—one woman in particular."

"Men are not so bad-looking either." She squeezed back, then again shook her head. "And to think that four people died because of these relics, murdered in cold blood."

"Deadly relics indeed," I murmured.

Holmes shook his head. "No, Henry. In the end it was not the relics that were deadly, but Signor Rafaello Pozzolo."

"But killing for them," I said. "That is sacrilege indeed."

Holmes sighed. "Yes, but to my mind, murder is always sacrilege. I believe the Catholic Church defines sacrilege as the violation or injurious treatment of a sacred object, and as Michelle suggested, what could, in the end, be more sacred than a human life? Even the life of the most mundane and humble person is a kind of miracle. It is one of the great mysteries that we are here and that we exist at all. To snuff out the existence of a fellow mortal—there can be no greater crime, no greater sacrilege."

"Well, let us hope," I said, "that the wild adventurous days for these relics are over and done with, that they shall now remain quietly on their shelves, acquiring dust, and stay out of trouble."

"Amen to that. As you know, I was reluctant to become involved in this case, but it has turned out rather interesting. It pains me to acknowledge the fact, but Pozzolo was one of the worthier opponents I have—" a smile flicked over his mouth "—matched wits with."

I was peering at the gold sculpted finger with the slots in the side. You could just vaguely make out the shape of the gray bone within. "I think you did the right thing, Sherlock—Saint Thomas's relic looks good as new. Or perhaps I should say good as old."

One of his black eyebrows rose slightly. "I think so too." His eyes shifted in the direction of the pews. "I am certain it does not much matter to anyone here."

"No," I said. "And I am with Michelle—the appeal is lost on me, but I suppose if it helps to make the saint real…"

"You two…" Michelle was smiling again. "Doubting Thomases indeed! It would serve you both right if that truly was the saint's forefinger."

Holmes smiled back. "It is... possible."

"Oh, let's go back outside—I have had more than enough of churches and relics for one day!"

"I couldn't agree with you more," I said.

We headed for the entrance, and I turned to take a last look at the chapel. Overhead were the spectacular mosaics, and the gold and silver of the reliquaries in their glass-fronted case glimmered faintly. On the opposite wall was the formidable statue of a brawny woman, Juno transformed into Saint Helena, now holding a massive cross. I suspected this might be my last visit to the chapel. It was not a place in Rome I would particularly want to see again. However, it was not in the same category as the Crypt of the Capuchins, a place where wild horses could not drag me!

We came into the church proper, genuflected before the front altar (when in Rome...), then started down the nave. Michelle again marveled at the intricate design of inlaid marble underfoot in the Cosmatesque style, which formed a pattern of repeated concentric circles, dark and light intermixing.

We stepped out onto the cobbled square into the bustle and hubbub of early evening. The sky overhead was dark blue, the sun out of sight, low in the sky. A mostly toothless old woman all in black sitting near the doorway raised her tin cup. "*Signori, bella signora, per favore—carita per una vecchia malata.*"

Michelle dropped a coin in the cup, and the clink on metal seemed to act like a magnet for the other beggars in the square.

I took her arm. "Let's get away from here. As Monsignor Greene said, we cannot help them all."

Holmes had his watch out. "It's close enough to suppertime that we can head for the restaurant. The monsignor and the others should be waiting for us."

A cart made of rough-hewn wood crossed before us pulled by a muscular brown ox; the driver wore a dark jacket and trousers, a feather in his strange hat. Next came an open carriage with a fat driver pulled by a skinny horse. We waited until both were past, then walked on, ignoring the other beggars. Michelle looked distressed, and I knew the poor thin children in tattered garments, their feet bare, must bother her the most. In the end, she touched a little girl on the head, then gave her a coin. No doubt aware that it could be snatched away at any moment, the girl bolted, some of the other children following her.

Michelle looked thoughtful. "Those fancy reliquaries could buy so many pairs of shoes for the children."

"Rome, perhaps even more than London, is a study in opposites," Holmes said. "You have the fabulous wealth of the churches with all their marble, gilt, and extravagant decor; you have the grand palazzi of the nobles; and then you have the ruined remains of buildings inhabited by many who live in dire poverty. In the end, it is much like London's terrible rookeries, slums such as Underton located not so far from the grand townhouses of the wealthy clustered around Grosvenor Square."

"But they should not put so much money into their churches at the expense of the poor!" Michelle said.

Holmes shrugged. "It is rather ironic: there is a school of thought that the outlandish schemes and the money-grubbing the Church employed to finance Saint Peter's were a major cause of the Protestant Reformation."

We went down a quiet, narrow street, one with battered old dwellings which had clearly seen better days. Attached to a worn brick wall was a shrine to the Virgin, a small wooden frame with a v-shaped roof. Inside the frame, the painting of Mary had bright blue robes; some artificial pink flowers were set before her. Such shrines were typical of much of Italy. Michelle pointed at it. "I think I like that one better than anything we saw in Saint Peter's."

We had attended Mass at Saint Peter's that very morning, a Sunday, and afterwards, in the early afternoon, the pope had granted us a final audience. Holmes had returned the pouch with the ransom, but by way of reward, his Holiness had insisted that he select one of the jewels, saying the Vatican could well afford to pay for a job so well done. He had seemed impressed with Michelle, especially when he discovered she was a doctor. Before we parted, he had given the three of us a final blessing.

I smiled at Michelle's comment. "You would have made a good nun in the order of the Poor Clares."

She gave me an ironic smile. "You know me better than that."

That made me think of Anna and Father Blackwell. "I wonder if Father Blackwell has come to any decision. He was certainly wavering. Pozzolo's kidnaping of Anna made him realize just how dear to him she was."

"If they join us tonight, we should be able to tell," Michelle said.

We followed a zigzag path through the narrow Roman streets, full now with people out taking their evening walk, men in dark clothing and bowler or cloth caps, nearly all of them sporting mustaches, and the women mostly in plain dresses. Bright silks like Michelle's electric blue were rare indeed. We passed many churches and small squares, some with fountains or statues of gods or nymphs.

The restaurant was the one where we had eaten our first meal after Michelle's arrival, and the balding proprietor with his grandiose mustache of black and gray greeted us as if we were old friends. He gestured with his big knotty hand toward the back, then led us to a table where Monsignor Greene rose to greet us.

His round ruddy face with the thin reddish hair up top had filled with a broad smile.

"Holmes, Dr. Vernier. And you, dear lady—a great pleasure indeed." He grasped Michelle's hand in his own plump hands, giving it an affectionate squeeze.

She gave him a dazzling smile. "The pleasure is mine, Monsignor."

We all sat down, and I noticed there were only place settings for four. "Aren't Father Blackwell and Signorina Antonelli coming?" I asked.

A faint, rather wistful smile pulled at Greene's mouth. "I'm afraid not."

"Oh, that's a pity," Michelle said. "I was so looking forward to seeing them, especially Anna."

"I have some news of them, but first let us have some wine and a toast or two."

The proprietor came to the table with a green bottle, skillfully twisted the corkscrew and withdrew the cork, then poured out yellow-white wine into our glasses. It fizzed over ever so slightly. Greene raised his glass.

"It is difficult for me to believe I have only known Sherlock Holmes and Henry Vernier for less than two weeks, because already they seem like the best of tried and true old friends. A toast to you both!"

Holmes raised his glass. "We might say equally the same of you, Monsignor. You have proved a friend indeed."

"Here, here," I said, and we all clinked our glasses, then sipped at the wine. It was cool, fruity, and delicious.

Greene nodded toward Michelle. "And I certainly consider you a friend as well, Dr. Doudet-Vernier."

She smiled. "The feeling is mutual, Monsignor."

Holmes showed a familiar, faintly sardonic smile. "And now, Monsignor, what news do you have for us?"

"Edward and Anna could not come tonight because they have left Rome together for England. They are engaged and hope to be married in the Church of England soon after they arrive."

"Good Lord," I murmured. "I would not have thought it possible."

Greene's thick eyebrows came closer together in the center, a faint wariness in his blue eyes. "I'm afraid I had something to do with that—a great deal to do with it, in fact."

"Afraid?" Michelle laid her hand briefly on his wrist. "Bravo, Monsignor! You brought them to their senses."

Greene looked pleased at her enthusiasm, but still wary. "That is one way of looking at it. However, I'm afraid my superiors would take an opposing view. Edward and I met for a long while yesterday morning. We talked and prayed together. Anna was much less torn than he."

"What convinced Blackwell?" Homes asked.

"Well, the solution was actually rather simple, although it had never quite occurred to Edward. The majority of Anglican priests are married, and we are all Christians. The two faiths have much more in common than they have dividing them. In the end, a belief in Jesus Christ, his life and resurrection, a belief in living a good life and loving your neighbors and your family—these are what is crucial, not the legitimacy of priests and bishops, the nature of transubstantiation, or the infallibility of popes. I reminded him that a parish priest has much the same duties in both churches, but of course, an Anglican one can also have a wife and children. Moreover, the Anglicans would be happy to have him."

Holmes was still smiling. "They certainly would. Both sides are always delighted to have someone come over from the opposition.

They are welcomed with open arms! Indeed, John Henry Newman was eventually given a red hat."

Greene laughed. "You understand us clerics perfectly, Holmes! Edward also has a distant cousin who is an Anglican vicar, and he can, no doubt, assist in making the transition."

"It's odd," I said. "As you say, it seems obvious enough, but it hadn't occurred to me either. In my case, perhaps it is because I grew up in France where, for all intents and purposes, there is only one Church. It is different in England."

The monsignor nodded. "Yes. There we are always very much aware that there is more than one Christian Church. The sects are often engaged in not-so-friendly rivalries. Indeed, the Anglicans themselves are somewhat divided into warring parties, high and low church, and the like."

Michelle sighed. "I wish they would have come tonight so we could celebrate together."

"They said for me to tell you they hoped to visit you soon in London after they are married. I think they are actually shy about the whole business, somewhat embarrassed, too. However, Edward left with me a note for you, Dr. Vernier, and Anna one for you, Dr. Doudet-Vernier."

He undid two buttons of his soutane, then reached inside and drew out two envelopes. Michelle and I both put them away to read later. Michelle stared at Monsignor Greene and bit at her lower lip.

"What is it, madame?" he asked.

"Could you not... could you not have, so to speak, taken the bull by the horns, and simply married them yourself?"

Greene gave a long sigh. "Oh, I would have liked that–although I would have needed to brush up on the ceremony! I have not performed a wedding in almost thirty years. All the same, I could not, in good conscience, do such a thing. I might have gone through the motions, but the Church would automatically consider such a marriage invalid and throw it out. The priesthood is an absolute impediment to a valid Catholic marriage. Then, too, the consequences could be grave for me. I would be in serious trouble, perhaps even in danger of degradation."

"Degradation?" Michelle said.

"An official name for the Catholic equivalent of defrocking. One is formally dismissed from the priesthood."

Holmes half-turned his wine glass. "And in the end, it would have been a futile gesture on your part."

"Exactly," Greene said.

Michelle sighed softly again. "So many rules and regulations. So many barriers against the most basic of human emotions."

"I would tend to agree with you, Doctor. Somehow, in my youth, when I was studying theology, this all seemed so simple. Real life is much messier. Then, too, I simply could not bring myself to see Edward or Anna as being bad people, as being people with wicked desires. Their love seems more a great blessing for them both, rather than a temptation or a curse. I knew if Edward turned away from her, he would regret it to his dying day. Then, too..."

He lowered his gaze, hesitating, but none of us spoke. "When I was a young man, I did not have the carnal fires Edward does. Celibacy was never so hard for me, but as I grow older, I have come more and more to question my choice. With age the flames of desire may die down, but the need for simple companionship and affection actually grows. Loneliness is the real bane of a priest's life. To share one's life with another, to have a loving woman at your side to face all the twists and turns, the tangles, the pains... That is what I am missing."

"Ah," Holmes said softly. "Well stated indeed, Monsignor."

Michelle gave him a certain mock-stern look. "Well, it is certainly not too late in your case, Mr. Sherlock Holmes!"

He shrugged. "We shall see." I was certain he was thinking of Violet Wheelwright.

Monsignor Greene's serious expression became jovial. "But then I was never anywhere near the same sort of Adonis as Edward! Who would have ever married such a plain stout wretch as myself?"

Michelle gazed at him intently. "Looks do not matter as much to women as to men. Surely there would have been someone who would have discerned your kind heart and generous nature."

Greene's cheeks flushed slightly. "You are very kind and generous yourself, Doctor."

I reached over to give her hand a quick squeeze. "That she is."

Greene sipped his wine. "I have decided to go back to England. True fellowship among the clergy here in Rome is rare. You cannot be friends with those with whom you are struggling for power and position—not that I ever wanted power or position. Then, too, there are none so conspiratorial in the Church as the Italians. After all, Machiavelli was Italian! I know so many priests but am close to very few. We all go through the motions of collegiality, but there is no real bond, no true amity. That is one reason I have so much enjoyed your company, gentlemen."

Holmes gave a brusque nod. "And we yours, Monsignor. True friendship is rare indeed. But will there be any difficulty with your superiors? Will they allow you to leave Rome?"

"I think so. I have been preparing the Holy Father for it for several years. I am tired of subterfuge and treachery, and he understands that. I want to go home and labor as a simple priest in a parish." He smiled again at Michelle. "It may not be the equal of having a wife, but a good priest can find solace amongst his parishioners. The country folk are simple, but they are true. They are not like so many of those who wear red or amaranth birettas! And of course, if I am in England, I can also see Edward and Anna regularly—and perhaps even take the train to London and visit my consulting detective and medical friends!"

"We shall look forward to it," Holmes said, and Michelle and I nodded.

Michelle appeared thoughtful. "Anna is so very young, but she has been through so much. She genuinely loves Father—I suppose if he becomes an Anglican, we can still call him 'Father Blackwell'— she does love him. I think they should be happy together."

I raised my glass. "May their marriage be as happy as my own!"

Michelle raised her glass, smiling. "And as mine!" She leaned toward me, and our lips touched briefly.

Holmes and Greene clinked glasses with us, and we all took a sip of wine. The proprietor arrived with a huge platter stacked with different cheeses and salamis, the smell pungent and appetizing, and he set it upon our table with a grand flourish.

Greene smiled. "After you all are gone, I shall go on a strict diet— no more gluttonous and fleshly pleasures!—but in the meantime…"

Holmes nodded. "As you know, I leave tomorrow, but Henry and Michelle have decided to stay on another week."

Greene stared at Michelle, his eyes faintly imploring. I smiled. "And we would very much like you to continue to act as our very own *cicerone* and guide, especially when it comes to food and restaurants!"

Michelle put her large smooth white hand over Greene's plump freckled one. "Yes, indeed!"

"Dear lady, there is nothing that would delight me more!"

About the Author

S am Siciliano is the author of several novels, including the Sherlock Holmes titles *The Angel of the Opera*, *The Web Weaver*, *The Grimswell Curse*, *The White Worm*, *The Moonstone's Curse*, and *The Venerable Tiger*. He lives in Vancouver, Washington.